ACID

The Richard Sullivan Prize in Short Fiction

EDITORS

William O'Rourke and Valerie Sayers

1996, *Acid*, Edward Falco

Edward Falco

University of Notre Dame Press
Notre Dame, Indiana

Published by the University of Notre Dame Press
Notre Dame, Indiana 46556

Manufactured in the United States of America

Stories in Acid have been published by the following journals: "Acid" in *TriQuar-terly*; "The Artist" in *The Atlantic Monthly* and in *The Best American Short Stories 1995*; "Ax" in *The North Dakota Quarterly*; "Drivers" in *Crop Dust* and in *Fish Stories*; "Geor-gia O'Keefe, Vision" in *Red Light, Blue Light*; "Gifts" in *The Missouri Review* and in *Plato at Scratch Daniels's and Other Stories*; "Petrified Wood" in *The Southern Review*; "Radon" in *The Virginia Quarterly Review*; "The Requirements of Flight" in *The Southwest Review*; "Smugglers" in *Ploughshares*; "Tell Me What It Is" in *Libido*; "Tests" in *Quarterly West*; and "Vinnie's Boy, Larry" in *The New Virginia Review*.

Library of Congress Cataloging-in-Publication Data

Falco, Edward.
    Acid / by Edward Falco.
       p.   cm. — (Richard Sullivan prize for short fiction)
     ISBN 0-268-00646-6 (hardcover : alk. paper). —
   ISBN 0-268-00647-4 (pbk. : alk. paper)
     I. Title.   II. Series.
   PS3556.A367A64   1995
   813'.54—dc20
                                   95-16887
                                     CIP

For Joe and Edith

CONTENTS

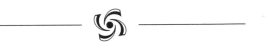

ACID

The Living Word was Jerome's bookstore. It was a cubbyhole, a small room jammed with Bibles, inspirational books, and cards for religious occasions; and it was located in a Long Island shopping plaza, between a record store and a bridal boutique that had gone out of business months earlier and was about to reopen as one of a chain of restaurant-bars that catered to college students. On the street outside the Living Word, Jerome stared through the restaurant windows as a crew of workers prepared for opening night. From the ceiling, King Kong hung vertically suspended, one huge hairy arm swiping at a biplane dangling from a rafter just out of reach. His other arm was wrapped around a red supporting column, as if he were leaning out from it, holding on to keep from falling. A scantily clad Fay Wray trapped in Kong's grip pressed the back of her hand to her forehead, on the verge of fainting.

From behind him, Jerome heard the sound of knocking on glass, and he turned around to find Alice waving for him to come into the record shop. Alice was the sales clerk and manager. At twenty-two she was only a couple of years older than his youngest daughter, but that didn't keep her from flirting. With the tip of her finger, seductively, she pushed her black, buttonless, boat top blouse down off one shoulder. Jerome put his hands on his hips and frowned at her. In response, she pouted elaborately, making her bottom lip quiver as if she were about to cry. Jerome laughed and went into the record shop.

"When are you going to stop playacting Jezebel?" he said, as soon as he pushed open the door.

"Don't start." Alice pulled her blouse back over her shoulder and glanced up at a large concave mirror suspended above her head like a satellite dish. There were no customers in the store. "I have a favor to ask."

"What?"

"Take me out tonight."

Jerome laughed again.

"I'm serious. Just for a couple of hours. Your wife'll never find out."

Alice sat behind the counter on a barstool, her hands in her lap, her black jeans and black blouse contrasting sharply with fair skin and platinum blond hair cut short as a man's. Jerome stared at her for a long moment, waiting for something in her expression to give her away, but she returned his stare unflinchingly, and in the end he couldn't tell if she were kidding with him as usual or if she were serious. He said, as if trying to understand: "You want me to take you out tonight."

She nodded, expressing exaggerated amazement at his lack of comprehension.

"Where?"

"Next door. The new place. I want to drop acid."

Jerome threw back his head and laughed loudly, folding his hands over his belly.

"Cut it out." Alice pursed her lips. Her slightly pointed nose in combination with short hair pushed back off her forehead gave her a birdlike look, her hair like a bird's cap.

"What?" Jerome said. "You're not serious?"

"You did it!" Alice's voice traveled up an octave. "You did drugs! You were wild!"

"That was twenty-five years ago," Jerome said. "I told you like a warning, not like you should try it."

"Well, that's not the way I heard it. I'm serious. I want you to take me out tonight."

Jerome went behind the counter. He stood in front of Alice and took her hands in his. Their image was reflected in the concave mirror.

ⓢ

Jerome was a tall, heavy man, bearlike in build, wearing a plain white shirt and blue jeans held up by bright red suspenders. His long graying hair was pulled back neatly in a ponytail, and he had a gold crucifix earring in his pierced right ear. Alice was sylphlike, dressed all in black, hunched forward on her counter stool. "Alice," Jerome said. "You don't want to drop acid. Believe me. Drugs will only make your life more of a mess."

"Bullshit," Alice said. "My life can't be any more of a mess."

Jerome knew what Alice was talking about. She was in love with a performance artist from Brooklyn who called himself St. John of the Five Boroughs. They had been going out for over a year when he abruptly dumped her. He said she was too bourgeois, too middle-class. This happened a few months ago, shortly after Alice mentioned the possibility of marriage. Jerome felt a twinge of guilt over this, since Alice had met St. John in the Living Word, where she had been visiting when he came in to buy a Bible and a crucifix for use in one of his performances. When he left he had Alice's phone number. "Look," Jerome said. "You're still pining over—"

"*Pining?*" Alice pulled her hands away. "Jesus."

"Forgive me," Jerome said. "I *am* fifty-two years old."

Alice said plaintively, "My father would be fifty-five if he weren't dead."

Jerome covered his eyes with one hand, and his chin dropped to his chest. "Alice," he said. "You're letting yourself get carried away."

"Am not." She jerked his hand away from his eyes. "All I want to do is drop some acid. I want to shake up my life."

"What do you need me for?"

"I trust you. You've got experience."

"Go with your mother." Jerome walked back around the counter. He glanced at the rows of CDs that filled the shop, at the brightly colored, rectangular packages. A mostly nude Prince reclined beside a rap CD that pictured four men totally naked except for the sawed-off shotguns and military attack rifles that covered their privates.

"My mom's in St. Thomas with her latest."

Jerome stepped between the two waist-high, black columns that would set off an alarm if he tried to leave without paying for a CD. "Alice," he said. "Stop feeling sorry for yourself. And don't be stupid and take a chance on screwing up your life." He pulled the door open halfway and a soft, electronic chime sounded.

Alice leaned forward to the counter and propped her chin up in her hands. "I'll be there tonight around midnight," she said. "I'll feel better if you're there. I mean, I'll understand if you can't. But I'm dropping acid tonight no matter. I already decided."

"Mistake," Jerome said. "Big mistake." He left the shop.

The rest of the day, Jerome straightened out and dusted off stock in the Living Word. He moved a new edition of C. S. Lewis's Narnia chronicles into the display window, next to a T-shirt that had a black handprint with a red circle in the center of the palm. At five o'clock, from behind his counter, he watched Alice pull down the metal gate over her storefront and insert and turn the keys that activated the alarm system. When she turned around and saw him looking at her, she mouthed the word *midnight*, winked, and crossed the parking lot to her car. As she walked away from him, Jerome's eyes fell to her legs. He noticed every crease in her jeans and the movement of her body within her clothes. His breathing slowed a little. He didn't turn away until Alice unlocked her car door and stepped out of sight. In front of him on the counter, a collection of art on religious themes was opened to a portrait of his namesake: da Vinci's *The Penitent Jerome*. He stared for a moment at the saint's wasted body before snapping the thick book closed with a loud clap.

Jerome was annoyed at himself. Noticing Alice, noticing her physically, produced a kind of heat inside him, a kind of heat that could only be released by touch. He had been married now for over twenty years. He had two daughters in college. He thought he had grown past the real desire for other women. He would always notice other women, he knew that. He would always be aware of their bodies, of the way they moved—but there was a line between noticing and wanting, and it was a line he didn't want to cross. When he was a young man, he had slept with every woman he could get into his bed. He had been a jazz musician, he played sax, and he lived for only two things: women and music. When he wasn't doing one or the other, he was doing drugs: mostly marijuana and hashish, but coke too, and some horse. He could still see himself walking along Houston Street toward the Village. He walked with a swagger, his sax in its case. He had a place way over on Broome Street and he'd cut across on Essex and walk down Houston into the Village, like there was a spotlight on him all the way. When he got to whatever club he was working, when he played his sax, he fell into a deep place. He'd play with the group, whatever they were doing, a lot of Dizzy, "A Night in Tunisia," "Groovin' High," a lot of Miles, and he'd be with them, one star in a cluster, one piece of light, and then something would happen, he'd break out, flare up, and the guys would back off and let him play. That's what jazz was like when it was good. That was why he did it. He'd be playing and then something just happened, he flew away, he'd be unconscious, flying, he'd get high soaring up to a place and then he'd level off and coast back in like gliding back down into his place in the cluster of lights, and the audience would applaud and the guys would throw him a nod, a little gesture that said yes, he had been out there.

That was the good part. But the good part was tied up with the bad part in a way he could never understand. Anger was the bad part. Something that was anger and more than anger. At first it was only there in the morning. He'd wake up with it. He'd get out of bed, his senses raw, like his nerves were all exposed, something heavy wrapped around him like a smoldering robe. He wasn't sure where it came from, he wasn't sure it mattered. There were his father and mother who hardly seemed to notice him. He was the youngest of six children, they didn't have time. There was his career as a musician, the next step just not coming, the recording contracts, the money and fame. That didn't matter, it was playing that mattered, still it weighed on him, seeing others move up while he stayed behind. But it was more than that. It was something inside him furious, something enraged. He couldn't rest, the anger pressed against his skin. It seeped into every part of his life. Then in 1972 he beat up a woman he had picked up after playing a club. He beat her up after having sex with her.

ⓢ

They had been lying together on his single bed. It was a summer night, the window next to the bed was open. There was a straight-backed chair beside the window, and it was covered with clothes: several shirts were draped over the back, and pants were hung over the shirts. The seat was piled high with dirty clothes. From his bed, where he lay on his side, knees pulled up to his chest, he stared at the chair and at the buildings beyond the window. There was no breeze. The air was heavy. The sheets under him were wet from the sweat of sex, thick knots of his shoulder-length hair stuck to his face and neck. It was near dawn: he hadn't quit playing till after 2 AM. The moon must have been bright, because he could see the buildings out the window clearly. He was thin in those days, thin and wiry. The woman who lay behind him was tracing the outline of his ribs with her fingertip. She followed the hard bone from the side to the center of his chest and back and then down to the next one. She lay behind him, so she couldn't see that his teeth were pressed together, that the corded muscles down his neck and to his shoulders were tight and hard. He had been doing blackbirds, thick amphetamine capsules, he couldn't remember how many. He was crashing, he told himself he was crashing, to hold on. Who was he? Who was the woman behind him touching him? Why did he want to slap her hand away, a minute ago he had been driving himself into her? Her touch was gentle and his whole being seemed to shrink from it. He told himself he was crashing, he told himself to hold on: who was he, he was thirty-two years old, he was floating away he was sinking under, he was a musician, he was in bed with a woman he had met a few hours earlier, she was tracing the outline of his ribs with her fingertip. He was crashing. If he could hold on. He wanted to cry and he had no idea why he wanted to cry. He told himself it was the speed, but he felt lost, even though he knew exactly where he was: in the same apartment he had lived in then for five years, on Broome Street in Manhattan, in walking distance of the clubs where he played. He felt trapped, locked up, even though he knew he was free to do whatever he wanted, he had the money he needed, he had the access to drugs, there were women to spend the night. His body began to shudder, as if he were chilled. When she completed the out-

ACID

line of his ribs, her hand went down lower, to touch him. She bit him gently, taking the flesh in the small of his back between her teeth. He turned around. Her eyes were glistening, playful. He hit her the first time when she leaned forward to kiss him. He said, "Don't touch me." She was more surprised than hurt. He hadn't hit her hard. He had slapped her. She said, "You . . ." and faltered. She hit him back, a half-slap half-push at his chest, and something huge inside him flared white and hot and he flailed at her, beating her, kneeling over her and striking until her body stopped resisting, the flesh went soft under his fists.

He spent a week in jail. There was no trial. His lawyer bargained with the city's lawyer and he got off with a suspended sentence. During his week in jail, he spent most of his time on his back, lying on his cot, looking out a barred window at the sky. The night of the beating he had crawled away from the bed on all fours. The nightmare image of himself crawling naked away from the bed was locked into Jerome's memory. It had never gone away, in all the twenty years since: the image of her startled eyes when he first slapped her, the feel of her body breaking under his fists, the animal explosion of grunts and screams from her and from him. Sometime long after she had stopped screaming, he crawled to the window. He had blood on his hands and face. He pulled himself up and looked out: the world was pulsing like the skin of a creature whose heart was beating hard. Color vibrated. The stars were white flames that flared like drumbeats. In jail it was different: colors settled, stars cooled.

After they let him out, he began taking long walks at night, and on one of his walks, he wound up all the way downtown, by the river. It must have been about 5 AM. He was cold, and he was coming up on Trinity Church. A thin, haggard man with long, windblown hair. The building was open. He entered through the central portal, and when he pushed open the inner doors and stepped into the interior, he was looking along the aisle toward the altar, where Christ looked down at him from the cross. He hadn't been in a church since he was a boy. He had been raised Roman Catholic. He had been baptized and had received communion, and that had been the end of it. Twenty, maybe twenty-two years since he'd been inside a church. He genuflected,

Ⓢ

crossed himself, and walked to the altar, where he knelt and laid his head on the chancel rail. He didn't know what he wanted. He was sobbing, and when he looked up again at the cross, he felt something warm and calming spread though him. He thought it might be the memory of himself as a boy in church with his family, kneeling in a pew between his brothers and sisters, watching the priest say mass, hold the gold chalice up to the light from a stained glass window, as if offering it to the light, offering the chalice up to the light as if the light were alive and might take the chalice from his hand. He had felt warm then and safe and that feeling returned to him there at the chancel rail in Trinity Church. But it felt like something more than memory, like his anger was being transformed: bile turned to honey. After that, everything changed. He started going to confession every week and receiving communion every morning. He quit playing the clubs. He quit taking drugs. He met Sylvia and got married. They opened a Christian bookstore on Sixth Avenue. When they had a child, they moved the bookstore to Long Island.

Jerome put the art book in the display window, next to the C. S. Lewis, and then closed up the shop and went home. He found Sylvia in the kitchen pounding a slice of beef with a wooden mallet. She was surrounded by food: a caldron of tomato sauce bubbled on the stove; in the half-opened oven, two apple pies cooled; on the counter beside her, bottles of spices were scattered among piles of raisins and pignoli. The tangy apple-pie smell overwhelmed the small kitchen. "What's this?" Jerome said. He put his hand on the counter and it slid over a slippery film of baking flour.

"This?" Sylvia pointed at the beef. "It's braciole."

"No. I mean all of this." Jerome clapped his hands and a little cloud of flour dust floated slowly to the floor.

Sylvia shrugged and made a gesture with her hands as if to say she didn't know why he would ask. "I'm cooking," she said. She rinsed her hands in the sink and dried them on a green dish towel that pictured a line of geese flying in formation. She hung the towel over the faucet, held Jerome by the shoulders, and kissed him on the lips. "Just because the kids are gone doesn't mean I can't cook anymore. I like cooking."

ACID

Jerome stepped around her and looked into the pot of sauce. "There's enough here for a month." He went to the kitchen window and looked out into the yard. In the reflection from the window, he could see Sylvia standing with her hands on her hips, looking at his back. Her expression wavered between anger and concern. In the twenty years they had been married, she had grown stout—not fat, but stout, almost matronly. She had turned fifty a week earlier, and last month, Beth, their youngest, had left for college: that, Jerome told himself, was why she was making a meal big enough for an army.

"Did you go to mass this morning?" she asked. "Did you receive communion?"

Jerome closed his eyes and leaned forward until his forehead touched the window. The glass was cool and wet.

"Did you?"

Sylvia claimed she could tell a difference in Jerome's behavior on the rare days when he missed mass and communion—probably not more than a dozen in the past twenty years. She said he got edgy and tense and hard to live with. He walked out of the kitchen without answering and sat in the recliner in front of the living room's bay window. The house around him was orderly and neat, as always, and as always he found that calming. The polished hardwood floors gave off a kind of warmth, and Jerome leaned back and settled into the comfortable familiarity of his surroundings.

From the kitchen, Sylvia called: "Do you want a glass of wine?"

He didn't answer. She was right about church: he began his day with mass and communion the way other people started theirs with coffee and the newspaper. If he missed mass, he was off balance the rest of the day. When he received communion, when he knelt at the chancel rail and extended his tongue and tilted his head to the priest, and the priest placed the wafer of the host on his tongue—when he received the body and blood of Christ into his own body, he felt transformed. He felt himself change as the wafer dissolved on his tongue: a warming light seeped into the dark places in his body. But he hadn't missed morning mass. He had gone at 6 AM, as always. He sat in his regular seat in the back of the church, under the stained glass window portraying Christ's heart surrounded by a fiery light, and he had received communion.

The bay window in front of the recliner was lined with shelves crowded with knickknacks. Jerome picked up a soapstone sculpture of a dolphin and held it in his open hand. He liked the soft, dough-like feel of the stone in his palm, the warmth it had absorbed from sitting under the window radiating into his hand. He touched the dolphin to his forehead and held it there a moment, his eyes closed. Then he put it back on the shelf and went into the kitchen. Sylvia was pouring sauce into jars. She had bright blue potholder mitts over both hands. "I'm sorry," he said. "I'm acting sullen."

"What's wrong?" Sylvia put the pot back on the stove.

He hugged Sylvia and kissed her on the cheek. "I think it's Beth . . . the kids being gone."

Sylvia nodded. Her eyes got teary.

"I think I'll go for one of my walks after dinner."

"It's getting cold out," she said. She returned to pouring sauce into jars.

Jerome leaned back against the sink. "Then maybe I'll go for a drive," he said, casually. "Later on."

After dinner, he watched television with Sylvia. When the eleven o'clock news ended and Sylvia started upstairs for bed, he told her he wasn't sleepy and that he thought he'd go out for that drive he had mentioned earlier. At first Sylvia continued up the stairs slowly, without replying. Then she joined him where he was sitting on the couch. "Are you sure you wouldn't rather talk?" She put her hand on his knee.

"It's not talk," he said. "You know how I get. A long walk or a drive soothes me."

"Okay. If you're sure." She kissed him on the cheek. "But try not to wake me when you come back in. You know what happens if I wake up once I've gone to bed for the night."

"I'll be quiet." He watched Sylvia walk up the stairs, and he listened while she prepared for bed. From where he sat on the couch, he could hear the floor creaking over his head, and each sound told him where she was in the bedroom and what she was doing. The silence meant she was standing in front of the dresser mirror in her night-gown, brushing her hair. The floor creaking again meant she was walking to the bed and pulling back the quilt. He waited until she was in bed a few minutes before getting up from the couch and getting dressed to go out. When he left, he pulled the door closed with a loud click, and he rapidly turned the key in the lock so that the dead bolt would snap closed loudly. By the time he started the car, it was midnight.

§

Jerome hadn't been inside the bar for more than a few seconds when he heard his name being called from someplace over his head. The place was jammed with kids who didn't look like they could possibly be twenty-one, though that was the drinking age in New York. Along-side him, two girls were holding each other at arm's length and squeal-ing with delight as they looked each other over and prepared to embrace. When he looked up, Jerome saw Alice leaning over a railing and waving to him. He smiled up at her just as a young ox shouldering his way through the crowd knocked him into a fortune teller in a glass case. Jerome would have grabbed the kid if the crush of bodies hadn't closed around him instantly. He leaned against the glass case as the fortune teller, apparently jolted into action by the collision, began me-chanically dealing out a hand of tarot cards, accompanied by an eerie, high-pitched violin music. He turned away from the black-clad, wiz-ened features of the gypsy-dummy and stood on his toes, trying to locate the stairway that led up to the second level. Before he could find it, Alice popped out of the crowd behind him and took his arm.

"I already dropped, I don't feel anything yet, I'm glad you came." She jumped up and kissed him on his forehead. "I thought you'd come," she said.

"Is there someplace to sit?"

Alice pulled Jerome through the crowd, toward the back of the bar. The decor of the place was overwhelming, a hysteria of clashing artifacts: a 1940s street sign next to a glass-encased statue of Elton John; Marilyn Monroe standing on a subway grating, her dress blow-

§

ing up as she tries to hold it down; a portrait of Charles Barkley wearing a T-shirt that advertised Nike sneakers and read: "The meek shall inherit the earth . . . but they don't get the ball." The place was packed with stuff that ranged from an antique Amoco gas pump to a full-size, red and white '57 Chevy with an Elvis mannequin in the driver's seat, to an old-fashioned round clock on a lamp pole, the kind you might have found in a railroad terminal or even on some town's main street before they were universally replaced with digital time-temperature displays. And overlooking it all was the massive King Kong, Fay Wray in hand.

As they made their way toward the back of the bar, the crowd thinned and the noise level decreased significantly. Jerome realized there was music coming through a PA system: Ella Fitzgerald was scatting her way toward the end of "Black Magic." By the time they found a place to sit, the Fitzgerald number was over and the Talking Heads were on. Jerome slid into a booth that was enclosed on three sides, like a small private room with a wall missing. Alice sat across from him. Over her head, light from an adjoining booth filtered through a round, multicolored, stained glass window. A waiter appeared almost instantly. Alice ordered an Irish coffee and Jerome ordered bourbon.

"So how come you came?" Alice asked, smiling. Then, before he could answer, she leaned over the table and her smile turned into a grin. "But I knew you'd come. I could tell."

"I came to talk you out of the acid."

"Uh uh," Alice said. "That's not it. Don't bum me out. I want this to be a good trip." She reached across the table and put her hand over his. "It's weird," she continued. "You look different in this place. We've known each other a couple of years now, right—but I've never seen you except in my shop or yours. You definitely look different."

"Who wouldn't look different here?" Jerome gestured toward a group of skeletons playing soccer.

"These are big tripping bars," Alice said. "That's what gave me the idea. I used to go to one of these in the city with John and everybody was always tripping."

"Not hard to understand."

꽃

"Well? Do you know why you came?"

The waiter showed up with their drinks before Jerome could answer. Alice put a twenty on his tray. "We're not staying long," she said. The waiter told her he'd be right back with the change.

"Alice . . ."

"What?"

"I don't know what you're thinking. I'm . . ."

Alice's Irish coffee came topped with a pyramid of whipped cream. She lowered her head and licked half of it away with one swipe of her tongue. "You wouldn't be here if you weren't interested. That's something John taught me. To cut through the pretense."

The waiter returned with the change. When he left, Jerome said to Alice, "I'm worried about you doing acid."

"I don't think so. I mean, maybe that's why you think you're here. . . ." Alice appeared to weaken slightly, as if some of her confidence were slipping away. Then she crossed her arms on the table and leaned closer to him. "Come on, Jerome. You've been staring at me for two years. I'm already tripping, so don't play mind games with me. I know you're interested. I can tell by your look. It doesn't matter what you say, you can act like my uncle all you want. Your eyes don't lie."

"But it does matter what I say."

"Bullshit. You can't hide your heart. You can't hide what's in your heart."

Jerome picked up his bourbon. "It's not my heart . . . I'm not trying to hide my heart."

"You're screwing around with me. You're playing with my mind." Her eyes got teary. "Now I'm getting scared. I'm getting bummed out."

Jerome reached across the table to touch her.

"Shit." She covered her face with her hands. "John does acid all the time. He says the world is like a mask that acid burns away. When he does acid he can see what's under the mask."

"What's he see?"

Alice shrugged. "I don't know. I'm getting scared." She took her hands away from her face. Her cheeks were wet and her mascara was smeared. Black lines ran down from her eyes like soiled tears. "I do acid once and I'm getting hysterical." She laughed and shook her head and covered her face again.

Jerome touched her arm and found her muscles tense. He tried gently to pull her hands away from her face, but it was like pulling on the arms of a stone sculpture. He moved around the table to sit beside her. "Alice," he said. He put his arm around her. "Are you all right?"

She shook her head.

Jerome took her wrists in his hands and pulled her arms down. Her lips were opened slightly and her teeth were pressed together. She appeared to be staring at something that wasn't there. Jerome held her face in his hands. He tried to turn her head to look at him, but she resisted.

"I'm scared," she said through clenched teeth. "I'm really scared."

"Of what?" Jerome leaned into the table, trying to get Alice to look at him.

"I don't know," she said, and then her eyes made contact with Jerome's, and some of the stiffness went out of her.

"Why don't we leave," Jerome said.

"Will you take me home?"

"Yes. I'll take you home." He put his hand under her arm and guided her out of the restaurant and to his car. It was a clear night, the sky bright with stars. Once Jerome was on the road, Alice lay down on the front seat and rested her head on his thigh. He stiffened at first. Then he saw beads of sweat on Alice's upper lip and her forehead, and he wiped them away with the palm of his hand. He asked, "Are you feeling any better?"

Alice nodded. "I don't know what happened," she said. "This feeling just came over me, like something terrible was all around me—like in nightmares when I was little and I knew something horrible was right behind me but I couldn't see it."

"Is it gone now?"

"Almost," she said. "It's melting away. I saw your eyes and it started. It's like melting away, it's almost all gone."

"You're high," Jerome said. "It's the drug."

☙

"It's different." She nestled her head into his thigh and stomach as if he were a pillow. "I don't feel high. I don't feel all messed up. I feel clear. It's like something warm is spreading through me, melting away everything bad."

"You're high," Jerome repeated.

Alice pointed up, out the windshield. "Look at the stars," she said. "How bright."

Jerome had to lean down a bit so that he could look up out the window. "There's nothing there. The light we're seeing, whatever made it, it was billions of years ago. There's nothing really there."

Alice looked up at Jerome and then back out the window. "What makes you so religious, Jerome? What makes you a religious man?"

Jerome was quiet. He looked down at Alice and saw that she was examining her hand. She held her opened hand in front of her face and moved her fingers slowly, as if she were playing a piano in slow motion. Her eyes were full of wonder. "I'm thankful," Jerome said. "I feel like . . ." He didn't know how to continue.

"Well," Alice said, still examining the workings of her hand. "You may be good . . ." She jumped up suddenly and knelt beside Jerome. She kissed him. "But we're going to be bad tonight," she said, "Just this once. We're going to be so bad we're good."

Jerome pulled into Alice's apartment complex, and she directed him to her parking space. Once they were out of the car and on the concrete walk that led to her apartment, Jerome put his hand on the small of Alice's back. "Are you feeling any steadier?"

Alice reached behind her and took Jerome's hand and slid it down into the back pocket of her jeans. She held her hand over his. "I like it better there."

Under his palm Jerome could feel the liquid smoothness and warmth of Alice's body moving. Energy flowed into him: his heart beat faster, his thoughts scattered and bounced, like molecules of water heating up in a bowl. His breathing changed, became more rapid, so that he knew if he tried to speak a whole sentence the final words would be clipped or chopped off entirely. He didn't speak. He kept his hand in her back pocket as they walked up a flight of stairs. Alice leaned into him, her head against his chest. At the door, she produced a key and sighed as if the mundane detail of having to unlock the door wearied her. When she had trouble getting the key into the lock, she seemed surprised.

Jerome steadied Alice's hand with his own. He unlocked the door, pushed it open, and stepped into her apartment. The place was small, essentially one room divided into a living area and a kitchen. There were two open doors off a short hallway beyond the living room: one led to a bedroom, the double bed unmade, sheets and bedspread crumpled on the floor; and the other opened into a bathroom.

"Sit down." Alice gestured toward a frayed couch strewn with clothes. As she pointed, a brindled cat darted out of nowhere, between her legs, and jumped up onto the counter that separated the kitchen and living room. The cat startled her, and she lost her balance. She would have fallen if Jerome hadn't caught her. "Whoa," she said. "Maybe I am stoned." She looked around. "Colors seem different. More intense." She squinted and looked at a spot on the wall over the couch. "Does acid build? Like keep getting stronger?"

"I can't remember," Jerome said. He was standing behind her now, letting her lean back against him. "It's been more than twenty years."

Alice was staring at the same spot. She said, "I think the walls are breathing," and then she laughed. "No," she said. "I'm okay." She turned to face Jerome and put her arms around his waist. "I don't feel stoned." She stood on her toes and kissed him on the lips. "Wait here." She walked off, down the hallway. With her hand on a doorknob, she stopped and turned around, and looked back at Jerome. The hallway was dimly lit, and in its shadows Alice's features seemed softer, almost flawless: her skin not dark in contrast to her white hair, but honey-colored, as if she were an exotic, a native of a tropical island. "I feel like . . . in harmony with things. I feel a . . . connection. . . . Like," she said, speaking slowly, each word taking its own good time, "right now I'm feeling like everything is a kind of moving quilt, and I'm one piece of the quilt over here, and you're another piece over there." She smiled, her eyes catching Jerome's eyes, and then she disappeared into her bedroom, closing the door behind her.

Inside his head, a voice asked Jerome what he was doing. Jerome said he didn't know. He pushed a terry cloth robe aside and sat down heavily on the couch. His heart was still beating hard. His skin felt prickly. Across the room, the cat was perched on the counter, watching him, its tail resting on what appeared to be a stick of butter. Again the voice inside his head asked him what he was doing, and Jerome answered again that he didn't know. It didn't seem possible that he would actually go to bed with Alice, and it didn't seem possible that he wouldn't. What's the truth? he asked himself, and he answered that he wanted to sleep with her, he wanted to touch her, he wanted to enter her and feel each movement of her body deep inside him, and he wanted her to feel him, he wanted her hands and lips to touch him. That's the truth, he told himself; and then he told himself that he wasn't going to. When he asked why not, he had no good answer. He wasn't the same man who once put a woman in the hospital, who once crawled away from sex with blood on his hands and face. That man was long gone. That wasn't what would keep him out of her bed. And it wasn't his wife or his family or his religion, though those thoughts were there: Sylvia sleeping on her side, her hands folded to her breast; the priest in the dark confessional sliding open the window between the chambers and waiting for Jerome to speak; his daughters as children, as young women now off in college, away from home. Those thoughts were there but they felt powerless, weak as sunlight at dusk. If he didn't do it, it would be because he just didn't anymore. It wasn't the way he lived. When this answer came to Jerome, he laughed at himself, and not a pleasant laugh but a laugh that carried a note of disdain.

Across the room, the cat leapt down from the counter, jumped onto a ledge, and slithered out a barely open window. The apartment was dead. Jerome realized that a long time had passed since Alice went into the bedroom. It occurred to him that something might have happened to her. He knocked on her bedroom door. When she didn't answer, he went hesitantly into the room. She was lying on a wide ledge under a long double window. She was on her back, covered by a single white sheet, looking up at the stars. In the flickering light from a red candle burning on top of a white plastic dresser, she looked like the woman in a magic act, the one the magician makes float up on thin air. When Jerome knelt alongside her, he saw that she was naked under the sheet, the thin fabric clinging to her body, taking on the texture of her skin. She was breathing very slowly, her chest hardly moving. Her eyes were fixed on the sky. Jerome touched her shoulder, and she whispered, barely audibly, "There's nothing there."

It took Jerome a moment before he realized she was talking about the stars, about the starlight.

She turned to look at Jerome. "You can touch me. If you want to."

He touched the palm of his hand to her cheek.

Alice turned back to the window. "I'm someplace special," she said. "I'm someplace strange."

"I know," Jerome said. He kissed her on the forehead and left her staring out the window, her eyes moving from star to star. Half an hour later he was back in his own bed, lying quietly under a spread next to Sylvia. Her body was warm and he edged closer to her. His heart was beating slowly now, steady and calm. His thoughts felt clear and solid. Alice was young. She was alone and drugged looking out her bedroom window at the stars. He was with his wife and sober, looking, now, out his own bedroom window, at the same stars. They were different and they were the same, the three of them, everyone, wrapped in urging bodies, under the dead light of the stars.

SMUGGLERS

By folding his legs so that his feet touched his thighs, Matt was able to completely immerse himself in hot water—water he had paid for shilling by shilling, dropping small English coins into a rusted metal box one by one to keep the water flowing until the bathtub was full. The tiny washroom was freezing and filled with roiling white mist. Matt held his breath until his chest began to hurt and then he popped his head above the surface just long enough to grab some air before sliding back under. It was three o'clock in the morning.

A half hour ago he had been fucking Janice. She was wiped out and crazy on some lunatic assortment of pills and coke and grass, and she had literally jumped on him and torn off his shirt and bit his shoulder. Janice was fifteen. He hadn't wanted sex, but there was no way to deny her. When he came, she was already asleep. He rolled off her and closed his eyes, and then—it seemed to happen instantly—he was dreaming. Uncle Mike, his father's brother, strode toward him in an open, empty place, no surroundings really, just his uncle taking a few steps toward him. He was dressed immaculately in white, like a movie version of a southern plantation owner, a crisp white suit tailored to his portly body. He wore a white, brimmed hat, and a white vest with a watch's gold chain dangling stylishly from a vest pocket. His hands were clasped in front of him and he said, "Matt. You'll never make it." Then there was a noise and the dream dissolved and Matt woke up with the image of his uncle vivid in his mind, his uncle who in reality was a ragged-looking, thin man with tattoos who always wore wrinkled clothes and who, his family guessed, had never run a comb through his long, greasy hair.

Someone had been knocking on the door: that was the noise that woke him. The clock on the nightstand said 2:46 AM. He had rolled off Janice at 2:30. The knock came again, three times, a little louder but still soft, as if the knocker had doubts about waking him so late at night. When he fully realized there was someone at the door, he sat up straight and his heart took off like a sprinter. His apartment consisted of a single room with a bed; a gas fireplace, which also worked by feeding coins into a meter; and a table and chair that served as a desk and an eating area. He turned on the nightstand light and checked the room. The cocaine was hidden, wrapped in aluminum foil inside his guitar case under the bed. A package of condoms sat in the middle of the table, beside a pair of airline tickets. He tossed the condoms and the tickets out of sight before answering the door. For a moment he had considered flushing the drugs down the toilet, but even half asleep he realized the Bobbies wouldn't be knocking so tentatively.

It turned out to be his landlady with a telegram from home. "It's urgent," she had said, her hair in curlers, her heavy body wrapped tightly in a wrinkled blue robe. "It's from the States." Matt thanked her and she walked away quickly, as if embarrassed. The telegram read: *Uncle Mike had heart attack. Died Tuesday morning. Wake Wednesday and Thursday. Funeral on Friday. Please come home for funeral. Please.* It was from his mother, and when he read it, sitting on the edge of his bed, he got suddenly light-headed. He was twenty-two and he hadn't been home in more than a year. The words his uncle had spoken in the dream came back to him as if through an amplifier: "Matt. You'll never make it." His legs and arms began to shake. In the morning, with Janice, he was supposed to smuggle cocaine into Paris. Janice had done it many times. They were to wrap the cocaine inside condoms and swallow them just before the flight. When they got to Paris, they'd take a laxative and the condoms would come out, the cocaine safe inside. He needed the money and he had flirted with Janice and cajoled her and insinuated himself into her favor, and then he had started sleeping with her, a crazy fifteen-year-old lost little rich girl—all so that she would let him in on her deal. And now he was sure he would never make it. His uncle had come back from the dead to tell him. The flight would take too long and the latex would break down in his stomach and the massive dose of cocaine would kill him.

Water clung to Matt's skin as he climbed out of the bathtub. When he saw himself in the full-length mirror on the back of the bathroom door, he was streaming clouds of mist. He dressed quickly, putting on heavy combat boots and jeans and a torn flannel shirt over a union suit that needed washing. Back in his room, the clothes that Janice had picked out for him, the cordovan loafers and khaki pants, the light-blue shirt with the button-down collar, and the London Fog overcoat—they lay neatly over the back of a chair, pressed and ready for the trip. Janice was sleeping on her side with her knees pulled up to her chest and her hands between her legs. Nights, out in the clubs, she looked like a teenage Shirley Temple gone bad, in torn blue jeans and a leather jacket, with a lingerie-model's body and a little girl's face, a bad little girl. Asleep she looked almost innocent, almost like a baby—but still wild, a wild innocence, even asleep, the way her wavy blond hair curled and tangled around plump cheeks and big eyes. In the morning she would scrub herself pink and pull her hair back into a ponytail before dressing up in a knee-length skirt and school-girl white shoes. That was her outfit for the Paris run.

Last time, Matt had helped her slide the condoms down her throat. She didn't need him to help, but there was something perversely erotic about it, pushing the cocaine-stuffed condoms down her throat while she sat on the floor by the bed, her head tilted all the way back and her eyes glittering with something that looked to Matt like craziness. Afterwards they had sex. Without asking, she had knelt by the bed, with her stomach on the mattress, and Matt had pulled up the knee-length skirt and pulled down the white cotton panties, and when he looked at her he saw that she was laughing quietly to herself, as if amused by his predictability—as if she knew the whole scene would turn him on because he was a man and she was amused that she was right about him, that she had him pegged. When he finished, Matt had felt frightened. He had felt frightened and uneasy for days.

He pulled his guitar case out from under the bed and unlocked it with a small key he kept on a chain around his neck. He opened it carefully, holding each of the metal snaps as he pulled them up one by one. Inside the case, his guitar nestled snugly against a plush red lining. The polished blond wood of the soundboard reflected the red and blue flames from the gas fireplace, and the hand-carved hummingbird on the pick guard appeared to move in the wavering firelight. Matt lifted the guitar and removed his wallet from a small compartment under the neck. He had two five-pound notes folded up neatly next to his long-expired visa. He put the wallet in the back pocket of his jeans, locked up the guitar case and slid it back under the bed.

Once on the street, he started for Stevie's apartment. Stevie sang for The Flesh Puppets, a band Matt had played with up until a couple of months ago. Matt had quit because he wanted Stevie for himself, and she wanted to do what she wanted, which included sleeping with women. After a few months, he realized anyway that her relationship with him was mostly for show. Really, it was other women that she wanted, lots of other women. So he left. But now, when he needed someone to talk with, someone to tell what had happened, to tell about his dream, he couldn't imagine who else but Stevie. Who else on the planet? He was twenty-two and there had been three women in his life, excluding his mother. There was Cathy from home, from Wisconsin, whom he had started dating in ninth grade and gone out with at least once a week up until the time he shocked everyone and bought the charter ticket to London. But he had never really been able to talk to Cathy. He might tell her about his dream, and she would listen—but she would be uncomfortable. She would feel like he was turning the tables on her. Cathy was supposed to talk. He was supposed to listen. Then there was Janice, but her communication, with him anyway, was mostly physical. That left only Stevie, and so Matt was headed for her building, which was only a short walk from his. With Stevie, the time of night wouldn't be a problem.

☉

When he arrived at her apartment, he found the door half open. A chokingly sweet haze of incense wafted into the hallway. Matt pushed the door open and found Richie and Dave sitting on the kitchen floor looking back at him with guitars in their laps.

"American Pie," Richie said, a clear note of relief in his voice.

"We been gettin' ripped off by the local scags," Dave said.

Richie opened a cabinet door under the sink and pulled out an ashtray with a couple of half-smoked joints. He placed the ashtray on the floor between him and Dave and took a long drag off a joint. "We heard you coming up the stairs," he said, his voice high.

Matt said, "I'm looking for Stevie."

"There's a surprise," Richie said.

Dave pointed down the hall toward Stevie's bedroom. "She ain't alone, Mate."

Matt said, "Is she ever?"

Dave turned back to his guitar. "Not often," he said softly, and he played a few chords and then looked up to Richie, who began to play along with him.

Matt followed the dimly lit corridor to Stevie's room. He stopped in front of the hanging beads that served as a door. The room behind the beads was lit by a single red candle on a curtainless window ledge, and drippings from the castle-shaped candle spilled over the ledge and down the wall to the baseboards. There was no real furniture in the room, only a mattress on the floor and some cardboard boxes spread around to serve as dressers and drawers. In the candlelight, Matt could see Stevie sitting up on her mattress, a sheet held over her breasts, her back against the wall, smoking a cigarette and looking at him through the bead curtain. She was a small woman, sylphlike in her movements, off stage; but when she sang, on stage, she moved in jerks, as if some great electric current regularly jolted her: first she'd be singing motionless, limp as the dead, then she'd suddenly fly in spasms around the stage, her arms and legs everywhere, as if she had lost her mind and all control of her body and the music had possessed her, as if she'd suddenly gone crazy—and usually the audience went crazy with

🌀

her. Matt hesitated on his side of the curtain. He could see another figure curled up beside Stevie on the mattress.

"My, my, hm hmm hmm," Stevie sang softly. "You just want to watch?"

"Watch what?" Matt parted the bead curtain and stepped into the room.

Stevie pulled back the covers on the girl sleeping next to her. She was young and smooth-skinned, her body sleek as an athlete's.

"Beautiful," Matt said.

She touched the sleeping girl's hair gently. "You want to join us?" she asked. "She'd be up for it. She's into good-looking men."

Matt sat on the floor beside Stevie. "Maybe," he said. He had tried that once before, sleeping with Stevie and one of her pick-ups. It had been strange in the beginning, in bed with two women, and even stranger at the end, when it was over—Stevie and her girl asleep cuddled into each other, and him on his side of the bed, alone. He felt like a sexual accessory. And he had been frightened, a kind of deep, unnamable anxiety shaking him up, keeping him from sleeping. In the morning, when he had told Stevie he wouldn't do it again, she had been disappointed. But now, with Stevie's offer, he could feel his blood moving. "I need to talk to you," he said. "Something incredible just happened."

"What?" She put out her cigarette and leaned toward him. Her interest was apparent in her eyes, which took on a vibrant, glittery quality when she was excited. "Really?"

Matt told her about his dream and the telegram.

"Was he sick?" Stevie asked. "Could you have known?"

"He wasn't old. He wasn't sick." Matt touched his forehead as if checking for a fever. "It's blowing me away."

Stevie grinned. She seemed pleased, as if something she already knew was now being revealed to Matt, something that would make them closer when they both knew. "You never saw him dressed like that? An old picture or something?"

"He was a slob. That's the last way. . . ."

Stevie said, "Then you know it was real."

☙

"But I need to know what it means."

Stevie slid down on the mattress and propped her head up on one hand. The sheet fell loosely over her breasts. "You want everything wrapped up," she said. "That's why we could never work."

Matt said, "What are you talking about?

"It happened. It's a mystery."

"It doesn't make you ask questions? Like, Where's he going? How come he was dressed like that? What happens when you die?"

She touched Matt's knee. "I'm not into controlling things. I'm into the music of it."

Matt closed his eyes and let his chin drop to his chest. He wanted silence for a moment. He wanted to think. Stevie and Richie and Dave—they thought of him as an innocent, as a boy. They called him American Pie, or Apple Pie, even though he smoked dope with them, and played with them, and slept with Stevie: no matter what he did, it didn't seem to change their perception of him. Partly, it was the way he looked. He had a round, boyish face that made him look even younger than he was, young enough that no one ever questioned him hanging around with a fifteen-year-old girl; and he had the straight, white teeth and the healthy skin of a milk-fed, well-cared-for child. He looked like a six-foot two-inch baseball player from Iowa—which is exactly what he had been in high school, except he was from Wisconsin. But he was twenty-two now, and he wanted something different. He wasn't sure what Stevie meant about *controlling things*, or *the music of it*, but he wasn't going to ask. "Me too," he said. "I'm into the music of it too, but—"

"What about what he said?" Stevie interrupted. "What do you think *that* means?"

"That's the scary part." The sheet over Stevie had drifted down, revealing most of her breasts and her back. Matt could feel his breath catching in his throat when he spoke. "Can I lie next to you?" he asked. "Would that be all right?"

Stevie lifted the sheet, inviting him to crawl in next to her. Matt looked at her for a long moment, taking in her body, the swellings and curves, the light and dark places. Then he lay down next to her, facing

ⓢ

her, and she covered them both with the sheet. Behind Stevie, the other woman stirred and then sat up and looked, surprised, at Matt. "What's this?" she said, not bothering to cover herself up, an edge of anger in her voice.

"He's a friend," Stevie said, without turning around. "We're talking."

The woman seemed to think about this for a moment. Then she smiled and said, as if excusing her momentary anger, "I'm still asleep," and she cuddled up into Stevie, wrapping her arms around her chest and snuggling against her.

"What's the scary part," Stevie said. "Just what exactly did he say?"

"What I told you. He said I'm not going to make it. He took like two steps toward me, and he had this concerned, like sad look on his face, and he goes 'Matt, you'll never make it.'"

"You think he meant as a musician, an artist? You'll never have any success, you'll never be any good? That way?"

Matt shook his head. "I'm supposed to smuggle some coke into Paris tomorrow with Janice. She's done it a couple of times to make money: you put the coke in a condom, you swallow—"

"You're not going to do it, right? Right?"

Matt didn't answer.

Stevie put her hand on Matt's neck, her thumb gentle against his cheek. "You know what can happen?" she said. "You know how long it'll take that much coke to kill you? About two seconds."

Matt laid his head on her shoulder. "I'm out of money," he said. "I've been out of money for weeks. If I don't do this, I've got to go home."

Stevie was quiet for a time. She stroked Matt's hair, running her fingers over the back of his head and his neck. "I see my father sometimes in dreams," she said. "He was killed in the Falklands war, which no one even remembers anymore."

Matt started to look up, but she stroked his head, signalling him to be still.

"I know it's not just a dream when we're standing under a big orange moon, because that really happened when I was very little. He held me on his shoulder under a moon just like that and told me always to remember it and the moment would never disappear. When we're standing under an orange moon like that, then he's visiting me and it's not just a dream."

"Do you believe that, really?" Matt pulled away from Stevie. "That the dead come back and talk to you?"

"Absolutely," she said. "You shouldn't go tomorrow. No matter what."

Matt stretched out and pressed his head into the mattress. "I told Janice I'd go with her," he mumbled. "She's expecting me to go with her." He felt sick. His stomach was jittery, on the edge of being nauseous.

Stevie laid her head on Matt's back. "What are you doing with that girl?" she asked, her voice not much above a whisper. "Do you even know what you're doing?"

Matt thought about Janice, about how he could explain her to Stevie. On the surface she looked like a brat. Her father was an earl or a duke, or some such title, and her family was wealthy—extravagantly wealthy. But she hadn't taken a cent from her family since she turned twelve. She had run away and been brought back time and again, until they just gave up on her. She had been making her own way for the last three years—mostly by smuggling drugs. She was fifteen. She had poems by Rimbaud committed to memory. She listened to Bartók and Frank Zappa. Matt had met her at a bar when he was still sleeping with Stevie and playing with the band. She had walked up to him and said, "Thirty-five thousand children die every day of starvation and my father has three homes." She was wrecked, of course. She was so high she probably had no idea what she was saying. Matt had laughed and then felt stupid when Janice appeared hurt by his laughter. She had stumbled away before he could think of anything else to say.

Matt closed his eyes and fell asleep without realizing it. When he woke up, it was light out and Stevie and the other woman were curled up together in a ball on the far side of the bed. The other woman was snoring lightly. He picked himself up slowly from the mattress, thinking he might have already made his decision, that Janice might already be in the air, on her way to Paris without him. He quietly left Stevie's room and entered the dark hallway. In the kitchen, he found Richie asleep on the floor, an ashtray full of roaches near his head and a gallon jug of wine held tightly to his chest, as if he were a child and the jug were a teddy bear. He looked around the room for a clock, but the walls were bare. The only furniture was a kitchen table, and the only thing on the table was Richie's guitar.

Matt stood quietly in the kitchen. He thought about what it would be like to call Cathy. She would be happy to get his call. She might not act that way at first, but she would be happy. When he left the apartment and went out to the street, he saw a husky old man unlocking the doors to a newspaper stand; and, behind the newspaper stand, a steady stream of people descending the stairs into the tube station. If he called Cathy, she'd book him a seat on a flight home. When he got off the plane, she'd be there at the airport, waiting. She'd tell his parents and they'd be there too, as well as her parents. It would be a party, a reunion, a welcome home: he could see Cathy standing there, picture her face, round like his own, her shoulder-length brown hair falling toward her back, the ends turned under in a satiny curl. She was not an especially attractive girl, though she certainly wasn't ugly. Matt thought of her as plain, a not very attractive girl. He had known her since she was thirteen. At the airport, her mother would cry. His mother would cover her mouth with her hands. The men would hang back. Then would come the embraces, the hugs and tears, the pats on the back—and he'd be home.

Matt asked the time at the newspaper stand. It was a little after seven. He started for his apartment. The Paris flight left at 8:15 from Heathrow. First he walked and then he ran, and when he opened the door to his room, he found Janice standing by his bed, glaring at him. She pointed to his guitar case, which was in the middle of the floor. "I broke the lock," she said. "I thought you'd just split."

Matt closed the door by leaning against it. "I fell asleep," he said. "I woke up with a dream that—"

"There's a cab on the way," Janice said. "I'm all ready. If you want to do this thing with me. . . ." She gestured toward the back of the chair where Matt's clothes were waiting.

ⓢ

In her navy-blue skirt and white blouse, with her hair pulled back in a ponytail and her face scrubbed clean of makeup, Janice looked like a child, like a little girl. For a moment, Matt didn't move. He stood there as though he were paralyzed. Janice stared at him, waiting, and the look in her eyes was a question: What's it going to be, Matt? What are you going to do? Matt's hand moved slowly toward the buttons of his flannel shirt. He imagined again the airport scene as he arrived home: his parents and Cathy's, Cathy walking toward him. Then he remembered a summer night when he was a senior in high school: both families had come to one of his baseball games to watch him play; he had his own cheering section in the bleachers. After the game, Cathy's two little brothers came running across the field to him, as if he were a hero. His parents went home and he went to Cathy's, where Cathy and her mother prepared dinner, while he drank a beer with her father and talked about the game. After dinner they all watched television, and after her parents went to bed, he made out with Cathy until they were both half naked and supremely frustrated, and then he went home, where his mother had waited up for him and wanted to know how the night had gone. The memory of that night felt like a great weight, or like a pressure suit—something that enclosed him and pressed against him. He undid the top button of his shirt and looked again at Janice, who was looking back at him now with curiosity, like a scientist observing the behavior of an animal.

"Matt," Janice said, her voice not angry. "Just tell me. Are you coming with me or not?"

Matt nodded.

"You're coming?"

He nodded again.

Janice pushed his hands away and began undoing the buttons of his shirt. "You're scared," she said. "I was scared the first time, too. I was terrified." She leaned into him and peeled the shirt off his back.

Matt wanted to tell her about the dream, but the words weren't coming. When she unfastened his belt and pulled his jeans down around his thighs, he sat on the bed and lifted his legs. She knelt in front of him and let his feet rest in her lap while she untied his shoe laces and pulled off his boots. Matt was watching Janice undress him, but he was thinking about his uncle. Once, when he was a boy of eight or nine, he had bicycled to his uncle's farmhouse. He hadn't told his parents, because this was a period of time when the talk about his uncle was all hushed and solemn. From hearing the grown-ups, he knew that his Uncle Mike had been to war in Vietnam. He had heard bits and pieces of things about drugs and shootings. He had heard some things about women. His uncle kept leaving town and coming back, as if the town were a prison and he could never manage a successful escape; and every time he came back he looked stranger. He had a beard. No one else in the family had a beard. He had long hair. No one else in the whole town, that Matt knew anyway, had long hair. This time when Matt bicycled to the farmhouse, it was one of the times when his uncle had just come back from being away, and everybody was whispering about him. Matt had bicycled the full ten miles out of town to the rundown farmhouse where his uncle lived, and he had found him asleep in his living room. He remembered that the house had been neat, but weirdly decorated: hubcaps were nailed to the wall in the kitchen and living room, and his uncle's sculptures that he made out of farm junk were displayed on tables and in nooks and crannies, places where anyone else in his family would have placed a lamp or a knickknack—and there was a closed-up wooden crate in the kitchen, hanging by a chain from the ceiling, the kind of crate that's made of wire and thin wood. A padlock was looped through the wire, so that you'd have to break the crate to open it. Inside the crate was a candle. It was round and it was big, the size of a carnival fishbowl. It was rust-red with a thick black wick that was lit and burning. Wax dripped down the sides of the candle and onto the crate and through the slats to the floor. Matt looked at the crate with the lit candle and he couldn't imagine why anyone would do such a thing: put a lit candle inside a locked wooden crate. He tiptoed into the living room, where his uncle was sleeping in a tilted back recliner with a bottle of whiskey on the floor beside him. He was wearing a crisp white T-shirt with *I*❤ *Wisconsin* printed beneath an idyllic picture of a farmhouse surrounded by barns and silos and cows lazily chewing grass in a pasture. He was

ⓢ

curled up in the chair, hugging his chest, his arms underneath the T-shirt, as if it were a straight jacket. Matt remembered being struck by the contrast between that clean white T-shirt and his uncle's haggard face and jaundiced-looking skin and long, stringy, unwashed hair. He had never told his uncle about the visit, his uncle or anyone else.

This was the uncle who had come to him in his dream. This was the uncle who had told him he'd never make it.

When Janice finished undressing him, Matt stood up and put on the cordovan penny loafers and the khaki slacks, the blue shirt with the button-down collar and the London Fog overcoat. Janice brushed his hair for him and kissed him on the cheek. "Don't be scared," she whispered. "We can do it," she said, and she took him by the arm, gently, and had him sit on the floor by the bed and tilt his head back, the way he had seen her do it, and open his mouth wide. First he closed his eyes; then he opened them and he watched her coat the outside of a condom with some kind of a gel before she lowered it into his mouth and began pushing it down his throat. He gagged the first time, and she told him to relax. Outside, the cabbie honked his horn. Janice opened the window and yelled that they'd be right down. Then she came to him again, and this time he closed his eyes and he imagined what they'd look like as they boarded the plane, like a brother and sister, like a couple of kids going off by themselves on a journey, and he relaxed and tried to ignore the pain as best he could, the feeling like he was being ripped open at the neck as she pushed the condom down his throat.

THE ARTIST

Jim had the rear-view mirror tilted so that he could see into the back seat, where Alice, his two-year-old daughter, appeared and disappeared and reappeared out of darkness as the car passed under streetlight after streetlight. He had been driving for over an hour trying to get her to sleep, and her eyes were still open. He located the dimmer control for the dashboard lights and increased the brightness just slightly so that he could read the time. "Daddy," Alice said dreamily. "Is it the fairy place?" "Not yet," Jim answered. It was almost nine. He dimmed the lights. "If you close your eyes, we'll get there faster." Alice closed her eyes, which surprised him. She was usually harder to fool than that.

A moment later, she was sleeping. Each time the light swept over her, she seemed to sink deeper and deeper into the car seat, her shoulder-length brown hair blending with the seat's brown, padded leather. Jim straightened out the mirror and turned the car around. When he drove Alice to sleep, he rarely traveled more than a few minutes' distance from his home, so he wouldn't have to waste time driving back once she was out. He was efficient. At forty-six he was father to three children, all under ten; husband to a doctor; owner of an advertising firm; and, finally, an artist, a video artist: he created pieces that were thought of by some as "experimental" films. He didn't think of them as films and he didn't think of them as experiments—but he used the term himself sometimes.

A set of spotlights came on automatically as he pulled into his driveway. He parked the car, lifted Alice from her seat, and carried her up a sloping walk surrounded by blossoming azaleas. The polished mahogany doors at the front of the house were open to let in the early summer, evening breezes. Jim opened the screen door and stepped into a house so quiet that it surprised him. Jake, his four-month-old, would be asleep by now, but Melissa, the nine-year-old, should have been up and around; and he didn't hear his wife, Laura, on the phone or running the dishwasher or doing something somewhere, as he would have expected. The house was just plain quiet, which almost never happened. He carried Alice up a short flight of stairs into the great room and noticed Melissa's sneakers and socks on the rug next to the baby grand. If he hadn't been afraid of waking Alice, he'd have called out for Laura or Melissa. Instead, he continued on silently toward the back of the house. He found his wife and daughter in the kitchen sitting at the table with a man who looked to be in his fifties. He had hair down to the middle of his back pulled into a braid. He wore multiple earrings and a gold nose ring. Where the top two buttons of his shirt were open, Jim could see the bright colors of a tattoo. From the way the three of them sat staring up at him from the table with grins on their faces, Jim guessed that he was supposed to recognize the stranger. At first he didn't. Then, little by little, he saw the boyish face of Tony Diehl compose itself within the weathered face of the stranger. "Tony?"

Tony touched his chest with his fingertips. "Who else, man?" He stood and opened his arms, offering Jim an embrace.

Laura said, "He came just a few minutes after you took off with Alice." Before dinner, she had gone jogging while Jim watched the kids, and she was still wearing her skin-tight Spandex outfit. She looked good. She was five years younger than Jim—and she looked younger than that.

Melissa said, "He's been telling us stories about you, Dad, when you were young."

Laura got up to take Alice from Jim. "Your father's *still* a young man."

ʕ

"Oh, please," Melissa said. "Forty-six is *hardly* young."

Jim handed Alice off to Laura. He asked Tony, "How'd you find me?"

Tony grabbed Jim's hand, shook it once, and then pulled him close and wrapped his arms around him. He stepped back and looked him over. "Christ, man," he said. "Twenty? Twenty-five years?"

Jim looked at Melissa and made a little motion with his head that told her it was time for bed.

"I want to stay up," Melissa said. "I want to hear about all the trouble you used to get into."

Jim said, "What have you been telling her?"

Tony answered, "None of the juicy stuff. Don't worry."

"Pleaaassse," Melissa said.

Laura, who had been standing quietly in the doorway with Alice, told Melissa to go get her nightgown on. "I'll get them off to bed," she said. "Why don't you guys make yourselves drinks downstairs and I'll join you when I'm done?"

Tony said, "Sounds good to me."

"I'm going to take Tony out to a bar." Jim put his arm around Laura and kissed her on the forehead. Then he directed Tony toward the living room. On the way to the front door, he said to Laura, speaking loudly and without looking back at her, "We have a lot to catch up on." When he looked up, he saw Laura still standing by the kitchen with Alice on her shoulder, her mouth open a little. He called, "I'll be back late. Don't wait up."

Tony waved to her. "Hey. It was nice."

Jim reached around Tony and opened the door, his body leaning into Tony's, nudging him out.

"Hey, man," Tony said, as Jim pulled the door closed tight behind him. "Are you hustling me out of your house?"

Jim had on his standard summer outfit: loafers without socks, light-weight khaki pants and a solid-color T-shirt. He said, "It's getting cool," and went to the back of his car, where a linen jacket was hanging from a hook above the side window. He put on the jacket and took out Alice's car seat while Tony watched.

꿈

"What?" Tony said. He opened his hands, as if surprised. "Are you pissed off at me? I should have called, right?"

Jim put the car seat in the trunk and pointed to the passenger door, indicating that Tony should get in.

"Jesus Christ." Tony got in the car. When Jim got in and started the engine, he said again: "Jesus Christ. Some welcome."

"What is it, Tony?" Jim started for the expressway. "Am I not being friendly enough?"

"Hey," Tony said. "We did hang out a lot of years." He flipped the sun visor down and looked at himself in the mirror. "Have I changed that much?" He pointed at the gold ring in his nose. "It's the nose ring, right? The nose ring's got you freaked?"

"You're a funny guy, Tony."

"What's funny? You want to see something funny? Here, I'll show you my tattoo." He started to unbutton his shirt.

Jim grabbed his arm. "Stop it. Tell me why you're here."

Tony leaned back in his seat as if he were suddenly tired.

Jim turned and looked at him. The boyishness he remembered was gone entirely. His skin had hardened and thickened: it looked as though it would feel ragged to the touch. His eyes seemed to have sunken into their sockets and he had small, fatty growths around each eyelid. He was forty-two, four years younger than Jim, and he looked like a man in his late fifties or early sixties, a man who had led a rough life. "So where am I taking you?"

"I thought we were going for a drink?"

"You want a drink?"

"Sounds good to me."

"Fine, I know a bar. You want to tell me what's up?"

"I'm insulted," Tony said. He was lying back in his seat, as if too exhausted to move. "After all the years we hung out, I can't stop in to say hello? A social visit?"

"What's the gun for?"

"The gun?" He touched the middle of his back. "I didn't think you'd see. I mean, I *know* your old lady didn't see nothing." He took a nine millimeter Beretta out from under the back of his shirt. He placed it on the console between them. "Let me tell you what's happening. You'll understand."

Jim said, "Isn't this a social visit?"

"You haven't changed, Bro." Tony sat up straight. "Actually, man. I can't believe you. Look at you! You look like Don Johnson, *Miami Vice*. Slick." He slapped Jim's stomach. "How come you don't have a gut, like me?" He held his belly with both hands. "And what kind of car is this, Jimmy?" He looked around the interior. "I never seen a car like this."

"It's a Rover."

"A what?"

"A Rover."

"What the hell's a Rover? Sounds like a dog."

Jim said, "Tell me what's going on."

"I've got a problem. Fuck the drink. You have to take me into the city." Tony stopped and seemed to think about how to continue. Then his thought process apparently shifted. "But, Jimmy, man," he said. "Look at you. Stony Brook, Long Island. This is like where the rich people live, right? You're like rich now. You got a doctor wife. You got your own business. You live in a fucking mansion. You look great, your wife's a piece of ass: I mean, what the fuck is this? You're unbelievable, man. Fucking Jimmy." Tony reached over and slapped him on the stomach again. "I'm proud of you, man. I'm still a small-time, drug-dealing screw-up, and look at you. I'm proud of you, Jimmy. I mean it."

Jim checked the side-view mirror as he picked up speed on the entrance ramp to the Long Island Expressway. He pulled the car over to the extreme left-hand lane and accelerated to seventy. "What kind of trouble are you in? What do you need?"

"Don't you want to know how I know all this stuff about you?"

"I haven't kept a low profile."

"That's the truth. *The Village Voice!* Not that I would have recognized you from the picture. Where's the curly hair down to your ass?"

"It was never down to my ass. Since when do you read *The Village Voice?*"

"I don't," Tony said. "Ellis showed me."

֍

Jim seemed surprised. "I thought Ellis would have moved on a long time ago."

"Oh," Tony said. "Like me, you're not surprised I'm still small-time—but Ellis. . . . Man, you don't know Ellis. Don't even think you know Ellis. The guy you knew, those years. . . . He's like completely gone. Totally. He don't even exist anymore."

"What happened to him?"

"Drugs. Twisted stuff. He's a sick puppy, man. If he's alive another month, I'll be surprised."

"Why? What's he got?"

"Not like that," Tony said. He pointed to his temple. "He's sick this way. He's out of his mind. He's not even human anymore, Jimmy. You won't believe the shit he's into. I tell you some of the stuff he's done, you'll puke right here, man. Right in the car."

Jim pulled into the slow lane, behind a tractor-trailer. He pointed to the gun on the console beside him. "Put that on the floor or something. I want to pass this truck." Tony put the gun on the floor in the back, and Jim pulled into the passing lane. They were both quiet for a long time then, driving in silence, in the dark. When they left Nassau County and entered the city, streetlights appeared above the road.

"Remember those two guys?" Tony said, as if the lights had suddenly waked him.

Jim didn't answer. He knew what Tony was referring to without having to think about it. "We're in the city," he said. "You want to tell me where we're going? You want to tell me what the hell I'm doing here?" Tony had slumped down in his seat and put his knees up on the dash. Jim knew that he was staring up at him out of the dark, checking out his reaction.

Tony reached down into his pocket and came up with a fat manila envelope. He opened the top. "Ten thousand dollars," he said. "I need you to give this to Ellis for me."

Jim took the money and held it up in front of the steering wheel. The bills stuffed into the envelope were held tight with a thick rubber band. He dropped the envelope. "What's this?"

෧

"It's Ellis's. Jimmy, my man. Ellis has got millions in his place. All in envelopes just like this. He's out of his mind."

"Millions?"

"You don't believe me." Tony put his right hand over his forehead, closed his eyes, and pointed to Jim with his left hand. He looked like a magician about to identify a card. "Look at the back of the envelope. What's the number?"

Jim looked at the back of the envelope. The number was written large with a black marker. "One hundred and sixty-two."

"You do the math."

"Ellis has got 162 envelopes stashed in his place, each with ten thousand dollars?"

"More. And he counts them. Two, three times a day. Religious."

"Somebody would have killed him for it by now."

"Jimmy . . . Ellis is . . . Everybody's scared of him. Everybody."

"This is the Ellis I used to play chess with? This is the Ellis was our supplier?"

"No, man. I told you. That Ellis is long dead. This is some other guy." Tony turned on the interior light. He said, "Look at me, man," and he leaned close to Jim.

Jim squinted and reached to turn off the light.

Tony smacked his hand away. "I'm serious," he said. "Look at me."

Jim turned to look at him and then turned back to the road. "I looked at you," he said. "Will you turn off the light?"

"Just listen a minute." He put his hand on Jim's shoulder. "I need you to do me this favor, but you have to understand about Ellis. You can't tell just to look at him." He paused for a moment, then turned off the light. "We're almost there," he said. "I'll tell you a few things."

"Thank you."

"Ellis owns this building; he lives on the top floor—the whole floor. He's got a freezer set up in his living room. He'll show it to you. He shows it to everybody. When he opens it, you're going to see a cop." He pointed out of the car, to his right. "Take this exit," he said.

Jim pulled the car to the right, slowed down, and exited onto a cobblestone avenue strewn with garbage. "Where the hell are we?"

"South Bronx. Just stay on this a couple of miles."

Jim slowed down to twenty miles an hour, and even then the cobblestones tested the suspension. The streets on either side of him were empty. Whole blocks had been gutted by fire. "A cop," he said. "He's got a cop in a freezer."

"A dead cop."

"Is this a joke, Tony?"

"I wish."

"You want me to believe this shit? Ellis has a dead cop in a freezer in his living room, a couple of million dollars scattered around in envelopes. . . . It's a joke. What else? Anything else you want to tell me about him?"

"Could I make this shit up, Jimmy? Really? Ask yourself, if I were lying, would I tell you shit this wild?" Tony clasped his hands behind his neck and tapped his foot. "I'm getting nervous just coming up here." He jerked around and retrieved the gun. "I haven't told you half of it." He put the Beretta into its holster behind his back. "He sleeps with little girls from the neighborhood. He pays their junky mothers with shit and they come over in the morning and bathe him— these three little girls. They carry water to his bath. I'm talking eight, nine years old. Same thing at night. It's like some sort of ceremony, some sort of ritual. They fill the tub and then. . . ." Tony stopped, disgust apparently overcoming him. "He wants me dead, Jimmy, and the guy's a stone-cold, pure-fucking-insane murderer. He's got this machete. . . ." Again Tony stopped. He pointed out the window. "Turn right here."

Jim turned right onto a wide, well-lit boulevard. The area seemed to improve some: the streets were paved, the buildings weren't bombed out, here and there people were sitting on stoops. Alongside him, Jimmy could feel Tony's nervousness. "Let me ask you something, Tony. If Ellis is so bad, why are you still hanging with him?"

"Let me ask you something first," Tony said. "How come it's different for you? You know what I mean? You tell me."

"What do you think? You think the gods picked me up and put me someplace else?"

"So tell me," Tony said. "All I know now is: one day no Jimmy. Twenty years later, they're writing about you in the paper. You're a big deal."

Jim looked at his wrist, as if checking a watch. "How long have I got, five minutes?"

"Give me the short version."

"The short version. . . . At twenty-five I split to the West Coast, hung out, met this crowd of people who were into art. They got me into school, I busted my ass, got my degrees, met my wife in graduate school, got married, had kids, moved back East. . . ." He stopped and looked at Tony. "Then you showed up."

"You know what I think?" Tony said. "I think the gods picked you up and put you someplace else."

Jim was quiet for a moment. "Okay," he said. "I'm not arguing."

"Amen."

"And you?"

"I don't know," Tony said. "Me . . . I got married once. It lasted a couple of years, I hated working. I lifted shit all day, I loaded trucks. Never had any money." He grimaced at the memory. "I don't know," he said again. "We couldn't have any kids, she wanted kids. . . . I screwed around a lot. . . ." He stopped and seemed to drift off.

Jim said, "So now you're working for Ellis again, and . . . ? What happened?" He picked up the money envelope. "You ripped him off?"

"Right," Tony said, mocking. "I ripped off envelope number one hundred and sixty-two, hoping he wouldn't miss it. Pull over here." He pointed to an empty parking space in front of an apartment building that looked seven or eight stories high. "We're here."

§

Jim parked the car. He turned off the engine and slipped the keys into his pocket. He turned to look at Tony, who was looking back at him intently. Tony picked up the envelope and handed it to Jim. "He gave it to me, Jimmy. He handed it to me, just like I'm handing it to you. Then he gets that fucking look that scares the shit out of me, and he goes 'You stole my money, Tony. You know what I got to do, don't

§

you?' I go, 'What money? This money?' I try to give him back the envelope. He turns around, goes into the other room, I hear him taking the machete down off the wall—and I split. This is last week. Now I hear from everybody on the street that I'm a dead man. Kill me, you get an envelope. Ten thousand dollars."

Jim leaned back against his door. "And you didn't do nothing, Tony. Nothing at all."

"What do you mean, am I an innocent? Neither one of us is innocent, Jimmy. But I didn't snake Ellis, that's what we're talking about."

"You want me to go up there and see this maniac and tell him what? For old time's sake, he should stop being a lunatic?"

"Listen—"

"If this guy's so crazy, why do I want to deal with him?"

"Jimmy, listen to what I'm trying to tell you." Tony stopped and looked up at the car's ceiling, as if pausing to find the right words. "Ellis is about to be dead—soon. He's like a guy who's reached the end of some kind of twisted road. It's hard to explain this, but I know. I'm sure. He's trying to wrap things up. It's all gotten too warped, even for Ellis. The guy wants to die."

"This is just something you know. Intuitively."

"Yeah, intuitively. But other shit too. Like, in the last month, he's been showing everybody his money. And he shows everybody the dead cop. Everybody. And he's been ripping people off, ripping them off big time. He hurts people, every chance he gets." Tony hesitated for a moment, then shrugged. "And he's wasted a couple of guys. Not street scum. These were guys with connections. With his own hands, with that fucking machete. I mean, Jimmy, he knows what he's doing. Somebody's going to kill him. He won't live out the month."

Jim picked up the envelope and held it in front of him. "So let's say you're right. Why's he going to take this back from me? If what you say's the case, he wants you dead. Like wrapping up loose strings. Maybe he'll want me dead too."

"He doesn't want you dead. He wants you to make a movie about him."

☙

"He wants what?"

"He wants you to make a movie about him. That's all he's talked about since he saw the article."

"I le wants me to make a movie about him?"

"It fits, man. It's like the end of his life, like his memoirs. He's been writing it all down, like a script. When he gets it done, he plans on coming out to see you."

Jim turned away from Tony. At the entrance to the apartment building, in front of the thick glass doors, someone had left a Mc Donald's bag with a cup and a fries container next to it. Jim said, "Tony. I don't make movies."

"You want my advice, don't tell Ellis that."

"And what am I supposed to tell him?"

Tony picked up the envelope and tossed it into Jim's lap. "Listen, Jimmy. I wouldn't ask for this favor if I thought it would screw you. You're an old friend. We were tight once. All you have to do is go up there, tell him Tony told you he wants you to make this movie about him, tell him you'll make it if he'll take the money back and let it be known he's not looking for Tony's head anymore. That's all you got to do. He'll go for it. I know he'll go for it. He asks you why, tell him old-times' sake. Tell him you been through some shit with me: he knows that anyway."

"But I don't make movies. The stuff I do, it's nothing like a movie."

"It don't matter," Tony said. "You're not listening to me. Tell him you're going to get Stephen Spielberg to direct the thing. Tell him Clint Eastwood's going to play him, and it'll open in a million theaters all over the world. Tell him anything. It doesn't matter. In a month, he'll be dead." Tony touched Jim's knee. "This isn't going to cost you, Jimmy. You keep me alive, and it doesn't cost you anything."

"Except," Jim said. "What happens if in a month he's not dead?" He looked through the dark car to Tony. Their eyes met. He said, "I'm sorry, Tony. I can't do this."

"Yeah, you can," Tony said, without hesitating. "Remember those two guys in Soho? Their friends got a long memory, Jimmy."

⑤

"You'd blackmail me?"

Tony took the Beretta out of its holster and laid it on the console. "Take this if it makes you feel safer. This is my life we're talking about. If you won't do it because it's decent, because you owe me at least something—then you force me to push a little."

ᔑ

Jim looked out the window, at the litter in front of the building. Then he got out of the car, holding the envelope. When he reached the glass doors, he found that they were locked. Beyond them, there was a small, empty space and then another set of glass doors leading into a carpeted lobby where a young man wearing a crisp white shirt, a thin yellow tie, and a light-weight navy-blue jacket sat at a desk. He was watching a portable television. Jim knocked on the glass and when the man didn't look up, he grabbed the handles and rattled the door. The man at the desk jumped, startled. When he focused on Jim, he looked him up and down a moment. Then he hit a button. Jim heard a click and he pulled open the glass doors. When he reached the second set of doors, they were locked. The young man grinned and pointed to a telephone hanging on the wall next to the doors. Jim picked up the phone. The man put a handset to his ear. Jim said, "Ellis Tyler. Top floor."

The man stared at him through the door as he spoke into the handset. "Who are you?"

"James Renkowski."

"James Renkowski don't tell me a thing, Ace." The grin had disappeared. "What do you want?"

"I'm looking for Ellis. I'm an old friend."

"An old friend," he repeated. The grin reappeared—more a sneer than a grin. He put the handset down on the desk and then pulled another phone in front of him by yanking at a gray wire. He punched a few numbers and spoke to someone. Then he hung up and stared at Jim unblinking until an elevator door at the back of the lobby opened and another two young men stepped out. Like the kid at the desk, they were dressed neatly, wearing white shirts and narrow ties under

ᔑ

summer jackets. When they reached the first set of doors, there was a loud click and they pulled the doors open. They both nodded casually toward him in the way of a greeting. Jim nodded back.

The ride up was quick. His two escorts stood one on either side of him. They were relaxed and quiet, and he didn't feel any pressure to speak. When they reached the top floor, the elevator opened onto a small carpeted area where two chairs bracketed a door that looked as though it were made of solid steel. One of the young men sat down heavily, as if tired, and the other opened the metal door.

Jim hesitated a moment and then stepped into a room that was dark and smelled of incense. His shoes partly disappeared into a plush black rug. The room contained a black leather couch and, positioned in front of the couch, a teak coffee table. Jim was about to take a seat on the couch when Ellis wandered into the room. He entered casually, his eyes on the floor, hands in his pockets, absorbed in his thoughts. When he looked up he appeared almost surprised to see Jim. "This is a shock," he said, his voice soft, close to a whisper. "You're one person I thought I'd never see again." While he spoke, he kept his hands in his pockets. He was dressed immaculately. His clothes—the dark blue suit and silk shirt buttoned to the collar—were tailored to a body thin and lanky as a marathon runner's. He was tall, six-foot something, and—just as Jim remembered—he stooped slightly, habitually, from the shoulders down, in the manner of a tall man used to dealing constantly with shorter people. His long hair was slicked back on his head and he wore glasses with thin lenses in a sleek frame. He said, "You've caught me at an awkward time, Jimmy. I have a business meeting coming up."

It took Jim a moment to respond. When he spoke, he was surprised at the ease in his voice and manner. "Ellis," he said. "You look different."

"You think so?" Ellis spread his arms and looked down at himself. Then he seemed to remember. "That's right," he said. He pointed at Jim and his eyes brightened a little. "You knew me in my fat days." Then he put his hands back in his pockets. "A long time ago, Jimmy."

"You look good."

"I'd invite you in. . . ."

"No," Jim said. "That's okay. I'm here because of Tony." He reached into his jacket pocket and took out the manila envelope.

Ellis touched his fingers to his temples. "I should have guessed," he said. Then he added, as if surprised at himself. "It didn't occur to me."

Jim said, "It wasn't a meeting I was prepared for either." He extended the money toward Ellis.

Ellis took the envelope, fanned through the bills, and tossed it onto the coffee table. He said, "Come in for a minute."

Jim followed Ellis through a series of dark rooms into a large, open area that appeared to serve as a combination living room-bedroom-dining room-bath. One wall was a line of open windows with a view of the Manhattan skyline. A line of crepe curtains fluttered in a breeze. The other walls were solid and barren: no art, no ornamentation of any kind. In one part of the room a teak dining table was surrounded by straight-backed chairs. In another part of the room, a queen-sized bed in a teak frame. Next to the bed, a free-standing, marble bathtub with brass claw legs. Next to the bathtub were three brass buckets the size of small garbage cans. As he walked past the open windows, his knees went loose and watery from the height. He glanced down at the street and noticed, several blocks away, a newspaper kiosk next to a public telephone.

Ellis said, "I'm sorry I can't be more sociable, Jimmy." He took a seat on the couch and motioned Jim to sit across from him.

Jim took a seat, and Ellis made a gesture with his hands indicating Jim should talk.

"He wants you to take the money back."

"What does he think, because we all used to be friends. . . ."

"Something like that," Jim said. "He asked me to cut a deal with you."

"A deal?"

"He thought you might be interested in having me do a movie. About you. About your life. He thought—"

꩜

"A movie?" Ellis said. "You don't make movies, Jimmy." He opened his hands, as if to ask Jim what he was talking about. "I've read about you. I saw your show. What you do, it's a kind of poetry."

"That's true," Jim said. "But I thought—"

Ellis put his hand up. "Stop, Jimmy. Don't embarrass both of us. Tony's not worth it." He turned around on the couch and leaned toward the windows, drawing in a deep breath of air, as if he needed the fresh air to help him breathe. He filled his lungs and exhaled slowly. Then he turned back to Jim. "The fool tried to steal from me. He took an envelope with ten thousand dollars and replaced it with one with a few hundred. He thought I wouldn't notice. If I ever see him again, I'm going to kill him. If anybody who works for me ever sees him, they'll kill him." Ellis leaned forward. "There's nothing you can do for him."

Jim said, "Ellis. . . ."

"Jimmy." Ellis's face tightened, a hard note came into his voice. "Come here," he said. "Let me show you something." Ellis put his hands on his knees and lifted himself from the couch as if it were an effort, and Jim followed him into an adjacent room with an eight-foot long and three-foot deep rectangular structure situated at its center like an altar or a cenotaph. The structure was covered with red drapery. At the back of the room was a worktable with a huge metal vise at one end. On the worktable, a chain saw rested next to a power drill and a set of pliers. A machete at least three feet long hung on the wall above the table. The blade was blood-stained, and there were lines of blood on the wall.

Jim said, "How long you been into woodwork, Ellis?"

Ellis looked at the worktable and then back to Jim. He didn't laugh. He pulled the red drapery off the structure, revealing it as a freezer with a thick black wire that trailed off into the black carpet. He said, "This is something I learned from you," and lifted the heavy white door of the freezer. Inside was a young man in a blue New York City police uniform. He looked like he wasn't yet twenty years old. His skin was an ugly, deep hue of purple. His eyes were open under bushy black eyebrows. Half his body was encased in ice, as if he were floating in it—his chest and face and the tops of his legs protruding above the cloudy surface.

Jim said, "You didn't learn this from me, Ellis."

"When you were just coming up, you cracked a guy's head open with a blackjack. Big public place, some bar. Everybody knew who you were."

"You've got the wrong guy. Never happened."

"No I don't, Jimmy." Ellis grasped the edge of the freezer with both hands and leaned over it, looking down at the frozen body. "I'll tell you something nobody else knows." He looked back at Jim, still leaning over the freezer. "I didn't kill him. He's like road kill. I found him. That's why the cops have no idea. There's nothing to connect me. I just saw him on the street, threw him in my trunk, took off. But I tell all the pieces of shit I have to deal with, all the small-time push-ers—like you used to be—that I wasted him. They come in here, see a dead New York cop in a freezer, they'd put an ice pick through their mother's heart before they'd screw me."

Jim turned his back to the freezer. Through the room's open door, he could see the living room windows and the lights of Manhattan.

Ellis said, "So now we don't have to talk anymore about Tony."

Jim didn't respond, and then Ellis was quiet for a time. When he turned around, he saw that Ellis was still leaning over the freezer, star-ing down at the frozen body, but his eyes seemed vacant. Jim said, "I'd better go then."

Ellis reached into the freezer and rubbed away frost covering the metal badge pinned to the cop's uniform. "Shield 3266," he said, and he closed the lid. Then he put a hand on Jim's back and led him out of the apartment, to the elevator, motioning the young men stationed outside the apartment to stay where they were. When the elevator doors opened, he put a hand on Jim's shoulder. "You got lucky," he said. "Don't let it get screwed up on you." Then he pushed him into the elevator and turned away before the doors closed. Jim watched him walk back to his apartment as the two young men stood on either side of the door, stiff as palace guards.

✿

Tony was waiting for him on the street, leaning back into the shadows of a small alley between apartment buildings. Jim had already walked past him when he stepped out of the darkness. "Jimmy," he said.

Jim laughed. He said, "You don't have to hide, Tony. It's straightened out."

"He went for it?"

"You're surprised?"

"No, I'm not surprised." He slapped Jim on the shoulder, a kind of congratulations or thanks. "I know Ellis, man. I know him like I know myself. What'd he say?"

"He's like a little kid. He's talking about who's going to play who, where we're going to shoot it, that kind of shit."

"And me? What'd he say about me?" He took Jim by the arm and pulled him back into the shadows.

Jim held Tony by the shoulders. "Look," he said. "I can't tell you he's happy with you. You have to go up and deal with him. You have to explain yourself to him."

"Shit. He's going to fuck me over, man. I know it."

"No," Jim said. "We have a deal. I make the movie, he doesn't hurt you."

"He doesn't *hurt* me, or he doesn't *kill* me?"

"He doesn't do anything to you."

"Are you sure, Jimmy? Because that fucking guy can hurt people so bad it's better to be dead."

Jim said, "No, Tony. This is a formality. This is for show. You got to go humble yourself up there. You know what it is. He'll make you grovel. He'll make sure the others see. You have to do it, Tony. Its for business."

Tony looked down at the ground, as if thinking things over. When he looked up, he said: "You sure about this, Jimmy?"

"Absolutely, Tony." Jim took Tony's hand and held it between his two hands. "It's cool," he said. "He wants Tom Cruise to play you in the movie."

Tony shouted, "Tom Cruise!" Then he laughed.

"All right, listen, can I go home now?" Jim reached into his jacket pocket for his car keys. "My wife'll be asking me questions for the next six months."

Tony stepped back for a moment, as if to look Jim over, and then embraced him tightly. "You saved my life, man. I got to thank you."

Jim whispered, "I just hope you're right, Tony. About Ellis not being around another month."

Tony stepped back. "Was I right about the movie?"

Jim smiled. Then he shook hands with Tony, and Tony hugged him one more time before walking away, out of the shadows and into the lights from the apartment building.

Jim watched from the driver's seat of his car as Tony waited for a short while on the street and then disappeared behind the glass doors. Within a minute or two, he heard the muted sound of shouting voices, one of the voices clearly Tony's. Then silence. He drove to the newspaper kiosk he had seen from Ellis's apartment and parked in front of the pay phone. When he stepped out of his car, he heard a scream, distinctly, but he couldn't tell for certain where it came from. He looked up and found Ellis's window. He kept his eyes on the window as he picked up the phone and dialed 911. He could see Ellis's apartment. The crepe curtains had been sucked out by the breeze. They fluttered over the street. He gave the operator Ellis's name, the location of the apartment building, and the apartment number. He told her about the dead cop. The operator didn't sound interested. She wanted his name. He told her the dead cop's badge number and hung up. He drove a block or two away and found another place to park where he could still see Ellis's window. A second or two after he turned off the lights and ignition, two police cars sped past him. Then there were police cars and paddy wagons and unmarked cars speeding down every street and through every intersection in sight, sirens screaming. Ellis came to the window and looked out. His hair was wild. He was no longer wearing his jacket and his shirt was open to the waist, as if the buttons had all been ripped off. The three young men came and one pulled him away while another closed the window.

🌀

They disappeared and a minute later the sound of gun shots crackled over the street. It only lasted a minute or two, but it sounded like a thousand shots were fired in that time. Then Ellis appeared again at the window, this time in the arms of a burly cop. Other uniforms seemed to be wrestling with the cop who had Ellis. It was like a brawl going on. The burly cop broke away from the others and the window shattered and half of Ellis's body hung out the window for a second—and then he was flying toward the ground, his arms extended as if he were diving. Jim got out of the car and walked to the entrance of the apartment building, where a crowd was gathering behind police lines. He waited until the ambulances came and men and women in blue coats began carrying away bodies in black zippered bags. After he counted five bodies, he left.

On the way back to Stony Brook, he practiced not thinking. He tried to concentrate on his home and family, on his life with his wife and children, on projects that engaged him. When a disturbing thought or image came to mind—Ellis flying through the window, the shattered glass around him like the surface of the water breaking, or Tony embracing him on the street, thanking him for saving his life— when such an image or thought came to mind, he'd stop thinking and make himself go numb until it dissolved. Then he returned to thinking about his everyday life. But for most of the ride home he was numb and empty of thought, and at one point he got shaky with the fear that something terrible had happened, that his life would change, that he wouldn't be able to go on living the life he had built with Laura, for Melissa and Alice, for the new baby, and for himself. He shook his whole body, like a dog shaking water from its coat, and he told himself that he'd do what he had to do, like always.

ᔕ

At home, he found everyone asleep. In their bedroom, Laura lay on her back, with the baby alongside her in a cradle. Alice had crawled into bed with her. She lay on her stomach with her head snug against her mother's breast and one leg flung on top of her mother's knee. Jim quietly removed a pair of pajamas from his dresser, went to the

ᔕ

basement to shower, and returned to join Laura and the children in bed. He checked the alarm clock on the headboard. It was only a little after midnight. In an hour or two, Melissa would wake up and try to get into bed with everyone else. At nine years old, she was in the stage of regular bad dreams, and most nights Jim would have to hold her and comfort her, and convince her to go back to her own bed. She'd tell him, usually, that she knew it wasn't right, but she was afraid of her bed, she was afraid that there was something under it. He'd take her back to her room and show her there was nothing under the bed, and then he'd lie with her for a while as she huddled close to him, careful that no part of her body extended over the mattress. This night, he thought, he'd let her sleep with them.

Alongside him, Alice moved slightly and he lay the palm of his hand on her small shoulder, her soft skin warm and comforting. He tried to close his eyes, but they kept opening, as if with a will of their own. He imagined he was lying on a raft, a raft of birch logs strapped together, and got to the point where he could feel the bed rocking, as if it were floating, and in his mind's eyes he saw the white logs of the raft as they drifted over a sea of murky water—but still, he couldn't fall asleep. It wasn't until hours later, when the quality of the light began to soften and the first few birds began to chirp and squawk, when he started working out in his mind the structure for one of his video pieces, when he began thinking about images and the way he might put them together, the image of Ellis flying from the window, the image of the young cop in the freezer, the bodyguards, Tony— when he began shaping and structuring the project in his mind, when he knew for sure that one day he would begin to work on it, then the tension in his muscles eased up some, and he closed his eyes, and when the sun came up, he was sleeping.

ᔖ

RADON

In the summer of '88, when my older sister turned sixteen and started dating a thirty-four-year-old Amway salesman, my father discovered we had unacceptable levels of radon trapped in our house. That was ten years ago, though it doesn't feel like it. It was a presidential election summer, and in addition to Howard, Julie's new boyfriend, my mother was upset about George Bush's campaign tactics, which she called Nazi-like and un-American. My father was worried that Michael Dukakis might win the election and ruin the economy, and he was also upset because his favorite TV preachers were all in trouble—Oral Roberts said God was going to kill him unless he raised four million dollars soon, Jim Bakker was being revealed as a bisexual, and Jimmy Swaggart had been caught with a prostitute—but most of all my father was going crazy about radon, which he was convinced would give us all cancer, soon. And everyone was worried about AIDS, which I heard one newscaster describe as a plague that could eventually wipe out half the world's population.

Luckily, no one was worried about me. I was fifteen, an average student, on the baseball, football, and basketball teams, and my two best friends, whom I hung out with constantly, were Mary Dao and Allan Freizman. Mary—a year younger than us and a grade ahead of us—was the smartest girl in the district, and Allan was another all-around athlete, like me. One night that summer my parents were in the living room arguing. They had started out discussing politics and eventually got around, as usual, to radon and Julie's boyfriend. My father wanted to spend four thousand dollars to seal up and ventilate the basement, and my mother wanted him to do something about Howard. "Honey," my father said. "Breathing the radon trapped in this house is the equivalent of smoking ten packs of cigarettes a day." "Honey," my mother answered. "Your sixteen-year-old daughter is sleeping with an Amway salesman." Upstairs, in my room, I was searching my closet for a dark jacket. Mary, Allen, and I were meeting at McDonald's. We were casing a house we planned on robbing.

I don't really know which one of us started the whole robbing thing, but that summer was the beginning and end of it. No one in the world would have ever suspected us. No one did. We must have robbed a dozen houses, all told. In the beginning it was a game. There's not a lot to do on Long Island, so we'd walk around, through the developments. Pretty much, we'd wind up in people's yards, where we'd sit and talk and drink beer and smoke grass when we could get it, and we'd keep an eye on the people through their windows. One night Allan brought binoculars, hoping to catch a peek of someone getting undressed. We didn't. It turned out to be an old lady's house where we wound up. We had a couple of joints with us and Allan wanted to go hunting for a better yard, but Mary just wanted to get stoned. So we compromised. We'd get stoned where we were, and then go looking for a better yard.

Mary's skin looked like it was always deeply tanned. She had big eyes and black hair slicked straight back (she claimed she'd rather die than wear bangs) and pulled into two little ponytails that made her look pixieish, along with being so frail. But God, was she smart. She spoke Vietnamese, French, and English, all fluently; and she always had a book in her pocket. Half the time, Allan and I didn't know what she was talking about, and she knew we didn't know and went on anyway. It impressed us and I think she liked impressing us. Allan and I admired the hell out of Mary, and we were both trying to get her to take off her clothes.

That night in the old lady's yard, Mary was explaining our philosophies to us. "Rick," she said, sitting cross-legged under a tree, slightly above me. She toked on a joint, held the grass in, and then spoke as she exhaled, her voice high and thin. "You're a materialist," she said, pointing at me, the joint between her fingers. "You don't care about what you can't see or feel—and maybe use. But if you can't see it or feel it, man—you don't give a shit about it."

"You mean," I said, "that's like because I'm always saying how I want a hot red Ferrari Testarossa and a big house on the ocean."

Allan took the joint from Mary. He said, "You been watching too much *Miami Vice*, man."

I must have been stoned, because I remember rolling on the ground laughing at that.

"What about me," he asked Mary. "What am I?"

"You, man—you're a grade A, number one, no-holds-barred nihilist."

"A what-ist?"

"A nihilist. That means you don't believe in shit. Nothing. Nada." Mary picked up the binoculars and looked at the moon.

Allan thought for a moment, then said: "How do you say that again, what I am?"

"A nihilist."

"And what about you," I asked her. "What are you?"

"Me?" She handed Allan the binoculars and took back the joint. "I'm an existentialist."

We both stared at her.

"That's like a nihilist who's into self-delusion. Sort of."

Allan checked out the house with the binoculars. "Hey," he said. "Look at this."

And that's when it started. Allan had seen the old woman take some money out of a bowl and put it in her handbag. A few minutes later, a car pulled up the driveway and a man took her away. I don't remember who said what first, or if anybody even said anything—but we must have all been thinking the same thing, because a few minutes later we kicked in a basement window, climbed up a flight of stairs, and ran out the back door with the money. Later, Mary said it was the most exciting thing she had ever done. The money came to a little over eighty dollars, which we split evenly. That was a couple of months earlier.

The place we were casing—Allan spotted it driving home with his dad. Allan's father's an ex-cop who owns a topless bar on Jericho Turnpike. Or he did then anyway. Now I hear he's retired in Florida. Allan always said he didn't hate his old man because it would take too much energy. He said his father was a stupid drunk who didn't care about anything but screwing the dancers who worked for him. His mother he didn't know. She had left when he was a child. Allan told us that she had moved to Alaska and married a Husky. He said he couldn't blame her for wanting to move up in life.

The house he spotted was only a few blocks from his own. An ambulance had just driven away and a police car was parked at the curb. Allan's dad stopped to talk to the cop, the way he always did, and Allan overheard that the man who lived there was old and three-quarters dead, and kept a loaded gun in every room. At the mention of the guns, Allan said he slunk down in his seat and acted bored while trying to hear every word. The old man used to be important—something about something in World War II, but Allan didn't get the details. Now he refused to live in a home or with his children. The whole thing was too good to pass up. Guns were easy money in the city: we knew a pawnshop that bought them no questions asked. All we had to do was sit in the old guy's yard and wait for him to leave the house.

I couldn't find the dark jacket I was looking for, so I settled for denim. In the living room, Julie had joined the argument. From the top of the stairs, I could see my father sitting back in his La-Z-Boy like a reluctant judge, while my mother stood on one side of the chair and my sister on the other.

"I won't have this!" my mother said, slapping the arm of the chair. "I want you," she said to Julie, "to bring him here tonight. And I want you," she said to my father, "to tell him we'll have him put in jail if this doesn't stop right now." She looked at Julie. "I won't have this," she repeated.

Julie talked to Dad as if they were the only two people in the room. "This is nobody's business but mine," she said calmly. "I'm grown up now. I'll make my own decisions and I don't need any help from anyone."

My father had lain back and crossed his arms over his eyes, as if bracing himself for a crash.

"Dad," Julie said. "Look at me."

He lowered his arms. Julie's hair was bright red and shaved at the temples, short over the top, and long in the back, where it was dyed blond. She wore a gigantic crucifix dangling from her right ear, and a "Jesus is My Friend" T-shirt that was too small on her: it left a few inches of her stomach bare and her nipples struggling for freedom. Her pants, she had slashed with a razor from top to bottom, so from where I stood I could see she was wearing neon pink panties.

My father said, "I realize you're grown up now, Julie—"

My mother sighed.

"But," he continued, "Your mother has a point—"

Julie groaned.

"Why don't we compromise," he said. "Bring him over, just so that we can meet him."

"I don't want to meet him!" my mother screamed. "I want you to shoot the son-of-a-bitch!"

"See!" Julie yelled.

My father jumped up, excited. "You know!" he shouted, quieting them both. "We didn't always used to argue like this, did we?"

I thought to myself: this was extreme, granted, but, actually, yeah— they did always argue like that.

"Did we?" my father insisted.

"What?" Julie said.

"What? Radon—that's what!"

My mother covered her face, and Julie turned her back to him. They both sighed.

"Go ahead!" he yelled. "Treat me like I'm mad! I'm telling you, this poison we're breathing is half our problem."

For a moment, everyone was frozen: my mother with her face covered; my sister looking at the wall; my father glaring at both of them.

§

Then his shoulders drooped forward, and he left the room with tears brimming in his eyes. He went out into the yard.

My sister went to her room. As she passed me, she said, "What are you staring at, jerk-off?"

My mother looked up. When she saw me, her face brightened. I've always had that effect on her, even now. She says I'm the best thing in her life. "Rick, honey," she said. "Come here."

"I'm meeting Mary," I said, on my way down the stairs. My mother loved Mary. When she came to visit, they'd often sit and talk for hours while I wandered in and out, pretending to be interested. My mother never questioned what I was doing, as long as I was doing it with Mary.

By the front door, she put her arm around my shoulder. "Five minutes for your Mom," she said. "I need to talk to somebody sane around here."

We sat down on the front steps, under the dim yellow light. Behind us, the bug-zapper was working overtime: I can still hear the pop and sizzle of bugs getting fried. "Really, Mom," I said. "I've got to go in a minute."

"Did you witness all that?" she asked. "The whole pathetic scene?"

With me, my mother was always dramatic like that—like I'm this pure thing besmirched by a dirty world. "Maybe Dad's got a point about the radon," I said. "Do you know what it is—radon?"

"Yes," she said. "It's wishful thinking."

I looked down at the steps. I always hated it when she said things that I guessed made some kind of sense if you were smart enough to figure them out—which I never was. I blamed it on the teacher in her. She was a high school teacher.

"Your father," she said. "Your father's a fool. You know I don't love him anymore."

"I know," I said. "You've told me."

She looked at me. I guess she heard something in my voice. "I shouldn't do that," she said. "I know. Talk to you about your father like that—about me and your father." She was about to cry. Tears were building in her eyes. "It's just that . . . I need to. . . ."

"It's okay, Mom." I put my hand on her arm.

〽

RADON

"Poor Rick," she said. "You have so much to deal with. It must be hard, growing up now: the whole world literally falling apart, society degenerating the way it is."

"Yeah," I said. "It's tough."

"This Willie Horton commercial," she said, perking up. "Here's a man climbing into the White House on the shoulders of a rapist. Could anything be more cynical, more devoid of morality? What's happened to ethics in this country?"

I said, "Yeah." Which is what I always say when I don't know what the hell my mother's talking about.

"Reagan," she said, "coming on the television and lying to the American public like that, lying through his teeth—with *such* sincerity. Liar. Liar. Liar."

I was tempted for a moment to ask her what Reagan lied about. I liked him. I thought he was a good guy. But the temptation only lasted for a second. "Mom," I said. "I have—"

"Go ahead!" She gestured as if she were talking to someone standing in front of us. "Pollute the water, foul the air, destroy the planet! Who cares, as long as you make a buck? God Bless the almighty dollar in whom we trust!"

I tried again. "Mom," I said. "Mary's waiting. Okay."

"Sure," she said. "You go have fun. Between this greenhouse thing, ozone holes, nuclear weapons everywhere, and, God help us, this new plague, this AIDS. . . ." She stopped suddenly and took hold of my wrist. "Rick," she said. "You're not. . . . You haven't started. . . ."

"No," I said. "I haven't."

"Well, you know about condoms, though? Right?"

I stood up. "Yes," I said. "I'll see you later."

She hugged me. "I didn't embarrass you, did I?"

I shook my head.

As I was walking down the steps, she asked: "Have you read about the hospital waste washing up all over the East Coast? It's unbelievable what they've found: AIDS-contaminated hypodermic needles, vials full of AIDS-contaminated blood, a stomach lining, chopped off body parts, eye—"

☙

"No. I missed that," I said, walking into the shadows. I called back: "See you later, Mom." Behind me, she stood there by the front door, under the yellow light, and looked out at our quiet suburban street, her face a mixture of disgust and fear, as if in the line of dark houses and neatly mown lawns she saw something repulsive.

I always liked walking on Long Island. There you are, surrounded by millions of people—but they're all locked up tight in their houses, and you could just as well be on the moon as you pass by the blue television light coming from their living rooms fifteen feet away. It's nice: private. I always liked it. A few weeks earlier, I had sneaked out of my house at three in the morning to go over to Mary's. It was dumb, really. We hadn't done anything: touched each other, seen each other, nothing. Then we just decided one night—I'm fifteen, she's fourteen—that we'd do it: have sex, sleep together. So I climbed out my window at three in the morning, and Long Island's something different at that hour. It's changed. The streets are dark and quiet, hardly any cars on the roads. You can hear natural things: the wind shuffling leaves and branches, a bird chirping, that kind of stuff. When I got to Mary's, she had left a ladder leaning against the house, and I climbed up to her bedroom where she was waiting, kneeling by the window in a white cotton gown that pictured Sylvester the Cat looking over a picket fence at Tweety Bird. I should have known she wasn't serious.

Even if she were, I don't know that I could have done anything: I was so nervous about being in her house, her parents asleep a few doors over. Mary's parents were tough. I'm sure her old man would have killed me had he found me there. He used to be a colonel in the South Vietnamese Army. Mary obeyed her parents, but she said she didn't respect them. Her brother Robert was gay. According to Mary, he had been all his life. She loved him, and she used to love having him around the house when he was a teenager, in high school, and his friends were over all the time. They practically lived there, especially between three and seven—after school and before their parents got home. Then, when Robert was sixteen and a junior, his parents found out and everything changed. They sent him away to school and forbade Mary to even mention his name. The parents paid his bills and pretended he was dead. And lost Mary's respect. She said her life had never been the same after Robert went away. She was never as happy as she used to be when Robert and his friends were always around the house. They paid attention to her, she said. They treated her like a princess.

In her room, Mary took me by the hand and led me to her bed, where we crawled under the sheets together. She had a flashlight there, and I had this feeling like I was seven years old again and playing Tent on a sleep-over. Mary was happy. I could see it. She smiled and held my hand and her eyes were mischievous and bright. I didn't know a lot about sex then, though I had seen enough of it on television to know I was going to have to get past Sylvester and Tweety before anything happened. Mary had started talking about the heat, which was unbearable that summer, in the 90s and 100s day after day; and everybody was talking about the greenhouse effect. Mary was getting into what was going to happen when the polar ice caps melted, flooding the poor, underdeveloped countries where the people were already suffering terribly. She said, "Thousands of children die every day from hunger. Right now. Imagine what will happen when their whole country turns into a giant lake."

I put my hand on her breast.

She smiled. "The industrialized nations," she said. "They'll have the technology to just pump—"

I tried to pull up her gown.

She pushed my hand away.

"Mary. I thought we said—"

"We did. But I'm worried about AIDS."

"Jesus," I said. "You sound like my mother."

"I like your mother."

"I know you do." She had been to the house a few days earlier and spent most of the evening talking to her. "Mary," I said. "We're both virgins."

Mary lay back on her pillow and let the sheet settle over her like a shroud.

"How can you be worried about AIDS if we're both virgins?"

She said, "You could have gone walking on the beach and stepped on a needle. It's possible."

"I'm going to kill my mother."

Mary grinned. "Mother-killing. I read about a primitive culture once. . . ."

Mary went on, but I stopped listening. Every once in a while I'd reach over and touch her breasts and she'd let me, but if I tried anything more, she'd just say "AIDS, you know," with this look like there was some kind of joke going on that I didn't get. I stuck around till daybreak anyway, and from then on after that I was always grabbing feels off Mary whenever I could get her alone, which I was constantly trying to do. Years later I found out from Allan that he had had about identical experiences with Mary, only she had never let him into her bedroom in the middle of the night—which I was unreasonably pleased about.

When I reached McDonald's, Mary and Allan were waiting in the fenced-in playground area, sitting under a ten-foot plastic statue of the hamburglar.

Allan said, "How come you're always late, man? You'd be late to your own funeral."

Mary said, "So what's up with Julie and her new dad?"

Mary had this thing that Julie was seeing Howard because Dad was a nonentity and she needed a father she could love. "Same stuff," I said. We left McDonald's and started for the old man's house. "My father's still got radon on the brain."

"Didn't you tell him," Mary said, sounding exasperated, "that radon's not a problem in this part of the country?"

"He says the tests show radon."

Mary put her hand over her eyes. "I told you," she said. "You can't trust those tests. They're rip-offs."

"But he had some professional radon guys check it out."

"Oh, great." Mary laughed out loud. "What are they charging him to get rid of it?"

"Four or five thou."

Allan joined in. "What are you saying, Mary? They're ripping him off?"

"It's a possibility." Mary rolled her eyes.

Allan thought for a moment. "You think we could pull off something like that?" He jumped in front of us. "Radon Busters! We be fast, radon be slow!"

"We're too young," Mary said. "You have to be an adult to work that kind of rip-off."

"Oh," Allan said. "Too bad."

When we got to the old man's house, we found all the lights off. In the backyard, we sat by a Mimosa tree. Thick clouds had sailed in, and we couldn't see much at all in the darkness.

"What do you think," Allan said. "You think he's out?"

"I don't know." We had been there once before when all the lights were out, and then just as we were about to break a basement window, the television went on. Loud. Very loud. We could hear it clear all the way out in the yard. "Don't forget last time," I said. "This guy never keeps the lights on. He's weird."

"I wish he had a car," Allan said. "Then we could just look in the driveway."

Mary said, "That's very helpful, Allan."

"I was just saying."

Mary touched my arm. "Go kick in the window. If he's home, we'll just take off. The hell with it."

"Oh, yeah," I said. "And I get shot in the back."

"That's not Wyatt Earp in there. The guy's a hundred and fifty years old."

"Shit." Allan walked casually to the house and kicked in the basement window. He just stood there.

I looked at Mary.

"He's showing us what balls he has."

After a minute or two when nothing happened, he slid through the narrow window and disappeared.

Mary ran to join him. I checked all the windows one last time, watching for any movement, and then joined them.

The basement smelled like no one had been in it for years, musty and damp. Allan was searching the place with his penlight, looking through cardboard boxes and inside closets. Mary and I took out our penlights and looked around. When Allan started up the stairs, we followed. At the top of the steps, a door opened on a dark corridor.

"Let's search the rooms together," Mary whispered.

"Over there." Allan pointed his light at an open doorway.

"This is the part I love," Mary said, almost to herself. "It's so exciting. You never know what you'll find."

Inside the room, I said in a normal voice, "How come you're whispering when we're the only ones here?"

Mary shushed me. We were in a den, and Allan was searching through the drawers of a roll-top desk. "Bingo," he said, and dropped a Colt 45 on the desk top. "This guy's a regular cowboy." He spun the barrel. "Loaded."

From the other side of the room, I heard a loud click and then Mary: "Holy goddamn shit," she said. "It's open." I turned to see her kneeling in front of a safe. The thing was three feet high and must have weighed five hundred pounds.

Allan said, "Won't be anything in it," and went back to searching the desk.

Mary grabbed the handle and pulled the door open.

I knelt behind her. Inside the safe was a small open area full of papers, and then a bunch of compartments with little round keyholes. Mary tried one and found it locked. "Shit," she said. They didn't look like the kind of compartments you could break into without plastic explosives. I reached around her and pulled the papers out. They were mostly insurance policies and legal documents. One was an 8x10 picture of an old guy who I guessed was the guy that lived there. He was dressed in all that long black Jewish gear. "Shit," I said and turned back to Allan. "I think this guy's a rabbi or something."

"So, man?" Allan sounded pissed. "I'm supposed to give a shit?"

Mary said, "He didn't mean anything."

"Hey!" Allan hurried around the desk. For a second I thought I had gotten him mad enough to fight me, but it turned out he had found a key inside an envelope. He crouched beside Mary and tried one of the compartments. The key turned and he pulled out the drawer. It was full of hundred-dollar bills. Mary whipped the drawer out and started counting, and Allan unlocked the other compartments. They were all stuffed with money—mostly hundreds, some fifties and twenties. "Oh my God," I kept saying. Mary said, "Jesus" every time Allan opened another drawer. By the time he pulled out the last compartment, Allan was laughing out loud, Mary was repeating "Jesus, Jesus, Jesus," and I was slapping them both on the back and whooping.

"Fifteen, twenty thousand," Mary whispered.

"Vacation in Vegas," Allan said. "Shit, we'll go to Monaco!"

"I'm putting mine in CDs," I said. "I'll be rich by the time I'm twenty."

Mary said, "You're such a—"

Behind us, there was a fourth voice. It was small and thin. "Bobby?" it said. "Rose? Is that you?"

We all three turned around slowly, and all three of us looked at the gun on the desk top. It was strange. We didn't yell, or make a sound out of fright, or jump for the gun—we just turned around slowly and looked. Perhaps it was because the voice was so small none of us were sure at all that it was really there.

In the doorway, an old man was bent over behind a walker. "Is that you?" he repeated, sounding a little frightened this time, and then he reached up and switched on a light.

Allan and I leapt across the room simultaneously and hit him so hard we knocked him the length of the hallway. He slid back and banged into a closed door. I shut off the light and in another couple of seconds Allan had pulled two trash bags out of his jacket, thrown all the money into them, and handed one to Mary. We went out the back door and tore through a trail of back yards until we neared Allan's house.

"Damn," Allan said when he caught his breath. He was smiling. "That guy flew like he had wings, man! He must have thought a truck hit him!" He laughed.

"Shit," I said. "I was scared to death. I thought sure the old son-of-a-bitch would be carrying an assault rifle or something! I thought we were dead, man!"

"He couldn't have hit you with a bazooka," Mary said. "Here. How come I'm carrying this?" She swung the bag of money over to me.

Allan said, "How much you think we got?"

Mary didn't answer. Allan and I got quiet, because when Mary didn't answer, it meant she was mad.

By the time we reached Allan's house, it was drizzling. The light was on in his father's bedroom, so we crossed around to the side of the house, toward the entrance to his basement, which was finished like an apartment. When we passed the kitchen window, we saw a naked girl by the kitchen table, and we froze because she was only a few feet away from us. She was standing there taking the last bites of a sandwich as calmly as if she were fully dressed in the privacy of a locked-up room and not stark naked directly in front of an uncurtained bay window. She had long blond hair and a body that made me stare, even though Mary was right there. The girl didn't look a hell of a lot older than us, and the letters LDB were tattooed once in a diagonal line across her right breast, and once again where her pubic hair should have been but wasn't. The letters were tattooed so low there that if she ever let her hair grow back they'd be covered entirely. She finished the sandwich, wiped her mouth with the back of her hand, and left the kitchen.

"Ouch!" I looked at Mary. I was trying to make a joke, because I was a little embarrassed about the way I had stopped and looked. "You think that tattoo hurt?"

Mary was standing with her hands on her hips. "I don't know," she said. "I heard branded cattle don't really feel it."

Allan said, "Another dancer—my dad's latest. Come on." Inside the basement, we emptied the money onto a poker table, and Allan pulled down all the shades and locked the door to upstairs. Mary sat at the table and started counting. Allan stood across from her. "So what are you so pissed about?" he asked.

"You didn't have to hit him so hard," Mary said, without looking up from the money. "You probably killed him."

"Get out of here!" Allan said.

I said, "We didn't kill anybody." It turned out later that I was right, though we did break the old guy's hip.

๛

"You still didn't have to hit him so hard," Mary said, counting faster.

Allan leaned over the table. "What are you, feeling guilty?"

Mary didn't answer.

"Shit," Allan said. "What's an old guy like him need it for?"

"All he's going to do is leave it to his kids," I said. "And I don't see them doing anything for him."

Mary looked up from the money. "Twelve thousand, four hundred."

"Man," Allan said. "I thought it was more."

"Me too," I said.

Mary divided the money into three stacks. She took one, wrapped it in her bag, and stuffed the bag into her jeans. "This is the last time for me," she said and started for the door. "I'm not doing it anymore."

I grabbed my money, bagged it, stuck the bag under my shirt, and hurried to catch up with Mary.

Allan threw himself across the table. "Hey, come on guys! Why don't you stick around awhile?" He gestured toward the ceiling, meaning he couldn't go upstairs because of his father.

Mary was halfway out the door. "Can't you just go up and go to sleep?"

"Too many funny noises." Allan grinned.

Mary hesitated, as if she might change her mind and stay—which I hoped she wouldn't because I was looking forward to being alone with her. Finally, she said, "Just go to sleep down here, Allan." She walked out.

"I got to go," I said. "I told my parents—"

Allan waved me off. As I closed the door he was counting his money.

I walked Mary back to her house. The clouds had blown over and it had stopped raining. We hardly said a word to each other until we reached her block. I always knew she was more sensitive about things than she let on because of how she talked about Robert, and because of that night I spent at Mary's: once when she had fallen asleep for awhile, I looked through a bunch of books she had lined up under her window, where she liked to lie and read, and they were all

ॐ

books on philosophy and religion, the kind of stuff I don't think any-body even writes anymore, and there was another book too, about the Vietnam War, something Mary never talked about, and when I opened it up, I found things underlined, including the number 13,500,000, which wasn't just underlined but circled, and it turned out to be the number of Vietnamese killed and wounded in the war—which surprised me, because I always thought it was such a small place that I wouldn't have guessed there were that many people in the whole country.

When we reached her house, all the lights were out. Mary said, "My parents must still be in the city. I thought they'd be home by now."

"Can I come in, then?" I asked. "Come on—we can just forget about tonight."

"Why?" she said. "Why do you want to forget about some old blind guy we just beat up and robbed?"

"He wasn't blind and we didn't beat him up."

"Christ," Mary said. "He was mostly blind—that's why the lights were never on in the house. And he was mostly deaf—that's why the TV came on so loud. He's probably a little senile too. I'll bet anything he thought we were his kids. I'll bet anything he's got children named Bobby and Rose. And I still won't be surprised if I read in the paper tomorrow that you guys killed him, you hit him so hard."

"We didn't kill him," I said. "All we did was knock him down the hallway so we'd have time to get out. You know," I said. "Nobody had to drag you into this. You liked the whole thing as much as we did."

"Because it was a game. We were stealing little shit. We weren't hurting anybody."

"Come on, Mary: insurance'll cover the guy's losses, plus he's got kids who can take care of him. Plus he's so goddamn old, what's he going to do with the money?"

Mary just looked at me. She said, "You don't believe in anything, Rick. Nothing at all."

I took a step back. Without thinking, I said, "What's there to believe in?" Then I added, quickly: "I know what I believe. I believe that you and I should make love, the way we said we would, because I don't know what the hell we're waiting for."

Mary nodded, as if agreeing with herself about something. She was quiet for awhile, and we both stood there on her doorstep staring at each other. Finally, in response to my proposal, she smiled and said, "AIDS, you know."

"Stop that shit." I moved closer to her. "We're virgins. We can't have AIDS."

She shook her head. "I'm not a virgin. I had sex when I was twelve with one of Robert's friends, and now I found out he has AIDS. So does Robert. That's where my parents are tonight. Making arrangements for him to stay in a hospice in the city."

My knees got that feeling, like they'd turned to water, and I felt shaky and chilled. I was thinking about the times I made out with Mary, how we'd stuck our tongues in each other's mouths. I didn't say it, but Mary knew what I was thinking.

She said, "You can't catch AIDS from kissing," and went into her house and closed the door. That was the end of it. I never saw her again, except at school, and she never said another word to me or Allan.

I walked home telling myself you couldn't catch AIDS by kissing, and by the time I got home I had myself pretty well convinced, but I couldn't help feeling a little nervous about it anyway. On the porch, I checked to be sure the money was well hidden under my shirt, and I tried to look casual as I walked through the front door. No one was in the living room, but the door to the basement was open, and Julie and Dad and a guy I guessed was Howard were all crawling around on their hands and knees. They looked like they were grazing. They didn't notice me and I walked by the open door and found my mother alone in the kitchen with the lights off, sobbing. I didn't know what to say, or if I even wanted to say anything, but she had seen me, and I couldn't just ignore her. "What's wrong?" I asked.

She shook her head.

I pointed to the basement. "Is that Howard with them?"

She nodded.

"What are they doing down there?"

"Looking for cracks," she hissed. "Howard sold your father some gunk to seal up the cracks and keep the radon out. The three of them are down there like a little happy family sealing up the basement."

"Oh," I said. I had forgotten about Dad's radon problem.

"You know what he told your father?" she asked, still hissing. "That they were just friends. That they had a 'platonic' relationship. That's what he said." She spit out the word. "*Platonic.*"

"Right," I said. Julie had been sleeping with the guys she dated since she was thirteen. At fifteen she had an abortion, and after that my mother put her on the pill.

"And he believes her," my mother said. She started crying again.

I left her there in the kitchen sobbing and went up to my room. I undressed and stuck the money under my pillow and got into bed, and for some reason that little time between getting into bed and falling asleep is what I remember best and sharpest about that night. It's a vivid memory—clear and troubling in a way I can't pin down. I think now that I was in love with Mary, and I remember that night because that was the end of it—but it's something more too. Like it means something, but I don't know what. I've never stolen anything since, and neither, I'd guess, have Mary or Allan. They both went on to college, as I did, and now Allan does something with some corporation, and Mary's married and has kids—so she didn't have AIDS after all. I never heard what happened to her brother, but I'm sure he's dead by now. I'm an engineer with Toshiba. I'm still single, I screw around a lot, but someday I want to get married. I never spent my four thousand from the robbery. It's mixed in now with a few thousand more, all in CDs. I can't say I ever really felt guilty about the robbery—so that's not what bothers me in the memory. It's something else. I'm in that bedroom waiting to fall asleep, the money's under my pillow, Mom's crying downstairs, and Dad and Julie and this guy Howard are crawling around trying to seal up the basement—and it all feels like it means something that it's somehow beyond me to understand. It's like one of those dreams when you've lost something important, when something tremendously important is missing, and you don't even know what it is.

ᔥ

PETRIFIED WOOD

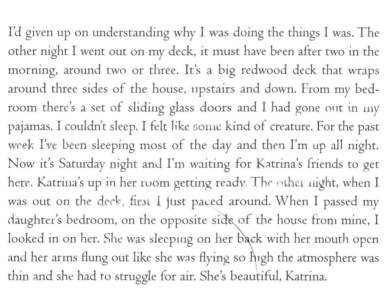

I'd given up on understanding why I was doing the things I was. The other night I went out on my deck, it must have been after two in the morning, around two or three. It's a big redwood deck that wraps around three sides of the house, upstairs and down. From my bedroom there's a set of sliding glass doors and I had gone out in my pajamas. I couldn't sleep. I felt like some kind of creature. For the past week I've been sleeping most of the day and then I'm up all night. Now it's Saturday night and I'm waiting for Katrina's friends to get here. Katrina's up in her room getting ready. The other night, when I was out on the deck, first I just paced around. When I passed my daughter's bedroom, on the opposite side of the house from mine, I looked in on her. She was sleeping on her back with her mouth open and her arms flung out like she was flying so high the atmosphere was thin and she had to struggle for air. She's beautiful, Katrina.

Her looks are only one of the miraculous things about Katrina. I'm downright ugly. I've got one of those W. C. Fields noses and black, bushy eyebrows that meet in a knot of hair at the bridge of my nose. Plus I'm short and I have a beer gut. My wife was no beauty either. Then here comes this kid who looks like an angel. Katrina has bright green eyes and thick strawberry-blond hair that she wears shoulder-length and is always striking the way it curls. She's twelve years old now, three weeks away from thirteen. When she was five, she turned

off some cartoons she was watching and said she would never watch
television again because it was violent and sexist. She got the sexist
from her mom. Katrina's never watched television since, but basically
she's just extremely bright and perceptive. Her little brother, Alex, used
to treat Katrina like his mom, even though she was only two years
older than him. Any time he had a serious question, he'd go to Katrina. It made her mom jealous.

We never talk about Katrina's mom and her brother. It's been five
years. I stopped thinking about it. That's another miraculous thing
about Katrina: how she's dealt with it all. She was especially close to
her mom. Alex adored her: there was none of the sibling tension you'd
expect between kids only a couple of years apart. Afterwards, I
thought Katrina would act up. The doctors said to look for it. The
way her seat belt restrained her may have kept her alive by keeping her
from being thrown from the car, but it also tore her up inside, her
inner organs. She was on the operating table for eight hours. She's fine
now. There was no permanent damage.

Katrina and me, we stayed alive.

I was uninjured, not as much as a bruise. I was the only one who
wasn't hurt at all.

We were coming back from a party. I was fooling around behind
the wheel, making everyone laugh, turning off the lights to make the
kids squeal, swerving to make them scream. Everyone was laughing.
We were having a good time. They trusted me. They trusted me
enough to let me scare them without really being scared—because
they believed I would never do anything really stupid, really dangerous.

But I did. I missed a curve.

Now Katrina wants to go out on a date. This request was followed
by the announcement that she's going steady with Jamie and that she
loves him.

She's twelve.

We were in the kitchen when she delivered the news, last Monday,
a school morning. I was at the sink, looking out the window. It wasn't
quite light out yet. The sky was the color of slate. The darkness
was fading out of it. To my left the microwave was humming, the

red seconds ticking down toward zero while Katrina's instant oatmeal cooked inside it. Katrina was sitting on a stool at the counter fiddling with a spoon.

She said, "Dad?"

I said "Yes," sharply, still grumpy with sleep, still looking out the window. There are deep woods behind our house, and I was watching the way the trees seemed to be slowly gathering shape as the sky grew lighter.

Katrina put her spoon down. She said, "Is it okay if I go to the movies Saturday night with Jamie, and then to a party at Linda's after?"

My first response was to the mention of Linda's name. She's this friend of Katrina's that I can't stand. Linda has been giving me heartburn since she and Katrina became friends, back in third grade. Why Katrina likes her is beyond me. She's a foul-mouthed, aggressive, arrogant, antisocial little miscreant. The kid hates everybody and everything—except apparently Katrina. She hates all adults. She loathes and despises teachers. She thinks her classmates are all idiots. The girl is a storm cloud on legs.

I said, "Linda's?" My tone of voice making my feelings apparent.

"Well, it's at her house. I think her parents will be there."

"You *think*?"

She said, "You know Linda."

"Absolutely," I said. I knew Linda. I had a bet going with Jeff, a guy I do some work for, that she wouldn't make it to fifteen without getting pregnant. I knew for certain, having eavesdropped on a couple of sleep-overs, that there wasn't a sex act on record that she didn't have at least six ways of describing. From age nine, as far as I could tell, the only things Linda had any interest in were sex and loud music.

"What's that mean?" Katrina said. "*Absolutely.*"

I turned to look at her, my arms crossed over my chest. "It means I don't like Linda." Behind me the microwave began a series of four loud chirps, its annoying way of announcing that the oatmeal was done.

Katrina whispered, "Microbird."

We called the microwave Microbird because Katrina, once, in first grade, had made eyes and a beak out of yellow construction paper and taped them to the machine's side. We left them on because Alex used to run into the room whenever Microbird chirped.

I said, "I heard it, Katrina. Did you think I didn't hear it?"

The way she was sitting behind the white counter, with both hands wrapped around a black coffee mug full of juice, she looked almost grown up, a young woman on her way to a lousy job or a boring morning class at college. The green of her eyes seemed especially bright, and at first I thought it was just the green blouse she was wearing, until I noticed the thin black line around her eyes. "Are you wearing eyeliner?" I asked, even though I could see it plainly.

"Just real light," she said. "Just a little bit."

"Don't I get asked about these things anymore?" I could hear my voice getting louder. I could hear the anger in my voice. I turned around to get the oatmeal.

Katrina's voice dropped down so that it was barely audible, the way she always does when she sees that I'm angry. She said, "I'm asking your permission about Saturday."

"That's good of you," I said, not looking at her, looking at my own reflection in the black glass of the micro. I noticed the way my gut was pushing at the fabric of my robe. I noticed the gray in my unkempt hair, and the loose and unhealthy texture of my skin. Katrina's skin was so smooth and bright it seemed to vibrate. "Given," I said, not looking at her, "that I'd be picking up Jamie and driving you to the theater, and then picking you up after and driving you to the party, and then picking you up from the party and driving you both home, it's good of you to ask my permission."

Katrina spoke so softly I had to lean toward her to hear. She stumbled over some words, which she's been doing a lot lately. "Jamie's brother'll tak— take us. He's in college. We're going to go the movies with him and his girl— girlfriend. They'll take us to the party. You only have to take us home."

I took the oatmeal out. It was in a glass bowl and the bowl was hot, as always. I snapped it down on the counter in front of Katrina. "You've got this all planned, I see."

᭦

Katrina's eyes were getting watery. She's always been like she could read my mind. "You can't go," I said. "It's bad enough Jamie's fourteen, but you're not going to the movies with college-age kids. Period!"

"It's his brother," she said. She was crying then. She pushed the oatmeal aside and started for her room, but she stopped at the stairs to look back at me. "I love Jamie," she said. "We're going steady now. And Linda's my best friend!" She wiped her eyes with her arm, defiantly, and continued up the stairs.

When I heard her door close, I threw her bowl of oatmeal at the wall. It shattered, seeding the rug with glass. Ugly brown gobs of cereal dripped down the wall. I took my car keys from their hook above the sink and drove away, leaving Katrina to catch the bus and go to school without so much as a good-bye.

That was Monday and Katrina and I just stopped talking to each other. I usually get up and make her breakfast, and at least that gets me out of bed—but I've been sleeping through her breakfasts all week. I've been sleeping through most of the day all week. I haven't had any work for months. I'm in graphic design, and computers are putting me out of business. That's something else I'm going to have to deal with. Right now, though, it's Katrina that's the problem. Me and Katrina. The other night when I was out on the deck, the moon was bright and fat and full. It looked like a hole in the sky, a pale tunnel. This was Wednesday or Thursday. The way Katrina looked lying in her bed, on her back like that, like she was flying, I thought of how young she was and all the things there were in the world that were still mysteries to her. It made me want to steal into her room and kneel next to her bed and touch my cheek to her cheek, the way I used to do all the time when she was a baby. But we weren't talking and I hadn't done that in ages—and anyway she was getting too old for me to be creeping into her room in the middle of the night and hovering over her bed. And her door was locked. I could see through the window that the push-button on the inside knob was pushed in.

There's a flight of stairs that leads down from the deck to our yard, which is really very small but looks big because our property backs up against a few miles of woods. I don't go down to the yard much. There's nothing there but broken branches that need picking up and a few azalea bushes clumped together where I once had the idea to make a garden plot something like ten or eleven years ago. But I went down to the yard that night. I don't know why. It's three o'clock in the morning and I'm standing in the middle of my yard in my pajamas in the moonlight. The moon was so fat and white I had the urge to lean my head back and howl. I had a strong urge to howl—but I didn't, afraid to wake up Katrina. Instead, I unbuttoned my pajama top and took it off. Then I slid out of the bottoms and my underwear. I was thinking to myself: you're a short fat guy naked in your yard in moonlight. I walked around a bit, stepping gingerly over twigs and rocks. I stood at the point where my yard ended and the woods began, and I stayed still and looked hard, hoping I might see something, a deer or a raccoon, which there are plenty of in those woods, but I didn't see anything. Nothing moving. Just the moonlight on the bark of the trees and the still shadows of leaves and branches.

I can't say why I took off my clothes except it felt good to be undressed and exposed to the night air.

I leaned against a tree and pissed on a clump of leaves.

I watched the water spill out of me in a straight dark line.

I rested my forehead on the rough bark of the tree I was leaning against and I closed my eyes and tried to feel the night air and the moonlight. I stayed there a long time like that, until I guess I got bored. Until whatever it was that got into me got out of me and I went back to where my pajamas were lying on the ground. I picked them up and shook them out, and while I was shaking them out I saw, under the scraggly azaleas, a couple of small ceramic elves and a piece of petrified wood the size of a man's fist. I had bought the elves at a local nursery, as decoration, when I was planning the garden. Actually Michelle bought them, my then-wife, Katrina's mother. She bought the elves and I pulled the petrified wood up out of the basement. I had been carrying that chunk of rock around with me all my life and I was pleased to have finally found a place for it.

Michelle thought I was kidding. She asked, "Why would you want to put that out here?"

I didn't know why. Things at that time in our life were going especially well. Katrina was less than a year old; and having her, which we hadn't planned on, had changed things between us. We had been married a couple of years at that point and for a long time the marriage had been rough. We didn't know if we loved each other. We didn't know if we even liked each other. We fought a lot—about housework, about who should do what, about who was spending whose money. But things settled down after Katrina. We seemed to settle into the idea of the three of us, the pattern of it. Katrina did something to both of us. She filled us up. She turned us into adults.

I didn't know why I had pulled the petrified wood up out of the basement, where it had been since we moved into the house. I had been dragging it around all my life in a box full of junk, always stashing it someplace. Then all of a sudden I went looking for it, hauling it up into the garden where I thought it would make a good decorative piece.

What Michelle knew about the petrified wood was that my father damn near killed me with it. My father was one of the most bitter and frustrated men who ever walked God's earth. It wasn't that he was bad or mean, not essentially, it was just that he was full of frustration and anger. It shined out of him like a black light. There were five kids in my family, plus my mother, and we were all afraid of him. My father never reached his hand toward me that I didn't flinch. I can't ever recall a kind word from him. It had to do with not having enough money, with not getting enough respect. He was angry. He was always angry.

The petrified wood incident, that happened on a trip from Los Angeles to Brooklyn. My father was born in Brooklyn and lived all his life there, except for the one trip to the West Coast. He was in his thirties then and out of work for the umpteenth time. He went to Los Angeles to take a job working for a guy he had met in the army, and the job went great for about two years before he decided he wasn't getting paid well enough or promoted fast enough. He wound up punching out the guy who had originally hired him. Then he packed up his wife and his five kids and a few possessions, all in the beat-up old Dodge, and started back across country to Brooklyn. It wasn't a pleasant journey. We made the trip in a little over seventy hours, with my father driving night and day. He had a bad back and it started acting up early. Before we made it out of California, he was driving in pain. His back hurt so badly, he had a hard time sitting up straight in the driver's seat. I can remember my mom tying him into the front seat with thick yellow rope, to keep him upright, to keep him from slumping over against the wheel. That's the way he drove across the whole country, roped into the front seat.

We ate in the car and we slept in the car. We stopped only for food and for gas and for bathrooms—and the one stop I pleaded for, the one in Arizona. I wanted to see the Petrified Forest. I was ten years old, and something about the words *petrified forest* set my imagination going. I don't know what I thought it would be like, I don't know what I thought I'd see, but I risked my father's wrath and pressed him to stop.

"We could just stop for a few minutes, Dad," I said. "Just so we could see what it looks like, the petrified forest."

He didn't answer. My dad never talked a lot. But then, to everyone's surprise, when we got to the Petrified Forest National Park, he took us in. I remember this huge petrified log lying like a bridge over a ravine that must have gone down a hundred feet, maybe more. Other than that there wasn't much. I don't know what I had expected: a big forest with rock trees or something, but there was just a lot of rock-strewn ground and a lot of the rocks were really petrified wood. I picked up a piece and my mother told me to put it down. You couldn't take any of the petrified wood out of the park. It was illegal.

I took a piece anyway. I smuggled it into the car when no one was looking and I put it under the front seat. We only stayed at the park twenty minutes at the most, just long enough to use the rest rooms and look around a little bit before my father herded us all back in the car and back on the road. Then that night, when we stopped to sleep awhile, he found the rock. Actually, my mother found it. It was pressing up into the bottom of her seat, and she felt it when she was trying to go to sleep. She reached around and pulled it out from under the seat. She said, "What's this?" and then I could see by the look on her face, once my dad looked over at her, that she wished she hadn't said anything. He took it from her. She had been holding it with both hands, and I remember that when he took it from her I noticed how his hand was so much bigger than hers, how he was able to hold it in one hand with his fingers grasping its stony edges. "It's petrified wood," he said, and he looked right at me. He wasn't tied into the front seat then: my mother had untied him so that he could sleep more comfortably. He leaned into the back seat and held the chunk of petrified wood in front of my face. A car went by and its headlights swept over the wood, lighting up the deep purple and yellow and rust-red quartz. "Didn't you read the sign?" he said. "Didn't your mother tell you?" He was leaning over me then and I was wishing that he was still tied up; and I was looking at the muscles of his right arm, the arm that was holding the rock. His arm looked huge. I said, "I didn't take it," and then this look that was a mixture of disgust and disdain came over his face. Disgust and disdain mixed with surprise.

Of course I took it. He knew I took it. Everyone knew I took it. He looked at me for just a second longer, and then he hit me with the petrified wood. It wasn't an especially hard blow. I'm sure he didn't mean to hurt me as badly as he did, but the quartz edges of the petrified wood were jagged, and he opened a gash in the side of my head and I blacked out instantly. Later, when I got older and thought back on it, I realized that he had knocked me out and given me a concussion. When I opened my eyes again, I was in the front seat, in my mother's arms, and she was holding a blood-soaked towel against the side of my head, pressing hard. My father was roped into his seat again, driving fast. I saw the speedometer hit ninety and ninety-five. I threw up a half dozen times that night, and every time we had to stop my father got furious and cursed me and my mother. I can still remember that night vividly, how sick I was, speeding through the desert in my mother's arms, my father roped into the front seat like a restrained animal. We drove all night and in the morning the sun rose up bright red.

And then there it was again, in my back yard, that same piece of petrified wood. I put my pajamas on and pulled it out from under the

☙

azaleas. My mother and father were both long dead. I hardly ever saw my brothers and sisters anymore, not since I stopped going to family gatherings because it was too hard without Michelle and Alex. I picked up the rock, and just holding it in my hands made me remember him. It was as if I could see him standing in front of me, his face dark with anger that was always right there, just under his skin.

I've wanted all my life never to be like him.

I hurled the petrified wood toward the trees, meaning to throw it out into the woods, but it didn't make it that far; and then I went back into the house and went to bed and fell asleep quickly and slept through most of the day.

When Katrina came home from school, I told her she could go out with Jamie Saturday night. I told her she could go to the party and that I'd pick her up after. She gave me a funny look, like she wasn't sure she could believe me. She said, "Thanks," and that was it. She put her bookbag in the closet and went up to her room.

Now it's Saturday night and I'm out on the deck. Fully dressed. I'm wondering whether I did the right thing, telling her she could go to the party. I'm wondering what's going on with me. I'm still not sleeping at night. Nights I wander around the house or out on the deck—though I haven't paid any more naked visits to the woods. I can hear Katrina upstairs running water in the bathroom. It's eight o'clock and Jamie and his brother should be here by now. I'm thinking that I wish the kid weren't fourteen and that it was his father instead of his brother who was taking them to the movies. And I'm wondering about Katrina, just what she's doing with Jamie. I figure they're kissing, but I wonder if maybe they aren't doing more. Is she even old enough to do anything more, to want to do anything more? How do I find out something like that? What am I supposed to do about it? I'm thinking about this when I hear a loud car roaring down our block. Loud, like the muffler's missing. I'm praying it's not Jamie and his brother, but then I hear the car stop in front of our house and the car doors slam, and I know it's got to be them.

A minute later the front doorbell rings. I take a deep breath and hesitate a moment, wanting to put off for just a second or two the social act: the pleasant father receiving in a kindly manner his daughter's date and her chaperone. Then, before I've even turned around, I hear Katrina yell "Bye, Dad!" and open the front door. I'm in the house in a flash, but the front door is already closed. By the time I pull the door open and step out onto the lawn, Katrina is already in the car and the back door is closing as Jamie gets in. An older boy I assume is Jamie's brother is just opening the driver's side door.

"Hey," I yell. "Wait up a minute!" I'm furious now. My face is red and my fists are clenched—but I don't want it to show. I don't want to embarrass Katrina, even though she's just embarrassed me, making me feel like some kind of jerk who would let his daughter go out without even meeting her date. I try a joking manner. "What's up?" I say. "Are you guys on your way to a fire?"

The older boy offers me his hand. It's early May and the air is still damp from a recent rain. The lawn feels soggy under my shoes. I'm standing on the lawn, the car is parked at the curb, the street is dark. It's dark inside the car, an old Thunderbird. There's no light on in the car, even though the front door is partly open. I shake the boy's hand.

"Mr. Hillman," he says. "Hello." He's being polite. He looks like your typical, All-American college student: tall, well-built, baby-faced handsome. He's wearing a white denim jacket over a black T-shirt, and he looks like he might be high on something, maybe pot. His eyes are red and he has the manner of someone being careful to appear sober.

"Did you lose your muffler?" I ask, smiling broadly. I have to look up to look him in the eyes.

He smiles back and doesn't reply. He looks a little nervous.

I step around him and lean down and look into the back seat. I can't see much because the car is so dark, but I see the shape in the back seat that is Katrina. She leans against Jamie, her arm linked inside his arm, and the sight of her leaning against him like that—like he's her protector, like I'm the bad guy, makes me want to reach in there and grab the kid by the throat and shake him till he cries like the baby he is. Katrina says, "Hi, Dad," and the other shapes in the car—Jamie and an older girl in the front seat—say "Hi, Mr. Hillman" simultaneously.

S

Such a polite group. They make it so obvious I'm the enemy, the unsympathetic unhip outsider carrying a list of rules and regulations. The father. "Gee," I say. "I can't see anybody," and I reach into the car and turn on the interior light. Katrina smiles at me, an intensely nervous smile, but I hardly recognize her. She's wearing a black leather mini-skirt that I didn't know she owned. It comes down only to mid-thigh. I notice the mini-skirt first and then I see that she's wearing nylon stockings that turn her little-girl's legs into a woman's legs, smooth and shapely. I don't know what to say. I'm bent over awkwardly looking into the back seat, smiling like an idiot, trying to think fast, to figure out what I should do.

Katrina doesn't even look like Katrina. I turn away from her for a moment, with a small awkward laugh. She's wearing makeup that's been applied much too heavily: the rouge on her cheeks is too bright. She looks like a clown. The black lines around her eyes are a quarter-inch wide. She's even done something to the shape of her eyebrows. She looks like a child who has gotten hold of her mother's makeup—which is exactly what she is. All these years she's kept her mother's makeup in her bottom dresser drawer along with her jewelry. When I look back at her I see that she's wearing a pair of earrings that I bought for Michelle on our first anniversary. They're jade, expensive.

"Kat," I say, calmly, still smiling. "I wanted to talk to you about something before you left. Can you come back in the house for a moment?"

Katrina begins to protest. Something about the movie schedule, but I'm not listening. I turn around and walk back to the house. It occurs to me that they could just ignore me and drive off, and I know for sure if I hear that car start I'll be in mine in a second and I'll chase them down.

But the car doesn't start. I go back in the house and cross my arms over my chest and wait in the hallway. A moment later Katrina comes through the door. She's crying. Her mascara is running.

"Don't ru— ruin my night," she says. Her voice is defensive. She knows she's wrong. It's in her voice. She's praying I'll let her go. She's praying that I won't humiliate her. That's in her voice too.

❦

What am I supposed to do? She looks ridiculous. Am I supposed to let her go out like that? She looks up at me and even with all the makeup I can see her child's eyes. "Kat," I say. "You're twelve years old."

"I'll be thirteen next week," she says. And now the tears are flowing. Black circles are forming under her eyes.

I look down and cover my forehead with my hand as if I'm checking for a fever. "Kat," I say, without looking up. "Just take the makeup off and get changed. Just wash off the makeup and get changed, quick, and then I'll let you go out."

"I'm not getting changed!" she yells. "You a— a— always do thi— this! You make me so miserable!"

"I make you miserable?" I shoot back, my voice loud suddenly. "Is that what you said?"

"Ye— Ye— Yes!" She screams, frustrated that the word won't come out, stamping one foot for emphasis, like a caricature of an angry woman. "You hate me," she goes on, shouting, her words fluid now. "You wish I were dead too!"

I lean toward her, wanting to shout something at her, something I can't even remember once her final words register. The words hit like a punch, like getting hit in the stomach.

Katrina grabs the door knob and starts to leave.

I lean my weight into the door, slamming it closed. "How could you say that?" I ask. "How could you say something like that?"

"Because it's true," she says. She's talking on some other level now, in some new place. "You never say anything nice to me. You're always angry at me for something. You wish I weren't here. You hate me. You're always trying to embarrass me."

I look at her now, and she seems to be changing in front of me. The softness of her face is disappearing. She's growing denser, harder. Her beauty is disappearing. She's ugly in her face paint and her whore's costume. Her green eyes turn black. "Do you believe that?" I ask.

She doesn't respond right away. She looks up at me and I can tell she's waiting for me to tell her it's not true. She's forgotten about her date. She's forgotten about the car waiting for her outside. She's waiting for me. She's waiting for me to tell her what she needs to hear.

"Go on," I say. My voice is like a stone speaking. "Go out on your date."

Katrina doesn't move.

I open the door for her.

She looks at me for another second, then runs out.

I watch her hurry into the car and I watch the car drive away.

When she's gone, I go around the house turning off all the lights. Then I sit in the dark for a long time. My head is empty. There's not a thought in it. After awhile I get up and go out on the deck and down into the yard. I move slowly toward the trees. One by one, Katrina's words replay. Katrina's words and my responses. At my feet I see the petrified wood and I pick it up. Katrina's words and my words are replaying in my mind. What she said. How I responded. I'm standing at the tree line looking out into the woods, not seeing a thing. I press the flat and smooth part of the petrified wood against my chest over my heart like a stethoscope. It's cool and soothing. I'm tight all over, in my neck and my back and my face, my face especially. When I touch my face, my lips and cheeks, I realize that I'm sneering, that my teeth are clenched under lips pulled back in a sneer. I realize that if someone could see me, I'd look like a snarling animal, all I'd need is the low growl, and it surprises me because I didn't know my teeth were clenched, I didn't know my lips were pulled back. I rock on my heels. I'm like an old Jew at the wailing wall, only there's no wall and no prayers, not a sound, not a word, only my body growing rigid. When I let Katrina back into my head, the same anger comes, and I know if she were here now I'd strike her, I'd slap those words out of her mouth. I think, *that she could speak to me like that,* and then I feel it again, I feel my teeth grating, I feel my lips pulled back. The snarl returns and sinks down and through and into my skin. It covers my face like a mask. I see myself here in these woods as if watching from someplace else: the texture of my skin glitters in moonlight, the mask that hides my face becomes gradually heavy and fixed. It's as if I'm buried where I stand and a mineral-thick water is filling up my cells, a heavy, fixing water that seeps out of the night sky like mist.

VINNIE'S BOY, LARRY

Larry worried about Sunday as his dad drove fast over the cobblestones on Bushwick Avenue. He pushed himself up in his seat so he could look out the window at trees speeding by. On the dashboard a thick red line that moved like mercury in a thermometer edged across black numbers toward 50 mph. Patches of snow and ice covered much of the street's blond cobblestones. Above him, the crowns of the trees were coated with frost, and in the bright light of the morning sun, against the clear blue sky, each tree looked like an explosion of whiteness. Larry imagined he was in a jeep, zigzagging along a road in Italy during the war. Each burst of light was an exploding shell. He pushed his elbow into the heavy cloth of his winter coat and felt for the butt of the toy German Luger tucked into his belt.

If his dad saw the gun, there'd be hell to pay. Uncle Joey had given him the Luger for Christmas, and Dad and Uncle Joey were fighting. Larry's dad was always fighting with one of his six brothers. He was a Bragoniri, and that's the way the Bragoniri family was.

Last night Larry had been sitting in the living room with Carl and Susan, his older brother and sister, watching the Sid Caesar show, when a knock rattled the front door. Sid Caesar was dressed up as a caveman. He had a tiger skin wrapped around him and he was jumping up and down, sticking his hands in his armpits like a monkey. Larry's mom picked herself up off the couch, and then the door cracked and the lock broke and then the door flew open. Larry and Carl and Susan looked up and saw their Uncle Joey standing in the doorway. It was freezing out, but all he had on was a T-shirt. He had big muscles, Uncle Joey, and they looked even bigger bulging out of his armless T-shirt. Larry's dad came running out of the kitchen and Larry saw his father's first punch knock Uncle Joey off his feet before his mother scooped up him and Carl and Susan and hurried them into the bathroom, where they huddled together and listened through the closed door as the walls shook.

When the fight was over, all the kids had to go to bed, even though it wasn't bedtime. The bedrooms were on the second floor, up a dark flight of stairs. Susan went to her room in the front of the house, and Carl and Larry went up to the room they shared in the back. Larry was seven years old, in second grade. Susan was ten, a small girl with curly brown hair and dark eyes. Carl was thirteen, tall and skinny, with long, lanky arms and legs; and he was hard to talk to. He was interested in astronomy and he had his own telescope set up on a tripod by the back window. Under the telescope, on a small table, were some astronomy books. Carl put on his pajamas and fooled with his telescope while Larry got undressed and into bed.

Larry had a school chess tournament coming up in the morning, and his father was supposed to drive him. Because of the fight, he was worried that his father would forget about it. He was also worried about Sunday afternoon, when his aunts and uncles drove out for dinner at Seaford, on Long Island, where his grandparents had a big house with a lot of land. Every Sunday, after dinner, his Uncle Frank—who had taught him how to play chess—would show him something new about the game, and then they would play. So far Larry hadn't beaten his uncle, but he had gotten good enough to be the best player in his grade except for David Cook, who was the principal's kid and who was good at everything—besides being the best-looking boy in the class and the nicest. Larry wasn't even close to being the best-looking boy. The kids said he was dopey-looking, and he guessed he was, with his big Dumbo ears with their long fatty lobes, and his big eyes that always made him look sad. Plus, he was skinny, though not as skinny as Carl.

Larry pulled the cover to his chin and closed his eyes. When he opened them again the house was dark and quiet, and his mother was kneeling by his bed. "Is Dad still going to take me in the morning?" he asked.

His mother straightened the blanket over him. "He said he would, didn't he?"

"Will we still go to Grandpa's Sunday?"

"I don't know," she said. "We'll see."

On the way to the chess tournament, as the red line passed 50 mph, Larry tried to gather the courage to ask his father about Sunday dinner. He sat quietly in the passenger's seat, trying to think of some excuse for asking about Sunday. His father was hunched over, holding the steering wheel with two hands. His short, dark hair stood straight up on his head in a crew cut, and his mouth was set in a grimace, as if he were thinking of something that made him mad. He was wearing a khaki work shirt with the cuffs folded back on his wrists, and you could see the thick muscles of his chest and arms through his shirt. Finally, Larry gave up and just asked. "Dad," he said, "will we still be going to Grandpa's Sunday?"

His father turned away from the road, "Don't we go to Grandpa's every Sunday?"

Larry didn't ask any more questions. At the front entrance of the schoolhouse, his father pulled the car over. Larry slid quietly out the door and didn't look back to see his dad drive away.

The chess tournament was in the cafeteria, and when Larry walked into the big room with the tables lined up in rows, he looked around for David Cook first thing. He had taken the German Luger to the tournament so that he could show it to David, who liked guns but wasn't allowed to play with them. His parents, David said, wouldn't even let him play cops and robbers with the other kids in the neighborhood. Larry always brought one of his guns to tournaments for David to see, and David brought something for Larry. That way they had stuff to do between rounds while they were waiting to play each other to see who'd win.

Larry was still standing by the entrance looking around the cafeteria when Mr. Cook came up and put his hand on his shoulder. "Are you looking for David?"

"Yes Sir, Mr. Cook."

Mr. Cook was wearing slacks and a sweater, which was how he usually dressed at tournaments; but Larry still thought of him as the principal, and it felt funny to see him without a jacket and tie.

"I'm afraid David's going to have to miss this one." Mr. Cook shifted his hand to the small of Larry's back and led him to a table.

"Is David sick or something?"

Mr. Cook sat down across from Larry at a long, pale blue table. There was a chess set between them. He moved the white King Pawn to King Four.

Larry looked down at the pawn.

"David was attacked by a dog yesterday afternoon, and he doesn't want anybody to see him yet. He's going to be all right, but he doesn't want anybody to see him."

"What kind of dog was it?" Larry asked. "Did it bite him?"

"It was a Doberman pinscher," Mr. Cook said, "and it bit David several times before its owner could pull it off him."

"Why'd it bite him?"

"Because David went into its owner's yard without asking, and its owner had trained it to attack anyone who did that."

"Is David going to be okay?"

"Yes," Mr. Cook said. "He's going to be okay, but I'm afraid . . ." he stopped for a moment, as if looking for the best word. "I'm afraid he's going to be scarred for a while. Until we can get plastic surgery. The dog bit his face, and . . . and he's going to look pretty awful for a while."

"Did he have to get stitches?"

"Yes," Mr. Cook said. "A lot of stitches." He added, "I hope that you'll be a good friend to David now. He's going to need some real good friends. The other kids may make fun of him. If they do, I hope you'll be his friend and stick by him. Do you know what I mean, Larry?"

"Sure," Larry said. "I'll be David's friend."

Mr. Cook stood up. He moved the King Pawn back to its opening position.

"Mr. Cook?" Larry asked, "Why did the man want his dog to attack kids?"

Mr. Cook looked thoughtful for a long time. Finally he said, "I'm sure he never meant for kids to get hurt. It was his property. He felt he had the right."

"Oh," Larry said, and nodded as if he understood.

Mr. Cook patted Larry on the shoulder and then went to the first table to make some announcements and begin the tournament. Larry took off his coat, careful to keep his back to the front of the room, so that Mr. Cook wouldn't see him hide the gun in its sleeve.

That night, with the First Place trophy under his arm, he followed Carl up the dark stairs to their room. Carl had been acting moody, as usual, and rather than try to talk to him, Larry took out one of his chess books. Carl turned off the lights.

"Come on, Carl." Larry was sitting on the edge of his bed, talking to Carl's back.

Carl knelt behind his telescope. "You know I need the lights out. I can't see any good with the lights on."

"Yeah," Larry said, "but what about me? How am I supposed to see my chess book?"

Carl said, "What do you need a chess book for? You're a little genius anyway, aren't you?"

"Am not."

Carl turned and stared at him. "Never mind," he said. "We'll trade nights. I'll get the lights out tonight, and tomorrow you can read."

Carl went back to his telescope, and for a while Larry sat quietly on his bed. The room was dark, and the way Carl knelt by the window, he looked almost as if he were wishing on a star, or praying. When he heard his parents beneath him, Larry crossed the room to lie on the floor and look down through the heating vent into the kitchen. His mother and father were sitting and talking at the table.

The heating vent was really just a square hole cut in the floor about two-by-two feet—with a wrought iron grate over it. Sometimes, at bedtime, if he couldn't get his shoes untied, his mother would make him take the grate off and dangle his leg down into the kitchen, so that she wouldn't have to walk all the way upstairs. He couldn't see the kitchen table through the grate, but he could hear his parents talking. Whatever they were discussing, they didn't want the kids to know, so they were speaking in Italian. Neither Larry nor his brother or sister knew any Italian at all, except for a few curses that everybody knew.

Larry liked to listen to his parents when they were talking in Italian: the sounds were a kind of music that almost made up for the other sounds that sometimes came up through the heating vent, the sounds of his father's shouts and his mother's screams, and the dull sounds that cut like glass when his father hit his mother, when his father was "slapping her around," which he had heard his uncles say you had to do to a woman every once in awhile. But this night they were talking quietly, and Larry floated toward sleep listening to their voices.

Once, when his father switched into English, he was talking about his older brother Anthony, who had enlisted in the army and died in the war, in the Normandy invasion. Larry woke up at the mention of the war, but then his father went back to Italian. Larry loved to hear war stories. All his uncles had fought. His dad was the only one of the brothers who hadn't served, and that was only because when the war came he was too old to be drafted and he had two kids already, with Larry on the way. Except for Anthony, his father was the oldest brother. Sundays, after dinner, when the women went into the kitchen to clean up, the men would sit around the living room and talk, and sometimes one of the uncles would talk about the war. Larry knew all the stories: how Uncle Robert was wounded at Pearl Harbor; how Uncle Carmine's ship was sunk by a German sub, how he survived two days in the water before being rescued and then got a medal for it; how Uncle Jimmy lost part of his foot in the battle for Cassino; how

⑤

Uncle David was in the first American convoy into Berlin; how Uncle Joey blew up a bunker with a hand grenade in Corregidor, which was a small island in the Pacific, where, Uncle Jimmy said whenever he mentioned it, "we took a hell of a beating."

Uncle Frank was the only one who never talked about the war. Larry was sure that something terrible had happened to him. All he knew for sure, though, was that Uncle Frank had fought in the Pacific, that he was the only survivor of an attack, and that he had been lost for a long time on one of the islands there and been reported dead. But Larry could tell by the way the uncles talked that underneath the story something else was hidden.

Larry lay by the vent, listening, until he felt Carl shake him by the shoulder, making him get up and into bed.

Sunday afternoon, on the way to Seaford, he carried the chess trophy in his lap. He was looking forward to showing it to Uncle Frank. For the ride out, he and Carl had the window seats and Susan was stuck in the middle.

"Don't forget you get the middle on the way back," Susan said. She pinched his leg.

"Quit it!" Larry yelled.

"I didn't do anything!" Susan answered.

Larry's dad took his eyes off the road and glanced into the rearview mirror. Larry and Susan stopped fighting.

Larry's mom said something in Italian and his dad answered angrily, "I'll be a son-of-a-bitch if I'm going to stay away from my own mother's house." He hit the steering wheel.

"Okay," his mom said, "but think of Mom and Dad. They don't need to see you two at each other's throats."

"I need you to tell me about my mother and father?" His dad took his right hand off the steering wheel and lifted it high, threatening her with the back of his hand. She flinched and Larry's stomach tightened. Then his father went back to driving and the car was quiet for the rest of the ride.

Once at his grandparents' house, everything went along as usual. The driveway was filled up with cars in a double line and the big house was packed with aunts and uncles and cousins. The kids were scattered through all the rooms, but mostly they were on the enclosed porch playing games. The aunts were in the kitchen and dining room preparing dinner and setting the table, and the uncles were in the living room, gathered around a news show on the television and arguing loudly about Truman and McArthur and something about Ike. Every once in awhile Uncle Robert would yell, "Would you all shut up and listen to what the man has to say!" Then it would be quiet for a few minutes until one of the brothers made a comment and the shouting started up again. Usually Larry's dad and his Uncle Joey were the loudest arguers, but this Sunday they sat on opposite sides of the room and didn't say a word.

Just before dinner, Larry's cousin Billy—his Uncle Joey's son who was about Larry's age—came over and shot him with a shiny Colt 45. Larry responded by taking the German Luger out of his belt and politely returning the fire. He didn't much like Billy.

Billy said, "My dad's mad at your dad."

"Your dad broke our door."

Billy stepped closer and whispered, "My dad says your dad's a bastard."

Larry didn't respond. He put his hands in his pockets.

The two boys stood there facing each other. Then their grandmother called, and they joined all the others in the dining room.

Sunday dinner was always served on two long tables placed side by side lengthwise. The grandmother and grandfather sat together at the head of the table, and then the aunts and uncles sat to the right and left of them in order of age. All the kids sat at the second table, also in order of age, the oldest ones closest to the adults. But this Sunday, for the first time, Larry's grandfather was too sick to come to the table. Grandpa had a disease of some kind that Larry didn't understand much about, except that it was serious, and because of it he stayed in bed most of the time. This Sunday, though his plate was where it always was, he wasn't going to come in for dinner with his children and grandchildren. While everybody was noisily going about getting into chairs, Larry's grandmother said to his father, "Vinnie.

🔄

Come." She pointed to Grandpa's seat. "Sit," she said. "You say grace."

Saying grace was Grandpa's job. When she asked Larry's dad to do it, the room got quiet very quickly. His dad hesitated, and everyone watched him. Grandma said, again, "Come! Sit!" and Uncle Carmine added, "What are you waiting for, Vinnie? Didn't Mom tell you to do something?" At that, Larry's dad stood up and took his father's seat at the head of the table. When he put his hands together, as if he were about to say grace, Uncle Joey got up and left the table.

"Where are you going?" his dad said.

"What business is it of yours?"

His dad said something, slowly, in Italian.

Uncle Joey answered, in English, "The day I listen to a lying son-of-a-bitch like you—"

He didn't get to say anything else before Larry's dad was out of his chair, and then everybody was yelling. It took several minutes to separate Larry's dad from his Uncle Joey. When they did, Uncle Joey's nose was bleeding, which frightened Larry. He jumped under the table, and from where he hid all he could see was feet. When things settled down slightly, he peeked out from under a chair and saw his Uncle Carmine and his Uncle Frank holding his dad on one side of the room, and his Uncle Robert and his Uncle Jimmy holding his Uncle Joey, who had a handkerchief pressed to his nose, on the other side of the room. Everyone was talking in Italian and he couldn't understand anything of what his father and his uncles were yelling at each other.

The shouting went on for a long time, and when it calmed down, they started talking in English again. After awhile they decided that Uncle Joey and his family had to leave because Uncle Joey had started the fight.

Uncle Joey said, "Sure! I'll go! Because he's the oldest brother! But don't anybody say I started this, because—"

"All right!" Uncle Carmine yelled. "We don't care who started it. One of you has to go, or there won't be any peace."

Uncle Joey gathered his family and quietly left the house—after going in to say good-bye to his father. When he was gone and things

VINNIE'S BOY, LARRY 93

began to return to normal, Larry crawled out from under the table. He stood up, straightened himself out, and saw that his father was looking at him angrily.

For a while, Larry remained fixed in his spot. He put his hands in his pockets. He knew his father was mad at him for hiding under the table, but he didn't know what to say or do about it. His mouth got dry as he stood there, and he felt tears beginning to build up, but he was saved from crying by his grandmother's voice once again calling the family to dinner.

This time the meal went along smoothly, though there wasn't nearly as much shouting and laughing as usual. When dinner was mostly finished and the adults were eating fruits and cracking nuts and talking, Larry asked his mother if he could be excused from the table. She nodded. As Larry got out of his chair and went into the living room, he saw his father watching him.

This was Larry's favorite part of the Sunday afternoon: the time he got to set up the chess set and sit hunched over the pieces as if thinking about a new opening or a difficult problem, when actually he was just waiting for his Uncle Frank to leave the table and join him. The chess set was under the coffee table in a shallow drawer, where it always was. He set up the board on the leather ottoman and pushed it in front of the couch. Sitting on the edge of the couch, facing the white pieces, Larry pushed the Queen Pawn to Queen Four. Then he went out on the porch and brought his trophy in. He put it behind him.

He was about to move another piece when his Uncle Frank started into the living room.

Hunched over the table, cracking a walnut in his hands, his father said, "Frank, why don't you get some gloves and teach the kid how to box. That's what he needs."

Uncle Frank stopped and said something in Italian.

Larry's dad said, "Did you see him hide under the table before, like a little scared mouse?"

Larry looked down at his knees. He turned to face the back of the couch and whispered, angrily, "Baloney." After he said it, he could hardly believe the word had come out. He had no idea what he meant by it.

"What was that?" his father said.

Larry didn't answer.

His father came and stood in front of him.

Larry turned around and said quickly and clearly, "I said 'baloney.' I'm sorry, Dad."

"You're not sorry yet," his father said. He smacked him across the face. "Now," he said, pointing his finger in the air, "now you're sorry."

Larry tried not to cry, but he couldn't help it. He covered his face with his arms.

"Go out on the porch," his father said, "and sit there till I tell you you can come in."

Larry slid off the couch, leaning away from his father, and walked stiffly to the porch. He heard his Uncle Frank say something to his father and his father say something back. They were talking in Italian again, but Larry heard curses on both sides. Then his father yelled, "You're telling me how to raise my kid?" and his Uncle Frank yelled, "No! Who can tell you anything!"

When Uncle Frank took a step toward his father, the other brothers got up and stood between them. Then Uncle Jimmy yelled something at Uncle Robert, and Uncle Robert yelled back, and after that the aunts were in the living room along with the kids, and everybody was shouting in English and Italian. Larry watched from the porch, his attention concentrated on his mother, who was flanked by Carl and Susan. She was screaming at Uncle Frank, yelling in a mixture of Italian and English that sounded like gibberish. Larry heard her shout "my husband!" and "my children!" several times, but he really didn't know what she was so angry about. Then, all of a sudden, the screams stopped and the whole house, in an instant, was as silent as a closet.

Larry's grandfather stood in the kitchen doorway, looking into the living room. He was wearing a white linen robe that only made the yellowness of his skin and the deep circles under his eyes more terrible. He raised his finger and said in a soft, scratchy voice, "Go home. Everyone go home." There was silence for awhile after that, and when Larry's dad tried to say something, his grandfather raised his arm with a quick, sharp jerk. The motion silenced Larry's dad instantly. When another few seconds passed and no one spoke, his grandfather turned and disappeared back through the kitchen.

Quietly, the families went about gathering their belongings. Larry's dad picked up the chess trophy, which had been knocked to the floor during the fighting, and carried it out to the car. Only after all the aunts and uncles and cousins were out in the driveway did some of them talk to each other.

By the time Larry and his family were halfway home, it was dark out. Larry sat in the back seat, between Susan and Carl. Susan had fallen asleep with her head leaning against the window. No one had said a word for a long time, but Larry could almost hear his parents thinking their thoughts in the front seat. Alongside him, to his left, his brother Carl was looking dreamily out the window at the passing lights. Larry twisted around to look out the back window at the long line of cars on the highway behind them, knowing that his aunts and uncles were out there in their cars, heading back to their neighborhoods. He got up on his knees to look out, and his father told him to sit down. Then he added, "You think your Uncle Frank is a big man? Because he knows how to play chess?" He turned to his wife. "I should tell him his uncle's a cannibal, his . . ."

"That's enough!" his mother said sharply. "What's wrong with you?"

"What's wrong with me . . ." his father repeated, shaking his head as if disgusted.

When the car was quiet again, Larry thought about what his father had said. The word "cannibal" was like the final piece of a puzzle, and as soon as he heard it, he knew the whole story about his Uncle Frank. Larry pictured his uncle killing the enemy the way he had seen in movies, crawling out of the jungle, sneaking up from behind, clasping one hand around a Japanese soldier's mouth and sticking a knife into his heart. He pictured his uncle actually doing this. Then he pictured

☙

him dragging the body back into the jungle and cutting off pieces to eat. "My uncle did that," he said to himself. Uncle Frank, who was the nicest of the uncles, who he played chess with on Sunday afternoons. Larry pictured it and thought about it until he was sick to his stomach and frightened and he felt as if everything around him were dangerous. Then he thought about David Cook. He worried about seeing him at school in the morning. He imagined his face scarred and torn. He was afraid he might look like a monster.

In the dark, he took the German Luger out of his belt and held it between his legs. With his thumb in front of the hammer so it wouldn't make any noise, he aimed the toy at his father's back and pulled the trigger. Then he placed it on the floor and pushed it with the toe of his shoe up under his father's seat. He did that without really knowing why. He just didn't want to see the gun. He didn't want to think about war. He sat back and closed his eyes. Under him, the wheels sped over the road and the whining noise of the tires seemed to him to sound like something alive being torn apart. He put his hands over his ears and tried not to hear—but no matter how hard he pressed, it was still there, the sound all around him whirling and spinning, filling up the dark.

TESTS

I couldn't see why it should be me. She's the one dumped a full ashtray
on me when I was undressed and sweaty, and I'm the one had to lean
over her sink washing ashes and junk out of delicate places. Then
James walked in, it was the middle of the night, the kid's ten years old,
sees me like that, the sink full of sooty water, and I can't imagine what
he thought. His mouth was hanging open as if he'd just walked in on
Count Dracula relieving himself in the bathroom sink. And I was the
one supposed to apologize. Plus, I was thinking at the time that all my
worrying was already killing me and I didn't need her adding one more
thing.

I was on my way to the hospital for tests, thinking about all this. A
Thursday morning, mid-May, southwest Virginia—and it's snowing.
A few days before, the temperature was in the 80s. I'm driving to the
hospital on a four-lane blacktop and mist is rising up off the pave-
ment. It swirls around in thin lines. Every once in awhile the sun
breaks through and then the snow looks like dust motes caught in
sunlight.

Molly wanted me to apologize because I lit up a cigarette right
after we made love, and she said I didn't look at her the whole time
or after.

I did.

I remember I looked at her once but she had her eyes closed. When
I told her that, that's when she dumped the ashtray on me—which I

think went too far. I was a terrible mess then, more crazy than sane, though of course nobody knew it—not my friends, my family, nobody. That's the way I am. Or that's the way I was. I don't know. But then, for sure. I tried to keep my relationships superficial. Molly claimed that anyone who knew me even remotely knew I was a mess. She thought it was funny that I thought no one knew. If they did, they didn't do anything about it. I could go weeks without a phone call. That included family. Even thinking back to those years makes me nervous.

On Tuesday night after the argument, I had an attack of something that kept me up the whole night. It started out like one of my normal stomachaches that I'd get regularly. They'd usually wake me up in the middle of the night and last a few hours before I could go back to sleep. I wrote them off to stress, nerves, who knows what—nothing serious though. But this one wouldn't quit. It lasted all night and into the morning. I drank dose after dose of Pepto-Bismol, went out driving to get my mind off it, took hot showers to relax. Nothing worked. By 7 AM I was at the doctor's, in line with all the allergy sufferers getting their morning shots. That's when I was told it might be an ulcer and to show up for tests on Thursday.

At that point I hadn't seen Molly for a few days already. She said flat out that she didn't want to see me till I was ready to apologize. I was ready to talk, but I felt she owed me an apology too for overreacting. And I wanted to wait awhile before facing James again, not to mention Billy, his older brother, who would have heard the story from James. Anyway, I was already half thinking about dropping the whole relationship. We were at the point where the boys would call me Dad every once in a while by accident, and then get all screwed-up over it and talk a mile a minute about their father, as if they wanted to make sure I knew they already had one and didn't need another. It all felt so complicated and difficult, and then she wanted me to start sleeping over some nights, think about making a commitment to the boys. That's what the argument was really all about. It didn't have anything to do with not looking at her when we made love—and we both knew it.

The doctor said it might be an ulcer, but I had it in my head it

TESTS

might be stomach cancer. I know that's pathetic. I had no real reason to think it, but five years ago I woke up one morning and my wife was gone. Not left me, not divorced—gone. No warning, no note, no nothing. Just one morning I woke up and she wasn't on the other side of the bed. She wasn't in the kitchen either, or the living room, or the basement, or the attic. She wasn't outside, down the block, at a neighbor's. She was gone. I was thirty-five. We had been married ten years. I had been happy, and I thought she was happy—up until maybe three months before she disappeared. At the beginning of that summer she said she couldn't stand to sleep with me anymore because I snored. She kept throwing me out of bed. Then a few weeks later she turned the den into a bedroom for herself and moved in. Meanwhile I'm begging her every day to tell me what the hell's going on. Then one night near the end of summer, she gets in bed with me like usual and I think the whole thing has finally blown over.

That was the last time I saw her. Police searched the neighborhood, dragged the pond behind our house, brought in dogs to sniff the yard. Nothing. I've never heard from her since. Neither have her parents nor any of her friends; and now, after all these years, I think she must have found a quiet way to end her life, though I'm never sure and for a long time I tried to stay close to my telephone. I bought one of those answering machines you could check on and I checked on it all the time. No one called. Every day I'd come home and there'd be a big red zero lit up where it recorded the number of calls received. When I finally got a divorce on grounds of abandonment, I got rid of the answering machine.

The fear of disease and dying set in about a year after she left. One morning I found a red spot on my chest, and I was sure it was a sign of cancer. The more I looked the more red spots I found, and every morning I found some more until I was sure they were multiplying daily. I kept a sheet of paper and a pen in the bathroom and I recorded every time I found a spot. Then one morning I had one of those dreams that you can't distinguish from reality, and in it I walked into the bathroom and looked at myself in the mirror and my whole face was a red spot. I looked like someone had painted a crimson circle

꩜

on my face. Next day I went to the doctor and showed her my red spots. She looked at me as if I were foaming at the mouth. After that, at her suggestion, I started seeing a therapist, where I learned that my fear of dying is an emotional reaction to my wife's disappearance. She (my therapist) explained it all. So that's why I was thinking I had stomach cancer.

When I arrived at the hospital, I had a hard time getting out of the car. I was scheduled for an ultrasound, and I was sure the technician was going to turn on the machine and look at the picture on the TV screen and then faint. I don't know what I thought: my insides would be dappled with red spots or something. I sat in the car and told myself that my fear was unreasonable, a psychological reaction, and when I was about ten minutes late for my appointment, I got out of the car.

I hate hospitals. I hate everything about them: the way they smell, the way they look, what happens to people there. Inside this hospital, it was the same story: antiseptic smell, corridors like bad dreams, long lines of doors that open onto things you don't want to see. It took me only a few minutes to find the right corridor, the right set of swinging doors; and when I did, there was a little waiting room with two green benches facing each other and a table between them with copies of *Time* and *Newsweek*. One of the magazines was open to a full-page, brightly colored diagram of Ronald Reagan's rectum, where apparently there had been some problems. Just past the benches, there was a nurse's station and two nurses who couldn't possibly have been as young as they looked.

As I approached the station, one of the nurses looked up from some papers. After I gave the requested information, she led me to a small room with stacks of what I took to be traditional hospital gowns.

"After you change out of your clothes," she said, pointing to a curtained cubicle, "please have a seat on the bench, and we'll call you when it's time for your test."

"Sure," I said, and I smiled at her as if I weren't even a little bit nervous. I really wanted to ask her if she were actually a nurse, because, honestly, she didn't look like she could possibly be any older than six-teen—but I figured she'd figure I was flirting with her, which I guess I would have been, sort of. At the time, I had this thing about young women: I needed to know if they still found me attractive. I was forty then, but I looked a lot younger; and when young women flirted with me, I felt a lot younger. But I didn't say anything. I had Molly—who was the same age as me—on my mind; and I was afraid I might have stomach cancer; and I was mad at myself for being such a pathetic hypochondriac. And I felt old. So I grabbed a hospital gown and went behind the curtain to change.

The gown, thank goodness, wasn't the kind that ties behind the back—the kind that always leaves a little bit of your rear exposed. I was thankful for that, but surprised that the thing only came down to mid-thigh. No way I'd be able to sit down. I rechecked the stack, but the gowns were all the same length, so I went out and stood beside one of the benches for awhile; and when I got tired of standing I grabbed a magazine and held it in my lap and sat down. The nurses kept looking at me and talking to each other. Then one of them came over and said, "If you'd like to put on the pants that go with that top, you'll find them in a separate stack, back in the changing room."

"Pants?" I said, "They didn't used to have pants, did they?"

She smiled and walked away, and I stood up—carefully—and went back to the changing room. I found the pants and put them on and stayed there until one of the nurses came back and got me and led me along several corridors to a small room with a bed and, alongside the bed, a bunch of machinery on a cart. She told me to lie down and then left me alone in the room. A few minutes later a neatly dressed older woman burst through the doors talking.

"How are you today?" she said. "This won't take us long. If you'll just pull . . . Here, let me do it." She pulled the gown up to my chest and began spreading grease all over my stomach. "Is that cold? It'll warm up in a second. This is just to facilitate—" She turned away from me, flipped several switches, turned on a monitor of some sort, and then turned back and began exploring my stomach with a small, cold disk attached to the machinery. "Oh, my goodness," she said.

"You have been sick, haven't you?"

"Excuse me?"

"You've been in a lot of pain, haven't you?"

"Not all the time. The other night, yes."

"Your gall bladder. It looks like pea soup in there."

"Pea soup?"

"You have gallstones. What the gall bladder does . . ."

She explained; and by the time I left the hospital, I had an appointment with a surgeon to see about scheduling an operation.

Outside, the weather's a lot less weird, but now I'm feeling major-league tense. I'm thinking about having my gall bladder removed, and no matter how I work it, I'm going to have to spend some time in the hospital. It's overwhelming, the things that can happen to you in a hospital. First of all, no one can guarantee the safety of the blood supply. I realize that the chance of getting blood infected with a serious disease is minimal—but it's there. Whenever I think about getting blood transfusions, I picture one of the down-and-out, terminal unlucky staggering into a blood-for-money place somewhere in Manhattan. It's unsettling. And then there's anesthesia. Going under is no problem, unless something screws up and you never come back out of it—which happens. Rarely, of course—but it happens.

By the time I'm a few blocks from the hospital, I'm sweating. I really want to go over to Molly's—but we've got this argument between us. Molly works out of her home. She's an editor for a publisher of high school science textbooks, and she's hooked up by computer to their offices in D.C. Within a few minutes I notice that my car is on automatic pilot and heading for Molly's all by itself. I understand clearly that I can't go to Molly's until I'm ready to apologize—but the car apparently doesn't care.

When I got there, I pulled in her driveway, and by the time I walked up the concrete path to the house, she was waiting behind the screen door. The morning had turned sunny by then, but Molly didn't seem much aware of the weather. She lived in a split-level ranch in a nice neighborhood; and she was wearing her regular outfit: ratty blue jeans and a T-shirt. This particular T-shirt had "Science Is Fun!" written across the chest in bright red letters. I found that strangely erotic.

"Morning," she said. She folded her arms in front of her and gave me this look that said she was waiting.

I said, "Good morning, Molly" and looked down at my feet. Then, when I looked up at her, I thrust my hands in my pockets. "Look, Molly," I said. "I might could apologize about this not-looking-at-you stuff, but we both know that's not what this argument's all about."

"You *might could* apologize?"

"I might could."

"You might could apologize to me. About this not-looking-at-me stuff." She paused, then continued: "What is this apology that you're thinking about offering?"

"Well," I said. "I'm sorry it all happened. I'm sorry we're arguing like this."

"That's your apology?" she said. She hitched up her jeans. "That's the apology you *might could* offer? That's the apology I've been waiting a week for?" She opened the screen door and stepped outside, and for a moment I thought she was going to hit me. Her teeth were pressed together so tight you could see dark lines running all the way up to her temples. "William," she said. "Whatever there was between us is done with. I don't want to see you again."

I considered telling her about the gallstones, but I didn't think I'd get much sympathy. "Look, Molly," I said, but I couldn't think of how to continue, so I just turned away from her and started for my car.

As I was opening the door, I heard her mutter, "Might could." Then she yelled after me: "You were born and raised in Brooklyn, you jerk! You *might could* apologize." She stepped into the house and slammed the door.

She had a point.

I dropped my head against the steering wheel and closed my eyes and stayed there in the driveway for a good five minutes before I finally started the car and drove away. I wasn't going to apologize, because an apology would have been stupid and worthless. What was I going to say: "I'm sorry I didn't look at you when we made love?" That wasn't what it was about. That was just what was on the surface. And what was under the surface? I don't know. I never could figure it out. Whatever—an apology wouldn't have meant a thing.

That was already the third or fourth relationship I'd been in and out of after my official divorce; and though I didn't know it then, I had another three or four to go before I'd finally give up and pack it in and learn to live by myself—and they all went approximately the same way. I'd date someone for a few months before she discovered I wasn't looking at her. Eventually the trouble just came to seem to outweigh the rewards.

When I got back to my house, though, after leaving Molly's, this odd thing happened: I reached the front door and froze. It was strange. You couldn't say I hesitated, or that I was having second thoughts about breaking up with Molly or anything like that. I froze. My hand would not reach out and turn the knob that opened the door into my house. I was still living in the same place I had shared with Kelly, my missing ex-wife. The front door was the kind with a big glass pane in the center of it, and I just stood there staring through the glass into the living room. It was like I was in a state of suspended animation. I didn't move. My living room was neat and orderly, the way I always keep it. You had to look close to see the dirt on the floor and under the sofa and around the edges of the rug. Except for the sofa—where I buried myself under a quilt in the evenings and watched rented movies or flipped through thirty or forty cable channels for hours on end—everything was covered with a thick layer of dust. It was weird out there standing in front of my house looking in. It was as if some kind of thought process was going on way down beneath the surface, on a level so deep I wasn't even conscious of it, but it necessitated so much bodily energy and concentration that I had to stand perfectly still and just wait. Which is what I did for a long time, and then, finally, I turned around and got back in my car and drove a few blocks away to a flower shop where I bought a bouquet of flowers.

I had it in mind to drive back over to Molly's with the flowers, hoping, I guess, that flowers might take the place of an apology—but

TESTS

I only had to drive a few blocks before I saw that wasn't going to work, and I turned around and headed back home. This time I made it into the house; but once I was inside, it started happening again, this strange stillness coming over me, and I wandered around my living room for a while with the bouquet of flowers in my hand, and then finally I dropped onto the sofa. I decided that what I needed right then was a nap and that when I woke up I could worry about meeting the surgeon and making arrangements with the hospital. I knew deep down that I wouldn't be the one poor soul who never came out of the anesthesia or who contracted a fatal disease from a blood transfusion. And I also knew that it was all over with Molly and her boys, that I wasn't going over there anymore, flowers or no flowers. I settled into the sofa, lying on my back with the bouquet clasped to my chest, and punched my head into the pillow and closed my eyes, and it occurred to me that to anyone looking through the front door I probably looked like the stiff in an old-fashioned funeral, where they laid out the corpse in the living room and stuck a bouquet of flowers in his hands. I lay there like that, thinking about that—that I looked like a corpse in an old-fashioned funeral—until I finally fell asleep, and all the problems, all the weight and difficulty and confusion, drifted mercifully away.

᭄

TELL ME WHAT IT IS

Ten steps back behind a pair of blue tents pitched side by side under thick trees on Cape Flattery, the ground ended abruptly at a thirty-foot vertical fall to the Pacific Ocean. A campfire in front of the tents had burned down to red embers. Alongside the fire, two card tables pushed together made one longer table topped with a battery-operated florescent lamp and a bright yellow plastic game board and crisp black tiles. Enclosed in the circle of light emanating from the lamp, two couples seated in folding chairs around the card tables were deep into a session of Acquire, a board game involving the placement of randomly selected tiles on a numbered grid. The tiles formed companies in which the players bought stock and either gained or lost money as their companies merged and grew or were taken over and disappeared. It was Barrett's turn to move and he had been staring intently at the board for several minutes. In the intense quiet of his concentration, the others listened to water lapping at boulders and rushing through sea caves that lined the shore below them.

Finally Barbara said, "For God's sake, Barrett, will you just merge Worldwide and end my misery?" She didn't have any stock in Worldwide and was almost out of money. If Worldwide were merged she'd be out of the game.

Barrett said, "What makes you think I have the merging tile?"

"Oh, please!" Barbara shouted.

Adam said, "Here they go." Adam and Adele were the second couple. Adam and Adele. Barrett and Barbara. They lived in adjacent apartments in Manhattan, and they referred to themselves as the alphabet couples, because of the unfortunate alliteration of their names—or sometimes they called themselves the As and the Bs, as in "Barrett, see what the As are doing tonight," or "Adam, see if the Bs want to come over for a drink." Adam owned The Body Works, a physical fitness center, and Barrett acted in *The Days of Our Lives*, an unending daytime soap opera. They were on vacation now, camping a few days on Cape Flattery, which was part of the Makah reservation.

"Do you think I'm an idiot? Do you think we're all stupid?" Barbara put her elbows up on the table and leaned toward Barrett. She was a woman in her early fifties who looked twenty years younger, easily. Some of her youthful appearance came from the fortune she spent on skin-care products and minor cosmetic surgery, and some of it was genetic. In any case, she looked good. Her naturally sandy blond hair was dyed a brighter blond, and it contrasted strikingly with her pale green eyes. She wore jeans and a sheer green blouse that showed off the shapeliness of her breasts. All of her beauty, natural and purchased, was at that moment, however, swallowed up by the anger that surfaced in her face. She shouted: "You've been buying stock in Worldwide for the last three rounds! You don't think we know you have the merger? You either think we're all idiots, or else you're an idiot for buying the stock!"

Adele laughed and said, "You guys. . . ."

Barrett placed the merging tile on the board. "Okay," he said. "Worldwide comes down." He smiled broadly at Barbara, his white teeth catching the lamplight. "Bye-bye, Barbara," he said, and he laughed out loud.

"You love it." Barbara pushed her chair back from the table. "Anything that screws me, you love."

Adam said, "Talking about screwing you, Barbara. . . ."

Adele reached across the table and slapped him playfully on the head.

"Yes?" Barbara said, perking up. She leaned seductively toward Adam.

⑤

Barrett said, "Let's do the merger first. Then you can talk about screwing my wife."

"Okay," Adam said. He pulled the bank toward him and began counting out money.

Barbara said, "I'm hot." For weeks now the Olympic Peninsula had been hot and dry—weather conditions almost unheard of in the region. She stretched, extending her arms over her head and pointing her fingertips to the sky. Her blouse rode up on her stomach. "I'm going to go take this thing off," she said, referring to the blouse, and she walked away from the table. As she bent to enter her domed tent, she pulled the blouse off, revealing a bare back and a quick flash of her breasts swaying in the pale outer reach of the lamplight.

Barrett said: "Too bad, Adam. You missed it."

From inside the tent, Barbara answered: "Go to hell, Barrett."

"What?" Adam looked up from a stack of hundreds. "What did I miss?"

"What did she do?" Adele said to Barrett.

Adele and Adam were a much younger couple than Barrett and Barbara, younger by more than twenty years. Adam had met Adele at The Body Works, where she had started working out at age thirty-two, when her daughter turned thirteen, entered junior high school, and started living behind a locked bedroom door. Her fourteen-year-old son had been living behind locked doors since he had entered teenage-dom some twelve months earlier. Adele couldn't blame either of them. She and her then-husband bickered constantly. Their principal forms of communication were the jibe and the insult. Adam, at thirty-four, was also married at the time, also with two teenagers. When he saw Adele, the first thing he noticed was her body—which was worth dying for, and which no one would ever believe had been through childbirth. Seeing her in a blue and red Spandex exercise outfit that clung to her like brightly colored skin, he offered immediately to be her personal fitness counselor. A year and two months later they were both divorced and remarried to each other.

Barrett said to Adele, matter-of-factly: "She pulled her blouse off before she got in the tent."

🌀

Adele turned to Adam. "And you missed it, Honey," she said, her voice dripping mock sympathy.

"Damn. . . ." Adam handed Barrett a pile of pink thousand-dollar bills and pale yellow hundreds. "Why didn't you nudge me?"

Barrett sorted out the money and placed it in neat stacks next to his black tiles. "Haven't you seen her tits before?" he said.

"No!" Adam said, petulantly. "I haven't. And I don't think it's fair. After all, you've seen Adele's."

Barrett and Adele laughed. Barbara came out of the tent wearing a bikini top. "Shall I strip?" she asked Adam. "Shall we even it up?"

"Absolutely!" Adam said. He pounded his fist on the table, making the tiles on the game board bounce.

"Hey!" Barrett said. "You're messing up the game."

"I'm sorry," Adam said. He pouted, sticking out his bottom lip.

Barbara sat down at the table. "You first," she said to Adam.

"I can't," he said. "I have a very small penis."

Adele laughed out loud, and Adam and Barbara laughed in reaction to her. Barrett just shook his head.

"I've heard about that," Barbara said. "Adele's told me all about it."

Adam grinned wickedly.

Barbara said to Barrett, "You saw, didn't you? Are the rumors true?"

"Like a horse," Barrett said. Barbara was referring to that morning, when Barrett had found Adam and Adele bathing in a tidal pool under a stone arch. He had applauded their naked bodies. Adam had looked taken aback for a moment. He had looked toward Adele, as if he might want to cover her. Adele, however, had appeared unconcerned, and Adam had wound up clowning as usual, doing muscle-man poses before Barrett turned and walked on. Now Barrett slapped Adam on the back. "Like a damn stallion!"

"Absolutely," Adam said. He touched one of his tiles and seemed to hesitate for an instant. Then he said: "Why don't we all go skinny-dipping?" He looked up at the sky, at a full moon that was about to disappear behind a long line of clouds.

"Fine with me," Adele said. "I love getting naked in the ocean."

"Are you two serious?" Barbara said.

"Sure," Adam said. "This is an Indian reservation, isn't it? Didn't the Indians used to bathe in the ocean?"

Barrett said, "I'm sure the Makah people bathed in the ocean—a hundred years ago, anyway."

"I'll do it," Barbara said. "Except the water's probably still cold—even with all this heat."

At fifty-six, Barrett was the oldest member of the group. He had been married three times before Barbara, and he had one child from each of those previous marriages. His youngest child, a daughter, was in her mid-twenties. He was still an attractive man, but his attractiveness didn't come from being in superb physical condition, as it did for Barbara, Adele, and Adam. Barrett's attractiveness was in his face, which was weathered and leathery, and in his eyes, which suggested an inner intensity. It was a look which many women over the years had found appealing. Women found his size appealing too. He was six-one, two hundred and twenty pounds. He looked up at the others and said, "You guys go. I'm too old and fat."

Barbara said, gesturing toward Adam: "You'd let your new bride go skinny-dipping with this sex fiend?" Barbara and Barrett had been married less than a year.

Adam said, "She's got a point, Barrett."

"You have to come," Adele said. "Otherwise you'll be the only one whose body's still a secret."

Barrett shook his head. He laughed as if he were nervous and a little shy. "I don't think so," he said. "You guys go. Really."

"Okay," Barbara said. She jumped up, rubbing her hands together with anticipation. "He's already seen you two naked," she added, with her back to the group as she ducked into her tent. She returned with two flashlights and tossed one to Adam. "Come on, Adele." She leaned down to Adele and whispered in her ear, loud enough for everyone to hear. "Not that I'm gay or anything, Darling—but I'm dying to check out your body."

Adam laughed and Barrett said, "You believe the libido of this woman?"

"You lucky dog!" Adam grasped Barrett by the neck and gave him a shake.

"Come on, come on!" Barbara took Adam by the arm and led him to the path that went down to the shore. "It's getting late and we've got that dumb fishing trip in the morning."

Adele hesitated at the table, looking across the game board at Barrett, who was watching Barbara and Adam as they made their way along the path. When Barrett turned to meet her eyes, she said: "You sure you won't come?"

"Believe me," Barrett said. "I haven't got the body to show off."

Adele laughed, dismissing Barrett's modesty. She smiled warmly at him, touched his fingertips with hers, and then joined Barbara and Adam, calling for them to wait.

Barrett put the game board and pieces away as he listened to the others descending the path to the water. For a long time, he could hear their laughter and the shrill, playful screams of the women. When, finally, the sound of their voices disappeared under the constant low whistle of wind through trees and the white noise of small ocean waves breaking over boulders that rose up out of shallow water all along the shore, when the only sounds left were the elemental ones—the fire, which occasionally popped and hissed, water leaving and returning ceaselessly, wind moving along the earth—Barrett carried the Acquire game into his tent, put it away, and came back out with a flashlight and an expensive pair of high-powered binoculars attached to a black graphite tripod.

Carrying the tripod on his shoulder as if it were a rifle, holding the feet in his right hand while the binoculars bounced along up over his head, and carrying the flashlight in his left hand, its beam trained on the ground, he followed the same path the others had taken, only in the opposite direction, up to the cape, to the point where the land ended and he could look out over Neah Bay to Tatoosh Island and the Pacific Ocean. Earlier in the day, Adele had taken his and Barbara's picture there as they stood on either side of a makeshift cardboard sign that read:

This is Cape Flattery
The northwestern-most point
in the continental United States

Now, as he walked along in the dark, he was watching for the sign. When he reached it, he would be close to the lookout point, where he planned on setting up the binoculars and watching his wife and friends as they undressed and went swimming.

Barrett approached the cape, amazed at himself. He was fifty-six years old and waves of sexual desire still pushed him along like so much driftwood. Desire swelled in him and still, now, at fifty-six, he didn't have the will to resist it. That morning, for example, his coming upon Adam and Adele bathing had not been accidental. He had been lying awake in his sleeping bag, looking out at the green canopy of trees through the netting at the top of his tent, when he overheard Adele suggest to Adam that they bathe at the shore. He had waited until he heard them leave the campsite before he got dressed quietly, careful not to wake Barbara, and he went down to the shore, hoping to come upon them. When he first saw them, they had their backs toward him. It was amusing to him that both Adam and Adele, at thirty-five and thirty-three, thought of themselves as old. To Barrett they were luminous with youth. Adam had the body you'd expect on a man who'd made a career and built a successful business around physical fitness. And Adele . . . Adele's beauty extended from the luster of her shoulder-length auburn hair, to the intelligence in her eyes, and the creamy glow of her skin.

When he came upon them, they were standing knee-deep in a tidal pool, Adam behind and to the right of Adele, his right hand on her shoulder, his left hand turning a thick bar of white soap in slow circles at the small of her back. While Barrett watched them, partially hidden by a pair of side-by-side boulders, Adam slid the bar of soap down over Adele's buttocks and then under her and through her legs. She laughed and turned around and they embraced and kissed. Barrett moved back behind the boulders and waited. He looked around, ner-

⑤

vous about getting caught leering at his friends. Getting caught would be humiliating and he was genuinely afraid of it—and that mixture of real fear and sexual excitement, that was one of the things that made him do it. It felt powerful, intense. He waited a few minutes and when he looked again, they were kneeling in the water, splashing each other playfully. Then he walked out from between the boulders and began applauding—as if he had just accidentally come upon them, as if their naked bodies were nothing more to him than an amusement, something which of course in his maturity and experience held no real power over him. Adam seemed taken aback at first, but Adele met his eyes and smiled—and then Adam, jackass that he was, began posing.

When Barrett reached the head of the cape, the shelter of the trees ended abruptly. The moon was just emerging from a bank of clouds, and it was bright enough that Barrett felt confident turning off the flashlight and laying it on a boulder. He walked carefully, testing the firmness of the ground with each small step. When he was close to the place where the land dropped away, he crawled on his hands and knees to the edge, where he lay on his stomach and looked down to the beach. Forty or fifty feet below him, Barbara, Adam, and Adele had just reached the water line and were standing in the surf with their shoes off and their pants legs rolled up. Barrett set up the tripod behind some bushes and a small tree, and he focused the binoculars on Adele. He had paid thirteen hundred dollars for those binoculars, and every time he used them he saw why: through their powerful lenses, Adele appeared to be a few arm lengths away from him. He felt as though he could touch her hair.

After several minutes of watching the threesome talking at the edge of the water, Barrett began to fear that they would chicken out and not go skinny-dipping at all. For a moment, he wished he were down there to urge them all out of their clothes and into the water. But, really, he didn't want to be down there with them. If he were down there, when they were all out of their clothes, he would have to pretend that it was no big deal. He wouldn't be able to leer and stare. He would have to pretend he didn't want to feel the weight of Adele's breasts in his hands, he didn't want to run his tongue over her nipples,

TELL ME WHAT IT IS

he didn't want to reach down under her the way Adam had. The truth was that he wanted to look, and he wanted to look with concentrated attention—not a pretense of amusement. And, if the relationship wasn't sexually intimate, that required distance and anonymity. So he preferred being up on the bluff, behind a tree, with his binoculars.

At home, in Manhattan, on the set at work, he was surrounded by stunningly beautiful women—all out of his reach, by his own choice, because he was married again. The tension was incredible. He wanted those women intensely and he didn't want them intensely—both at the same time. He was fifty-six years old, with three grown children, a veteran of three failed marriages. He was lucky to have Barbara. He knew it. He knew it absolutely. And yet, whenever an attractive woman came near him, something happened in his blood, something over which he had no control. It was as if his blood heated up, the surface of his skin grew electric, his breathing changed. He didn't know if it was like that for all men, all the time—but he was determined, absolutely, this time, with Barbara, to stay in control. He had slept with so many women over the years. And he knew now, knew absolutely, in his heart, that what he really needed to be happy was *one* woman. He needed Barbara. In the years he was single before he met her, in those years when he moved constantly between one woman and the next, when his life felt like a habitual swirl of movement, he suffered from anxiety attacks, terrible attacks that on a couple of occasions included hallucinations. Since he married Barbara, he had been fine. He needed to stay with her, to stay with one woman, with Barbara. He needed to learn to stay still. He needed to learn to value what he had and to resist the desire to move from woman to woman to woman.

Barrett knew what he needed. . . . And yet, some nights, he still found himself out at Flashdancers on West 21st, where dozens of mostly-undressed girls filled the room and the runways. All the women were beautiful, and varied in form: with light skin and dark skin; with big breasts that floated over taut but ample skin, and small breasts tight to the rib cage; with small pink nipples on white white skin, and large oval nipples, brown or nutmeg on darker skin; with asses that were round and asses that were long and flowed into youthful thighs: beauty everywhere on the pedestals of table tops, and what he desired was to look at it, what he desired was to see what was every day all around him hidden from his view.

In a sense, Barrett's voyeurism was a kind of compromise. He chose looking over acting. He was going to leer at Adele, but he wasn't going to make a pass at her. Adam was a jackass, but he was his friend. He liked betting on football and basketball games with him, and playing poker with him on Friday nights, gambling being another source of intensity in Barrett's life. He didn't want to sleep with his friend's wife. Even though his relationship with Barbara had been strained for the last few months, he didn't want to mess up the marriage by sleeping with another woman. But of course he wanted Adele. He wanted to see her, to touch her. He wanted her. He didn't want her. It was maddening and confusing. It had always been maddening and confusing.

Down on the beach, Barbara slipped out of her bikini top, and Adam's loud whistle floated up to the cape. While Adam and Adele watched, Barbara stripped out of her jeans and then her panties, slowly, with an equal mix of seduction and play. Watching from the cape, Barrett felt the familiar tingle of sexual excitement—and it surprised him. He had seen Barbara naked on a daily basis for almost a year now, and he had thought that she no longer excited him—not even when she put on the flaming red teddies, or the exotic black garters, or the Frederick's-of-Hollywood panties with the crotch cut out. Now, here he was watching her secretly from a distance through binoculars and feeling that old, recognizable tingle in his groin. When Barbara was fully undressed, she trotted away into the water, where she watched Adam take off his clothes, her head bobbing on the surface, as if she were just slightly jumping up and down in the water. Adam got undressed quickly and yelped as he dove dramatically into the waves. Then Adele turned around and looked up at the cape, looked up directly at Barrett.

Barrett moved away from the tripod and took a step back behind a tree trunk. His heart raced wildly. He said to himself, "She can't possibly see me." Then he wondered if she had perhaps seen the glint of moonlight off the lenses of the binoculars. Or maybe he was wrong, maybe his body was somehow silhouetted by the moonlight and she knew he was up on the cape watching her. He slid down and sat on the ground behind the tree, and he was filled with wildly chaotic feelings of shame and guilt and anger and remorse. Why did he do things like this? He was a fifty-six-year-old man. He had a career. He had a family. Why was he hiding in the bushes like a pimply teenager peeking at girls? For God's sake, he repeated to himself, and he was filled with a ragged humiliation. Then he told himself he was over-reacting. So what if they knew he was up here watching? Hadn't he been perfectly welcome to join them down on the beach? He'd make light of it if they knew. He'd turn it into a joke.

When he went back to the binoculars, he half expected to see Adele wave at him. Instead he found her reaching behind her back to unsnap her bra, still looking up at him, looking directly at him, as if she were engaged in a staring match and resolved not to be the first one to look away. She had already taken off her pants and blouse, and when the bra came off, she smiled, the same warm smile she had given him just before she left the campsite. Then she took off her panties and just stood there for a long moment, looking up at the cape, before she turned around and walked slowly into the water. Barrett watched them all the time they were in the water, and he watched them get out and get dressed, and then he hurried back to the campsite and put the binoculars and tripod away, and got undressed and into his sleeping bag.

By the time Barbara came into the tent, Barrett was almost asleep. He had listened to the exchange of good-nights through a sleepiness that was like being drugged. He heard the zipper to Adam and Adele's tent open and close, and then Barbara was climbing into their tent, almost stepping on him.

"Barbara?" he said, exaggerating the confusion in his voice, as if he were waking from a dream.

"Go back to sleep," Barbara said. She bent over him and touched his cheek gently with the back of her hand before pushing a strand of hair off his forehead.

"How was it?" he asked, turning onto his back and looking up at her.

〽

"Fun," she said. "They have beautiful bodies. . . ." She paused and bent to kiss him on the forehead. She whispered, "But I'm happy to be with an older man, someone with character and real strength."

Barrett laughed softly. "Are you putting me on?"

Barbara didn't answer. She kissed him again, gently, told him she loved him, and then pulled her sleeping bag close to his before she got in it and went to sleep.

Barrett was better able to relax once he was sure Barbara didn't know he had been watching them. For a long time he lay quietly thinking about the next morning's fishing trip, trying to remember what was exciting about holding a pole for hours while you waited for a fish to bite. Then he started thinking about himself, about who he was, about his relationships with others. Did Barbara really believe he had strength and character? He guessed she did. That was his image, the image he projected out into the world. He was an *actor*. He was a man of experience. He had suffered and he was world-weary. He was a man who lived with the knowledge of the nothing at the center of everything. That was the image he had been working on and refining from the time he was a boy. But who he was, who he was *really*, that was both his image and something more—and that something more. . . . He wasn't sure what it was. It was shaped by the people and places in his life, but it was something more. It was his angry father and the Brooklyn of his youth. It was the wives he had gone through, one after the other, and discarded or been discarded by because he was unhappy or unfulfilled or unsomething, or she was. It was his children, all grown now and into their own lifetime of trouble. But it was also something more. It was his experience and his thought and something more.

But Barbara believed in the image within which everything came wrapped. As he lay in his sleeping bag, not seeing the dense bright stars in their patterns so infinitely complicated they were like a complex, visual music, he tried to think about that something more that he never had been able to apprehend as anything other than a feeling, an idea that there was something under the images he invented and rendered for others—but he wound up feeling as though he were floating loose of the earth. He wound up feeling as though he were drifting. If no one knew you, who were you? And how could anyone know him if he wouldn't stay still long enough to be known? Outside his tent there was an amazing variety of noises—but Barrett's thoughts made him deaf long before sound truly disappeared in the deafness of sleep.

ᔕ

At four-thirty in the morning the sky was an unbroken mass of dark clouds. Adele stood in a circle of lamplight staring out over a fleet of fishing boats to the black water of Neah Bay. Adam stood behind her, looking the other way, back to a small building, a glorified kiosk, set at the edge of a gravel parking lot. Through an uncurtained window, he could see Barrett and Barbara standing in front of a desk cluttered with papers, while behind the desk an elderly woman typed some figures into an adding machine with her right hand and opened a desk drawer with her left. Barrett handed her some money, and Adele took the slip of paper that had issued forth from the adding machine and been ripped off precisely by the old woman. Adam said, "We shouldn't have let them pay for this. It's probably expensive as hell."

Adele grunted softly, a sound that meant nothing beyond acknowledging that Adam had spoken.

Adam went on: "Barrett makes me feel like a little kid sometimes, the way he's always picking up the tab. I think I may have a tendency to let him take too much control. Probably because he's so old."

"He's not that old," Adele said. She laughed quietly, as if to herself.

"Are you laughing at me?" Adam said.

Adele didn't answer. She was wearing white shorts and a bright yellow sleeveless blouse. A hooded, red vinyl rain slicker was folded over her right arm. She had taken the raincoat just in case—even though the weather report had called, once again, for clear skies and a temperature in the nineties.

Barbara nodded toward the raincoat as she approached Adele. She was carrying two Styrofoam cups of black coffee and she extended one to Adele. "You must be psychic, Honey. The captain's mom says it might rain."

"Shit," Adam said. "Will we still go out?"

Barrett, who had been following behind Barbara, carrying two more coffees, handed Adam a cup. "We're just waiting for the couple that's going out with us. Captain says they're on the way."

"Is this latté?" Adam asked, looking down at his coffee. "I like a lot of foam."

"Right, latté," Barrett said. "And the captain's serving croissants and apple scones on the flying bridge at seven."

Adele stuck her hand out, palm up. "Is it starting to rain?"

Barrett looked up to the sky, as if he might be able to see the rain falling. "I don't feel anything."

Adam said, "I think it's just misting."

"There," Barbara said, and she gestured to the village's single blacktop road, where a station wagon had just come round a curve. As they all watched, it pulled into the gravel parking lot and a middle-aged couple emerged. The man was shaped like an egg, with a small chest and a huge stomach that sloped down to skinny legs. He was wearing a camouflage outfit. The woman was also heavy, but her bulk was solid and seemed evenly distributed from her shoulders to her feet. She gave the impression of a living rectangle.

"Good God," Adam said, as the couple approached them and the captain emerged from his office at the edge of the parking lot. "I hope this boat's solid."

"Stop it," Adele said, turning her back to the couple and giving Adam a look.

The man in the camouflage approached the group with his arm extended for a handshake. Barrett switched his coffee to his left hand and shook the man's hand. "Joe Waller," the man said to Barrett. He extended his hand to Barbara and he gestured to his wife. "This is my wife, Lady," he said. "Would you believe twenty-five years?" Lady nodded, confirming what he said. "Married twenty-five years yesterday, two kids through college and married, one in college, one in high school." He said this as he shook Adam's hand and moved on to Adele. "Can you believe it?" he said to Adele.

Lady said, "And we're only forty-three."

"No kidding," Adam said.

"Hey!" Joe exclaimed, turning around to face the captain as he approached them slowly, carrying a large white bucket in each hand. "We going to catch some salmon today, Captain Ron?"

The captain was a Makah. His skin was dark and lined with myriad creases and folds. His eyes were solemn and deep. "I hope so," he said, and then continued on toward the boats, the large white buckets dangling from his hands like balancing weights.

Adam said, "I guess we follow him."

"That's Captain Ron," Joe said, putting his hand on Adam's back. "You ever been out with him before? Where you folks from, anyway? The wife and I are down from Alberta. . . ."

Joe went on as the group followed the captain down the rickety boat ramps and over the narrow docks to The Raven, Captain Ron's fishing boat. Behind them, the village at Neah Bay was quiet and dark. The only lights came from the Thunderbird Motel, which overlooked the water and was bracketed by gravel parking lots, one of which housed the small rust red building out of which Captain Ron ran his charter fishing boat business. When all six passengers were on board, the captain jumped off the boat, undid the mooring lines, and then hopped back on and climbed up to the bridge. He backed the boat out of its slip and onto the bay. From below deck a young woman came up dressed in boots, denims, a blue and gold Notre Dame sweatshirt, and a heavy, yellow rain slicker. Her eyes were watery and her short, dark hair was pressed flat against one side of her head, as if she had just a moment ago been sleeping. She introduced herself as Tina, the captain's daughter, and explained she was working this trip as First Mate, which meant she'd be the one untangling lines and helping with the tackle. Then she looked at Barbara, who was dressed in shorts and a summer blouse, and said. "You're going to freeze like that, M'am. Want to borrow a sweatshirt?"

§

Barbara shook her head, although she was already hugging herself and shivering slightly. "It's supposed to get hot later," she said.

The girl laughed. "Not on the water," she said. "Not this morning." She disappeared below deck again and came back up with a ratty gray sweatshirt, which she tossed to Barbara. Barbara put it on and continued hugging herself and shivering.

By the time the sun came up, everyone was fishing. The captain had taken the boat out past Tatoosh Island, onto the Pacific, and within forty-five minutes everyone had pulled at least one salmon on board. The Canadian couple had each caught two big sockeyes in rapid succession, and Tina was kept busy unhooking everyone's catch and getting their lines back in the water. In minutes the deck had grown slippery with fish slime, and the pervasive stink of fish grew so intense it was as much a taste as a smell. The sun had risen on a gray, chilly, misty morning, and the ocean swells regularly lifted and dropped, lifted and dropped The Raven, as one after the other the fishers yelled out "fish on!" and Tina came running with a net or a gaff, depending on the degree of bow in the pole tip.

Barbara was the first to get sick. Then Adam, Adele, and Barrett joined her. The Canadian couple were fine. They stood side by side in the stern of the boat, and it was as if their mass and bulk created a solid, unmoving place in the midst of a rolling, perpetually moving ocean. They kept fishing away, pulling in salmon after salmon, while one by one Barbara, Barrett, Adele, and Adam made trip after trip from the deck to bathroom, from the deck to bathroom. After a while they gave up trying to fish and each descended the short stairway to the cabin belowdeck, where they lay on benches and cushions, trying to maintain some control over the awful sickness in their stomachs. It was no use. They kept having to carry themselves to the bathroom, where the smell of vomit and diarrhea mingled with the ubiquitous stink of fish.

On one of his trips back from the head, Barrett sat next to Adele, at her feet, and across from Adam and Barbara. The cabin was a tight, dark place with only two small portholes to bring in light. Benches followed the contour of the boat's hull. They were covered with thin, dirty cushions, and the tops of the benches were hinged and apparently opened up to create storage space. Barbara and Adele were stretched out on the benches, curled up into fetal balls. Barrett was sitting with his head between his legs.

"Barrett," Adam said. "Can you die from seasickness?"

Barrett's voice was harsh. "Damn," he said. "What I'd give for solid ground."

"Jesus," Adam went on. "I'm serious. I really feel like my stomach's bleeding or something. I think I saw blood last time I puked."

Adele said, weakly: "Nobody dies from seasickness, Adam."

"How do you know!" Adam snapped back at her. "Are you an expert or something?"

Adele opened her eyes and lifted her head from the bench. "Adam," she said, firmly. "Your stomach's not bleeding. Once we get on land, you'll be okay."

"Are you sure?" Adam said. He dropped his head down between his legs and clasped his hands over the back of his neck. When Adele didn't answer, he asked again, sounding close to tears: "Honey? Are you sure?"

"I'm sure." Adele looked over her knees, to Barrett, who was sitting up straight now, with his back against the hull. When she caught his eye, she shook her head, as if exasperated.

"Barrett," Adam whined. "Will you go talk to the captain? Maybe he'll take us back in."

Barrett was silent a long moment; then he pulled himself to his feet. "What the hell," he said. "It's worth a try."

"Really," Barbara said, opening her eyes for the first time. "You think he might?"

Barrett made a face, indicating that he doubted it, seriously. Then he climbed the stairs to the deck and a metal ladder to the bridge, where he found the captain fiddling with the electronics. He asked him to take them back in, and, as he expected, the captain refused, explaining he'd have to refund the Canadians' money, and that would make the day a loss. Barrett offered to cover the captain's losses, but he just shook his head and looked out over the bridge to the ocean. Barrett returned belowdeck, defeated. Along with the others, he lay around in misery for

ဌ

another hour before the Canadians softened, having anyway caught the boat's limit for salmon, and allowed the captain to take them in. When they finally made it back to the campsite on Cape Flattery, everyone crawled into a tent and immediately fell asleep.

§

It was late afternoon when Adele opened her eyes. Alongside her, Adam lay stretched out on top of his sleeping bag. He lay on his stomach, naked except for the bright red briefs that clung to him tightly as a tattoo. His body was covered with a sheen of perspiration: a pool of sweat had gathered in the small of his back, and his hair looked as though he had just stepped out of the shower. Adele was also soaked. She ran her hand over her chest and stomach, and sweat ran down her sides in rivulets. She sat up and let herself awaken slowly to the sounds and sensations around her. It was quiet. And it was hot. Very hot. She pulled on a pair of cutoff denims and a T-shirt, and she crawled out of the tent.

The campsite and the surrounding woods seemed eerily still. There was no breeze, and the heat, even in the shade of the forest, was palpable: she could feel it on her skin like standing close to a fire. The only sound was the constant, faraway murmur of the ocean. It didn't take Adele more than a few moments of standing in the heat to decide she wanted to go for a swim. She retrieved a pair of sneakers from her tent and started down the trail to the shore. When she approached the beach, she found Barrett crouched in the surf. He was sitting on his haunches, wearing a blue bathing suit, looking out over the ocean as water rushed back and forth over his feet and ankles.

At Adele's approach, Barrett turned around and smiled. "You believe this heat?" he asked.

Adele knelt alongside him, immersing her calves and thighs in the water. She threw her torso forward as she pushed her hair up over the back of her neck and submerged her face and hair in the surf, rubbing the cooling water into her scalp and forehead and eyes. She came up shaking her head, getting Barrett wet. "Oh God," she said. "That was good. I think I roasted in the tent."

§

Barrett laughed and wiped the water away from his face. "Are Adam and Barbara up yet?"

Adele shook her head. "Still cooking," she said. "At least when I left they were."

"Poor Adam," Barrett said. "He thought he was going to die out there."

"He's such a baby." Adele turned around so that she was facing Barrett. She sat in water up to her waist. "Do you mind if I ask you something?"

"Go ahead."

Adele hesitated. She was sitting with her legs stretched out and open in a V, and she swirled the water between her legs with a crooked finger. "I'd better not," she said, and she looked away and then back, as if with that motion she had turned the page in a book and was now reading from a new script. "I got so sick out there," she said, referring to the fishing trip. "For a while, out on the water, it felt like I was blind. Do you know what I mean? It was like I couldn't see: up and down, up and down, drifting, moving. . . . Do you have any idea at all what I'm talking about, Barrett?"

Adele was being cute, and Barrett smiled in response. It was an honest smile. "I think I know what you mean. So?"

"So, what?"

"The question," Barrett said. "The question you wanted to ask."

Adele's expression changed suddenly. Her eyes in an instant grew watery.

Barrett put his hand on Adele's knee. "What is it?"

"Adam and I are not going to last," she said. "I mean, I doubt we'll be together another month after this vacation."

Barrett looked off, past Adele, his face taking on an appropriate expression, a world-weary look of sadness for the unfortunate ways of this world. The rate of his heartbeat, however, picked up slightly. "I'm sorry," he said. "I didn't know things were bad between you."

"It's not that things are bad," Adele said. "I doubt Adam has any idea. It's just that. . . . He's such a little boy. He's sweet, but it's like being married to a child. You heard him on the boat." She looked up at Barrett, as if wanting confirmation. "He was whimpering, for God's sake. I mean, if someone had taped that exchange in the cabin, it could have been a ten-year-old boy talking to his mother." Adele touched Barrett's hand. "Am I inventing all this?" she said. "Isn't that how it sounded to you?"

Barrett rubbed his eyes with his fingertips, hiding his face momentarily. Of course Adam was boyish. It was the way he was. Adele's complaints against Adam threw Barrett back into his own refuse heap of complaints—his wives' against him and his against his wives—complaints that had wrecked one marriage after the other. The problems were many, the details numerous, but after three marriages all Barrett really remembered was the process by which things fell apart, the faults real and invented that led to arguments followed by unhappiness followed by separation. It wasn't that the specifics, the details of the complaints, had disappeared; it was just that now they seemed unimportant in comparison to the process of coming apart, a process he had been through three times already. So Adam was boyish. That was Adele's complaint. What was his complaint against Barbara? There were several, none of which seemed very important at the moment.

Barrett removed his hands from his eyes in time to see the emotion gathering in Adele's face, building second by second as he failed to respond. "Of course," he said. "That's something about Adam. He's like a kid sometimes."

Adele looked up at the cape and closed her eyes for a long moment. Then she turned to Barrett and stared at him intently, waiting to read his smallest gesture.

Barrett had been here many times before, at this moment. It was the moment when he had only to touch her and she would lean toward him and they would embrace. He could kiss her now. He could touch her. She wanted to be kissed and touched by him. This was the moment when it might begin, whatever it would turn out to be: an affair, love, a sexual adventure. He stood up and extended a hand down to Adele. "Let's walk a little," he said.

Adele took his hand and lifted herself from the water. She walked alongside Barrett in her dripping cutoffs and soaked sneakers. Her

T-shirt too had gotten wet and it clung to her, the shape of her breasts and the color of her skin revealed almost entirely through the thin fabric.

Barrett looked away, toward the green hills that sloped down to the sand. They were walking toward a place where three boulders formed a semicircle on the beach and three more out in the water completed the circle.

"Can I ask my question now?" Adele said.

"Sure. Go ahead," Barrett answered without looking at her.

"You and Barbara," she said. "Are you going to last? Are you two going to make it?"

Barrett's heart was beating fast. He didn't answer. He looked down at his feet and folded his arms over his chest as if contemplating a response.

They had reached the circle of boulders and Adele stopped and looked around. The boulders formed a small private beach, a place protected from the casual view of others. "I'm going in here," she said, and she pulled off her clothes and waded into a deep tidal pool that was still connected by a flowing stream of water to the ocean.

Barrett had watched her as she tore off her clothes and tossed them in a heap on the sand, his eyes searching out the soft and shadowy places, the slow curves and sloping angles of her skin. He followed her into the tidal pool. When she turned around to face him again, standing waist-deep in water, he stepped close to her, took her hands in his and said, "No. We're not going to make it." When he spoke, he heard his voice change, the timbre turning just slightly more resonant, the tone dropping a note. It was his best acting voice and it had emerged out of nowhere, on its own. It surprised him, as did the tears welling in his eyes.

Adele brushed the tears away with wet fingers. "I didn't think so," she said. "You act as though you don't even like each other any more."

"She doesn't understand me," Barrett said, and he bowed his head and covered his eyes with his hands, and as soon as he did it, the gesture seemed fake to him. He half expected to hear a director yell *cut!* He pushed on. "I feel empty," he said. "We're married . . . but I feel. . . ."

ᔕ

He heard himself speaking, but he could hardly believe what he was hearing.

"I know," Adele said, and she embraced Barrett, wrapping her arms around him and holding him tight against her. She repeated: "I know. I know exactly."

Barrett pulled away and held Adele at arm's length. "I have a question for you," he said, allowing a note of urgency into his voice. "The other night, when you went swimming with Adam and Barbara, did you know . . . Did you know I was watching you?"

"From the cape?" she said. "With the binoculars?"

"Yes," Barrett said. "How? How did you know?"

"I didn't. I mean, I didn't know—but I imagined it. I imagined you were up there watching. . . . And it was like I could feel you, I could feel your eyes on me."

"But what made you think . . ."

"It's your eyes. . . . They're hungry. Everyone sees it in you. It's just, like, a hunger about you . . ."

"It's crazy," Barrett said, "because . . . I felt this connection between us then. It was like something real between us. I felt filled up by it. I can't explain, really. . . ." He leaned forward, as if he were tired of stumbling for words, and he embraced and kissed Adele, his lips pressing hard against her lips, his tongue pushing into her mouth.

Adele returned the kiss, letting her hands move over his back, clutching and releasing his shoulders—but when his head moved lower, to her breasts, and he tried to pull her down to the water, she resisted. "Not here," she said. "Barrett. Not now." She stepped back from him. They had moved, while kissing, into shallower water, and Barrett was on his knees, looking up at her. She ran her fingers through his wet hair.

Barrett took her hand and pulled her toward him. "Yes," he said. "Here. Now."

Adele shook her head and remained standing. "Someone might come by. Barbara or Adam. . . . They're probably up."

Barrett looked at the sky, at the wavering, late-afternoon light. "No one can see us here," he said, and he ran his hand along the length of her thigh. "Adele," he said. He leaned forward and kissed her leg, high, above the knee. "Listen," he said. "There's nothing to life but moments like this. Intense moments like this." He touched his chest. "My heart is racing," he said. "I'm looking at a beautiful woman, and my heart is a drumbeat: it's pounding in my chest." He took Adele's hand and held it over his heart. She came down to her knees in the water. She knelt in front of him, her hand pressed flat against his breast. "We'd regret it forever," he said, "if we let this moment pass." He embraced her and kissed her and turned her body around, moving them both toward shallower water, where he lay on his back and pulled off his swimming trunks, and moved his body under Adele's, threading his legs between her legs. He had, then, only to thrust his thighs up and they were joined. Above him, Adele's head blocked out the bright yellow circle of the sun, the heels of her hands pressed against her temples, her fingers buried in her hair. She appeared, from the angle where Barrett looked up at her, to be floating away from the earth, attached to nothing, not him or the ground or the water; and in the pleasure of the moment, Barrett too felt as though he were floating—into a place of pure sensation, rising free of the gritty earth. Then he moved his hips, pushing into the heat of Adele's body, and the seasickness from earlier in the day came back with a rush. He felt as sick as he had at any point on the boat trip.

Barrett tried to hold himself steady to let the sickness pass, but Adele was moving rhythmically, the palms of her hands flat against his chest, pushing him down into the sand and water. He held Adele's wrists, and behind him, from someplace beyond and above the boulders, he heard a sound like a rock might make being kicked in the sand. He wanted to turn around and look, but he was afraid of what he might see. He feared that Barbara and Adam were above them on the beach looking down at them in the water. He closed his eyes and told himself these feelings would pass in a moment if he remained calm. His mind swirled and his nausea swelled, but his body kept properly functioning. Adele appeared to have no idea there was a problem. When he felt her hair brushing his chest, he opened his eyes and found himself looking into a rip in the fabric of the sky, a shift-

ↄ

ing blaze of energy and light. He threw his forearm up over his eyes, and the motion sent him spinning, as if he were spiraling up and away. With his other hand he grasped blindly for Adele, and when he found her shoulders he pulled himself up and wrapped his arms around her.

"What?" Adele said. "What is it?"

Barrett didn't answer. His eyes were filled with a mosaic of color, blinding him to the solid coastline that might have steadied him; and the blood rushing in his ears made him deaf to the music of water and earth and wind that might have calmed him. He was sick. His body was tumbling through light and space. He held on tight to Adele, as if her body could anchor him.

"Barrett?" Adele said. She wiped away the sweat gathering at his temples. "Barrett," she repeated. "Can you tell me what it is?" And when Barrett didn't answer, when he continued mutely clinging to her, she tried to calm him by saying, again and again, soothingly, "Tell me, Barrett. Tell me. Tell me what it is."

AX

Ax laid his head on top of the classroom desk and looked out at the campus. Beyond a pane of glass dripping with condensation, ice encased tree and shrub: it hung in frozen pendants from wires, it glazed the grass on the quad. At the front of the room, the professor finished his lecture. It was the first day of the spring semester. He crossed his arms over his chest and looked worriedly toward the back of the room. "Ax," he said. "I haven't bored you, have I?"

The class laughed.

Ax sat up straight. He ran the palm of one hand slowly over his shaved head until it came to a ponytail wrapped tight in a rubber band: silky blond hair protruded straight out from the back of his head for a couple of inches before falling in a neat twist down the length of his neck. He held the ponytail in his fist. "Professor Crowder—"

"Jim," the professor interrupted. "I prefer to be called by my first name—as I announced at the start of the class."

Ax hesitated, uncomfortable with calling Crowder by his first name.

"I know it's hard," Crowder said. "Perhaps if I changed my name to Hammer, or Spike. . . ." The class roared. With a wave of his hand, the professor dismissed them. He pointed to the blackboard, to the quote: "the seen walls of lost Eden could not have been more beautiful," and said, "Read the Ruskin assignment for the next class."

Ax slid out of his chair and hoisted a black bookbag to his shoulder. Over the noise of chattering students and chair legs grating against the tile floor, the professor called out to Ax and motioned for him to come to the front of the room. While Crowder answered the questions of several students standing around him in a semicircle, Ax leaned against the light green cinder blocks of the classroom wall. Crowder was sitting on the front of his desk with the palms of his hands over his knees. When the last student left, he turned to Ax. He was silent a moment and the room filled up with the buzz of fluorescent lighting. "Alex," he said, finally, his voice diving lower. "It's good to see you back."

Ax looked down at his pants legs, at the frayed and ripped fabric at the knees. "Thanks," he answered. Last year, his sophomore year, Ax had been good friends with Bill and Charlotte Everwine, English Department professors, a married couple in their early forties. He had met them in the fall semester and moved into a room in their house in the spring. He did work on their property, twenty-five acres of mostly wooded land, and around the house, in return for room and board. During the time he lived with them, he got to know most of the faculty in the department, including Professor Crowder. Then, a few weeks after he had left for summer vacation, Bill Everwine committed suicide: he hanged himself from a tree behind their house. Fall semester, Ax had stayed home and worked for his father. The knowledge of all this was in the tone of Professor Crowder's voice. Ax said, "I didn't know if I was going to, come back to school. It shook me up, everything."

"Of course," Professor Crowder said. "I think everybody understood that." He slid down off the desk. He was wearing thick corduroy pants, and he pushed his hands into the pockets. "Charlotte would like you to stop in and see her. She's in her office."

Ax looked away, toward the classroom door.

"Charlotte thinks you're avoiding her. You didn't go to the funeral. You didn't come back to school." Crowder hesitated slightly, as if he were suddenly unsure of himself. "You should talk with Charlotte," he said. "It'll be good for you."

🌀

"She's in her office?" Ax said.

"Go see her." Crowder offered his hand and Ax shook it.

In the corridor, Ax moved among knots of students. While he lived with the Everwines he had . . . What? Had an affair with Charlotte? No. It wasn't an affair. It wasn't passionate or romantic. It was something different, something he hadn't understood then and didn't understand now. The first time was soon after he moved in. He had been working in the greenhouse with Bill. The greenhouse was a large room attached to the family room. It extended out into the yard, under the kitchen. Bill had knocked out the wall himself and attached the double-insulated sheets of glass to a hardwood frame. Ax had worked with Bill for most of the day, and when they were done his hands and face were grimy. Bill pointed him to a makeshift shower in a corner of the greenhouse and left him alone. Ax stepped inside a circular curtain, undressed, and showered. While he was drying off, he looked up. Then or now, he didn't know what made him look up, but when he did, he saw Charlotte leaning over the kitchen sink, looking down at him through the top of the greenhouse. When he saw her, he looked away quickly. When he looked back, she wasn't there. He got dressed and went to his room.

Dinner that evening, Bill told stories, as usual, and Charlotte made her usual joking comments. They were both more than twice Ax's age, but he felt comfortable hanging out with them. They were smart. They seemed to know something—a lot—about everything; and they were good company, certainly better than his parents, who frowned whenever he was around, unhappy with his shaved head and ponytail, with the tattered clothes he wore. The Everwines were different. They approved of the way he looked. And he liked them: Bill, with his mile-a-minute chatter, his perpetual motion; and Charlotte with her cynical sense of humor, even if she could be mean when she wanted.

By the time dinner was over, Ax had quit thinking about the shower. So what if Charlotte wanted to check him out? If the situation were reversed, he might have done the same thing. Who could be sure he wouldn't have? No big deal, Ax decided. Besides, he didn't believe in convention and tradition anyway—as he had announced to both Charlotte and Bill any number of times. What were clothes but a societal convention? Why was it okay for women to see men's breasts, but not for men to see women's breasts?

When Bill finished his last mouthful of broccoli, chewing elaborately to indicate his pleasure, he pushed his plate away and burped.

Ax looked embarrassed.

Bill pressed his hands to his cheeks. "Oh my God," he said to Charlotte, sitting directly across the table from him. "Have I offended?"

"Not that I can see," Charlotte said.

Bill leaned toward Ax, half lifting himself out of his seat. He was tall and thin, and he didn't have to lean far to hover over Ax where he sat at the center of the table. "A burp, my friend, is a way of complimenting the cook—in this case, me." He remained hovering over Ax, staring at him. "Not to burp after a meal," he said, "is an insult."

Charlotte joined Bill in staring at Ax.

"What?" Ax said.

"Burp," Charlotte said.

"Burp?"

Bill said, "You don't want to insult the cook, do you?"

Ax burped.

Charlotte applauded.

"Thank you," Bill said, touching his heart with his hand to indicate his sincerity. Then he hurried away from the table. "Chores," he announced. "I've got to go meet with a student whose thesis is stuck."

"Better hurry," Charlotte said. She began clearing the table.

"I'll help." Ax picked up his and Bill's plates, and started for the sink.

"You clear the table," Charlotte said, "and I'll go give Mr. Bill a kiss for the road."

Ax said, "Fine," and when he turned around from the sink, the kitchen was empty. From the front of the house, he heard the squeak of the screen door opening, then the murmur of hushed voices and a long moment of silence, during which he imagined Bill and Charlotte were kissing. Before the screen door closed, Molly, the family dog, a white and tan springer spaniel, trotted into the house and made a beeline for Ax. Ax knelt and roughhoused with the dog, who promptly lay on her back and offered Ax her stomach to rub. Ax patted her. When he looked up, Charlotte was leaning against the kitchen door, watching him.

"Molly's tracking mud." Ax held up a paw to illustrate.

Charlotte was smiling slightly. "She adores you," she said. Like Bill, Charlotte was tall—for a woman at least. She must have been five ten or so, the same as Ax, but from where he was on the floor, looking up at her, she seemed taller. She was wearing the kind of dress that wrapped around her and was fastened with a belt. There was a long moment of silence while Ax just stared up at her, unable to think of anything to say. Then she undid the belt and the dress fell open. She wasn't wearing anything under it. "Ax," she said. "Interested?"

Ax didn't answer. He looked away for a moment. When he stood up, he could feel the color draining from his face. He felt light-headed. When he looked at her again, his glance fell on her breasts and traveled down the length of her body. Charlotte's eyes were lined with wrinkles—she had crow's feet that extended to her temples—but her body was youthful, her skin tight and smooth. She stood on her toes and leaned back against the wall. When she came down, the kitchen light switched off. In the semi-darkness, she crossed the room slowly, dropping her arms and shoulders so that the dress fell way, floating down off her back to the floor. Moonlight came into the kitchen through the window over the sink, and in that softer light, she grew younger, sylphlike. She put her hands on his chest and then slid them around to his back as she laid her head on his shoulder and dropped slowly to her knees, her cheek sliding down his shirt, over his belt buckle, her hands sliding down his back. It was over in a few minutes, almost before he fully comprehended what had happened. She wiped her lips with the back of her hand and kissed him on the forehead. After she was gone, after he heard her bedroom door click shut, he realized he hadn't said a word.

When he started straightening himself out, arranging himself, he saw that his arms and legs were quivering—as if his muscles were suddenly, just slightly, out of control. He went up to his room and lay on

ʕ

his bed with the lights off. In the darkness, he berated himself. He shouldn't have let it happen. He should have found a decent way out of the situation. Then, a moment later, he was seeing Charlotte again: crossing the kitchen in moonlight, her dress falling off her shoulders. While Ax lay there in the darkness, Molly pushed the door to his room open and jumped up on the bed. She pushed her snout up under Ax's armpit, and Ax stroked her head gently. The dog made him think of his late-afternoon walks with Bill and Charlotte, when they'd take Molly and follow one of the many trails through the woods behind the house. While they walked—with Bill usually holding forth on one subject or another—Molly hurried in front of them like an enthusiastic child, anxious to see what was around the next bend, but not wanting to venture too far from home base. Ax liked being part of Molly's home base. He wondered if things could be the same after what had happened.

The next morning Bill got him out of bed early for a greenhouse project. By 6 AM, they were all in the kitchen. While Charlotte made apple pancakes, grating unnaturally red grocery-store apples into a premixed batter, Molly lying at her feet with her eyes following her every move, hoping for a crumb to fall her way; and while Ax sat hunched over a hot cup of black coffee, Bill entertained them both by mocking his graduate student's thesis on the influence of Chinese pictographs on Ezra Pound's poetry. "Sweet Jesus," he said. "You should have seen the look I got when I told her Pound couldn't read Chinese. Her face went white, she shrunk about two inches, and she kept saying 'but . . . but . . . but . . .'" At the sink, Charlotte, who knew and didn't like the student, doubled over laughing. By the time breakfast was done, everything seemed to be back to normal. If Bill had noticed any nervousness in Ax, he hadn't mentioned it. For the rest of the spring, that was how things went. Ax had sex with Charlotte once or twice a week. He never said anything. Mostly, she came into his bed late at night. It was almost as if the sex happened in some other dimension, some other branch of reality. It was like a dream: a kind of experience that didn't have any real-world consequences. Except, a few weeks after Ax went home for the summer, Bill hanged himself.

☉

As Ax approached Charlotte's office, he wondered what he would do if he found out that what had happened between him and Charlotte had something to do with Bill's suicide. All he knew for sure was that he wished he didn't have to think about it. He wished he could avoid knowing. In his heart, he felt it had to have something to do with him and Charlotte. All that last spring, Bill had been full of projects and ideas. He had been a habitual swirl of movement and talk. Why all of a sudden? It had to have something to do with him and Charlotte. He knew, but he didn't know for sure—and he didn't want to. That was why he didn't go to the funeral. That was why he didn't return to school in the fall. What was going to happen now? What if Charlotte said, "Ax, when I told him about us, he couldn't take it"? Ax had envisioned this meeting a thousand times, and his imaginings ran from the dramatic—"Alex. He thought of you like a son"— to the cynical: Charlotte wanting to take up where they left off. He was also afraid that she would be angry with him. He hated it when others were angry with him. It was not an emotion he understood well. He hardly ever felt it himself. It was as if that emotion had somehow been muted in him. What Ax wanted was for the whole thing to go away. He was twenty years old. He was too young to carry such a weight.

At Charlotte's office, he didn't hesitate. There was no way around seeing her again, not as long as he was a student. He knocked on the door and waited. When she opened the door and he stepped inside, all thought went out of his head. She looked older. And she seemed angry. He crossed the room and sat in the chair beside her desk, while she closed the office door. When he realized he was smiling and that he must look inane, he quickly altered his expression, putting on a solemn face. "Charlotte," he said.

Charlotte interrupted, as if surprised: "Just the two of us, and you speak?"

Alex ran his hand over his head and grasped his ponytail. His eyes brimmed.

"For God's sake," Charlotte said. "Don't cry. And let go of your ponytail. Bill always said you hold onto that thing like a kid holds onto his dick."

§

Ax let go of the ponytail. He rubbed the tears out of his eyes; then clasped his hands together, fingers interlocked, and rested them on his knees. He looked up at Charlotte, his teeth clenched, as if readying himself for another blow.

Charlotte's expression softened. The office smelled strongly of chemicals, the sharp odor of mimeograph ink. She sat at her desk, her chair swiveled toward the wall. "*Ax*," she said. "Where the hell'd you get a name like that anyway? It makes you sound like some kind of object." She pushed a stack of silk-screened posters onto the floor. "I think the smell of these things has got me stoned." She shook her head as if to clear it, and then turned to Ax. "Look," she said. "Why I wanted to talk to you, it's got nothing to do with me or Bill—or you. Not directly anyway. That's up to you. If you want to disappear, Ax, that's fine. I'm not going to cause any problems."

"I don't want to disappear," Ax said quickly. He saw that Charlotte was waiting for him to go on, but he couldn't think of anything else to say. He looked around the room, at books piled on the floor, at two empty garbage pails sitting in the midst of stacks of papers and overflowing file folders. On the wall, a nail had come loose and a large bulletin board dangled diagonally.

"Place is a mess," Charlotte said.

"It's not like you."

"This is not a place to talk, anyway. I wanted to see you because I need a favor." She crossed her arms under her breasts. "I want you to help me shoot Molly. I have to kill her."

Ax laughed. When Charlotte didn't indicate immediately that she was kidding, he sat there looking stupid, a dumb grin on his face. He said, "You're not serious, are you?"

"She's got cancer of the mouth." Charlotte spoke slowly, as if she were tired.

"When?" Ax said. "How long has she had it?"

"A few months." She fingered a stack of papers on her desk. "Her mouth's a mess."

"There's nothing anybody—"

"Sure," Charlotte said, a touch of anger returning to her voice. "It's not the kind of cancer that will kill her. It'll just make her miserable for the rest of her life. It hurts her to eat or drink. And if I don't scrape the dead tissue and God-knows-what shit out of her mouth every few days, she'll starve to death because she won't eat at all. Are you willing to take care of her?"

"I'm not willing to shoot her," Ax said.

"I should have guessed." Charlotte's anger appeared to flare up. Then it disappeared. "Okay," she said. "It's not a big deal. She's a sick dog. . . . I'm not looking forward to it either."

Ax stood up. His stomach was fluttery. "Can't you just take her to the vet?"

"Is that what you'd do, Ax? Drop her off in some antiseptic-smelling office and then leave?"

"Is it better to take her out in the woods and put a bullet through her head?"

"Yes," Charlotte said, "If you were the dog, which would you prefer?"

Ax tried to think. He was sweating, and he wiped the moisture from his forehead and upper lip. "I can't do it," he said. "I'm sorry."

"It's all right, Ax." Charlotte took him by the arm and showed him out of her office. She opened the door for him. "I shouldn't have even asked." She smiled and closed the door as he stepped out into the hall.

Ax was already in his dorm room before he remembered he was supposed to be on the other side of campus, that he was about to miss his next class. He flung his bookbag onto his desk and sat on the windowsill—after clearing a small space for himself by knocking away a pair of sneakers with socks draped over them. He hadn't had to get too close to the sneakers and socks before realizing why they were on the windowsill, under a slightly opened window. His roommate, whom he hardly ever saw, was prohibited by his religion from ever picking anything up off the floor or doing laundry more than once a semester—or so he claimed. The room bore testament to his convictions. The desk tops, the bunk beds, the floor, every inch of surface space in the room was covered with towels, sheets, crumpled papers, books, boots, shoes, sporting equipment, soda and beer cans, wine and liquor bottles, food wrappings, and, in one corner, a long-forgotten, half-eaten pizza, still in its box. Ax knew he couldn't stand it much longer and soon he'd have to clean it himself. So did his roommate.

Outside, the cars in the parking lot were the only things not coated with ice. It was late in the day, and most of the cars had already been driven someplace and back. Ax considered taking a nap, but his roommate, for some reason, had emptied the contents of two dresser drawers onto his bed, and it felt like too much trouble to get up and clear it off. When he lived with the Everwines, he had a room to himself. He kept it neat. Ax found clean clothes, neatly pressed and laid in place in a dresser drawer, soothing. He liked housecleaning. He liked the feel of warm water running over his hands as he washed dishes. He loved the warmth of clothes right out of the dryer, their fresh smells and clean, bright colors. When he was folding newly washed and dried clothes, he would often stop a few moments and hold a warm piece of clothing against his neck or cheek. He was comfortable amidst order.

The Everwine house had been the only place he had ever lived entirely to his liking. Their house was beautiful. The hardwood floors of the living and dining room were buffed to a high polish. The walls were painted a soft off-white. Huge skylights in the living room and kitchen filled the house with natural light. The downstairs family room had a big, brick fireplace, and one wall was glass with a long sliding door that opened into the greenhouse. By contrast, his own house, his family house, was never in good repair, and without him around it was a pig sty. His mother had never liked cleaning. When Ax thought of his mother, he saw her sitting in the darkened living room, the blinds closed and the curtains drawn, smoking cigarette after cigarette as she lay back in a ratty gray recliner with her eyes closed. She claimed it was headaches brought on by women's problems that confined her to dark rooms. She claimed that movement and light brought on migraine headaches. Ax's father claimed she was lazy. He said she had given up on life, and he'd shout that at her again and again when they argued, year after year, about the dogs pissing on the rugs, about dishes going unwashed, about Alex going unfed and uncared-for, about her not being a good mother.

Alex couldn't remember when he started taking care of himself, making his own meals, washing and ironing his own clothes—but he was young, seven or eight. By the time he was a teenager, he was making the meals for all of them, washing and ironing everybody's clothes. Part of him felt as if, somehow, he was responsible for his mother's headaches, for her fights with his father. He felt as though, if he could only keep things neat enough, if he could keep things clean enough, if his mother didn't have to worry about him, about being a good mother or keeping a neat house, then the headaches would go away, then his father would stop fighting with her. But it didn't work like that. No matter how much Alex cleaned, no matter how much he tried to keep the house in order, his mother's headaches continued, she remained in darkened rooms smoking cigarettes, and his father insisted that she had given up on life. The only obvious consequence of Alex's self-sufficiency was that his name no longer came up when they fought.

As he sat on the windowsill, looking out into the parking lot, Ax's sleepiness made a compromise with his reluctance to clear off the bed: he crossed the room, slid his hands under the mattress and flipped the whole thing over. He wrestled his blanket free, wrapped it around his shoulders, and flopped down onto the bed. A few minutes later, he was asleep. When he woke, the room was dark and he was hungry. Somewhere on his hall, someone was playing Pearl Jam—loud. Eddie Vedder's voice moaned. Music was also coming from the room above him, though Pearl Jam drowned out everything but the repetitive thud of the bass. In the light of a full moon coming through the uncurtained windows, he got up and opened the top drawer of his desk, where he found his car keys. He stretched and yawned and noticed for the first time the faint odor of incense—which meant that, as usual, somebody on the hall was smoking dope. He bundled up, putting on his long winter coat, along with hat, scarf, and gloves, and stepped out into the hall, where the fluorescent lighting was so bright it hurt his

⑤

eyes. It was like stepping out into a spotlight. He hurried down the long hallway and out the heavy fire doors to the parking lot.

His car was neatly encased in an envelope of ice. He kicked the trunk with the flat of his foot, and a sheet of ice slid off the car and shattered like glass at his feet. He got the scraper out of the trunk and started to work on the car windows. After he had chipped the ice away from the windshield, he unbuttoned his coat. It was cold, but there was very little wind, only an occasional gust. Under his coat, he was sweating. When he finished with the windows, he got in the car, let the engine run for a few minutes, and then drove to the drive-thru at Wendy's. A freckled teenager with a surly expression slid open the delivery window and handed him his bag of food. He ate on the way to Charlotte's.

Every once in a while, as he drove out of town and onto the familiar back roads that led to Bill and Charlotte's house, he'd shake his head, as if he couldn't believe what he was doing. He hadn't ever killed anything bigger than a bug, and he wasn't anxious to start with Molly—but he couldn't stand the way Charlotte had looked at him as she showed him out of her office. Her face had been full of disdain. Her smile as she closed the door had held something close to disgust. All those nights in the spring, when she came into his bed—sometimes she had seemed disappointed because he wouldn't speak to her, sometimes her disappointment turned sharper, into something more like anger. He had wondered what would have happened if she had pushed him, if she had insisted he respond, instead of just asking a question, waiting, and then filling in the answer.

At Charlotte's house, he drove slowly up the driveway and then sat in the car for a few minutes after parking and before turning off the engine and the lights. He had hoped she would hear the car and come to the door, but when he stepped out into her front yard, there was no sign of movement. Ice cracked under his feet as he walked across the lawn. He stopped and crouched for a moment and pulled the ice covering off a slip of grass. It came off neatly, a small, hollow ice sculpture. He held it up to the moonlight.

"Very romantic," Charlotte said. "'Ax Appreciates Nature.'"

〽

Ax couldn't locate Charlotte's voice. He looked over the house again, searching the windows, but didn't see anything.

"Good grief," Charlotte said. "Over here."

She was sitting on the bottom limb of a tree, off to the side of the house. She was wearing several layers of outer clothes. Ax could barely see her eyes peering out from between a knit hat and a wool scarf.

She slid off the tree limb and walked toward him. "I saw you coming. When you didn't get out of the car, I thought you were just going to turn around and go home, change your mind."

Ax shook his head. "No."

"Then you're just in time." She touched his arm, indicating that he should come with her, and they started for the back of the house. "When I saw your car coming, I was waiting out here, trying to get my nerve up. Molly's in the shed."

Ax walked silently beside Charlotte. When they reached the shed, she undid a latch and they both went inside. The shed was a fairly large wood structure—like a small barn. It housed the lawn mower–tractor and a variety of outdoor tools. In one corner, an old electric space heater rattled loudly, its circular red coils pushing heat toward a blanket where Molly lay curled up in a small circle.

Molly lifted her head and twisted around—only mildly curious at who was entering the shed. When she saw Ax, she leapt up, bounded across the space between them, and jumped onto his chest. Ax spoke to her and patted her head.

"She always adored you," Charlotte said. She reached down toward the foot of the tractor and came up with a rifle case.

Ax watched her unzip the case, drop something inside it, and zip it up again. "She doesn't look sick at all," Ax said. Molly had rolled onto her back and Ax was rubbing her stomach.

Charlotte started for the shed door, carrying the rifle case by its handle. "Look in her mouth."

Ax moved around in front of Molly and knelt at her head. When he tried to open Molly's mouth, the dog let out a high-pitched squeal and backed away from him.

ᔥ

"She's fine," Charlotte said, "as long as she doesn't have to eat or drink." She pushed the shed door open with her shoulder and motioned with the rifle for Ax to lead the way.

On the trail into the woods, Molly followed at Ax's side, rather than running ahead the way Ax remembered. "She doesn't seem as perky as she used to."

"No," Charlotte said. "She's not. Sometimes she's in a lot of pain. You can see it."

Ax noticed that Molly's legs seemed stiff as she walked over the icy path. "What about a shovel?" he said. "Are we going to bury her out there?"

"I dug the hole a month ago. It's under the tree where Bill hanged himself." She smiled sweetly at Ax. "You don't think I'm being too sentimental, do you?" Then she laughed a short, bitter laugh.

Ax stopped for a moment, then hurried to catch up.

She turned to look at him. "You could have at least sent a god-damned card."

When Ax felt his eyes filling with tears, he remembered how Charlotte's telling him not to cry in her office stung him. He looked away from her, gritted his teeth, and blinked the tears away. To his surprise, when he spoke he sounded angry. He said, "I suppose I felt guilty. I guessed what we were doing, what happened between us, it had something to do with it, with Bill killing himself." He had to stop. He reached behind his head and touched his ponytail, and then quickly pulled his hand away.

"What is it that you think happened between us?"

Ax didn't answer. They had reached a small clearing in the woods. Charlotte stopped and motioned toward a tree, where a mound of dirt was piled against the trunk, over a hole that must have been three or four feet deep and equally long. The dirt and the tree were covered with a casing of ice, as was everything else in the clearing: the branches, the leaves on the trees, the grass under their feet. Molly planted her front paws at the edge of the hole and looked down into it, sniffing.

Charlotte put the rifle down near the hole. She looked up at a thick branch extending out from the tree, reaching over the clearing.

೯

Ax crouched at the foot of another tree, across the clearing, and Molly came and lay at his feet. Charlotte crouched in front of him, so that her knees were touching his. There was hardly any wind. There was hardly any sound. "What happened between us, it had more to do with Bill and me than with me and you."

While Ax waited for her to go on, he noticed again how much older she looked, though he couldn't place what it was that made her look older—something in her eyes, something in the dullness of her skin.

"Bill always knew," she said. "You were his idea from the start. He knew you'd just let things happen to you. He knew you wouldn't resist."

"He knew about us?"

"Alex," Charlotte touched her temples with her fingertips, as if her head suddenly ached. "We were both, just . . . You and me having sex, he thought it might be a good idea. Because he didn't want to. With me. That's all. That's all it was." She looked up at Ax. "You're angry," she said. "You should be."

"What about you?" Ax could feel the redness showing in his cheeks. "Was I just . . . I mean . . ."

"I'm sorry," Charlotte said. She closed her eyes. Her face seemed to harden. When she opened her eyes again, they were fiery. "You thought I didn't love him," she said. "You thought I betrayed him." She laughed. It sounded like a horse snorting. She stood up quickly and took a few steps away. "It was the other way around," she said. "It, was, exactly. . . ." She stopped talking. She crossed her arms under her breasts and walked away from him, out of the clearing.

Ax remained crouched with his back against the tree, listening. He heard her footsteps crackling over the ice all the way back to the house. He heard a door close. Molly nudged his ankle, as if to ask why they too weren't leaving. Ax patted her roughly on the head. Then he got the rifle. He unzipped the case and found two loose bullets inside it. He didn't know anything about guns, but this was an old bolt-action rifle and it wasn't hard to figure out. He pulled back the bolt, inserted the bullet, and slammed the bolt closed, his hands shaking slightly. He cursed, not knowing what he was cursing at. Molly watched from the tree. Ax knelt by the dog and patted her neck. When she turned over on her back, he rubbed her belly. Then he placed the rifle barrel under her neck, aiming it toward the back of her head. He squeezed the trigger slowly. When the rifle fired, it surprised him. Molly had barely moved. She had just flopped over on her side. Ax lifted her up and he saw the bloody mess on the ground under her head. He carried her to the hole, and he had to lay down on his belly in order to place her in her grave. He found the shovel where it lay on the ground behind the mound of dirt, and he kicked it and banged it against the tree to knock the ice off. He put one foot on the mound of dirt, and with the point of the spade, he broke through the crust of ice and into the dark earth under it. He cast a few shovelfuls of dirt into the hole and then he stopped and sat down on the wet ground beside the grave. He didn't know what he was feeling. There was a knot in his throat. While he sat there, a gust of wind came up: a long, slow rising of the wind. It blew through the trees and set off a sound that was at first a soft, chimelike tinkling and then grew into something loud and wildly musical as ice broke from trees and splintered onto the ground. Ax covered his head as ice shattered around him. When the wind stopped, ice was heaped all through the clearing. Ax went back to filling up the grave, but as he worked he thought about the music of the ice as it cracked and broke, and he had to stop, just to look at it, to look at the moonlight reflecting off it. In the distance, he heard a door open. Then Charlotte called his name. She was calling him Alex. He didn't answer. He stood silently in the clearing and listened as the sound of his own name filled up the woods. He said it once himself: *Alex*. Then he continued filling up the grave, thrusting the shovel into the black earth, flinging down shovelful after shovelful of dirt, working urgently, almost as if he were digging through to something trapped on the other side of the mounded earth, something that might still be alive.

A X

DRIVERS

Buster Crain's silence is legendary: we were married two years before he started talking to me. At Cornell University, where he teaches, his colleagues call him the Iceman. The name has nothing to do with the Eugene O'Neill play. It's the press's nickname for a tennis player who never shows his emotions on the court. Buster Crain is like that—a scientist who never shows his emotions and never speaks unless spoken to. Except for his limp, which he always told me he got in a car wreck when he was a kid, he also looks like the tennis player: same wiry build, same icy blue eyes.

I met Buster when I was a grad student in the English Department. I took his biology course as an elective, and after the last class I asked him to lunch. He said "That sounds nice" and two months later we were married. Buster and I were a perfect match. He didn't know how to talk and I couldn't shut up. I didn't have any friends and I was away from my family and I was always a natural talker anyway. After I'd spend a night and morning alone in my apartment and a day listening to lectures among strangers, I'd explode at the sight of Buster, words flying out of me. Buster couldn't have gotten a word in if he wanted to, which made him comfortable. He'd be with me, attentive, his eyes showing he cared, and I'd go on and on. There were a lot of things I needed to talk about then, and I talked about them, and he never seemed to tire of listening.

But our relationship was defined: I talked, he listened.

Then, after we were together almost two years, Buster's sister called to tell him she was getting married. I watched him with the phone to his ear. He looked down at the rug, shaking his head slightly. Finally he said, "You can't expect me to be happy about it." Then he was silent again and I could hear his sister's tinny voice rattling through the receiver. When she started shouting, he looked away for a moment and then hung up. He went into the kitchen and stared out the window.

I put my arms around his waist. I asked, "What was that about?"

"Jean is getting married. She wants us to come to the wedding."

"She's marrying the same guy?"

He nodded.

I was quiet awhile because I knew about his sister, though I had never met her. She lived in the Brooklyn neighborhood where Buster grew up, and she was his only family. Both his parents and an older brother died before I met him. She was a couple of years younger than Buster, and she'd been living on and off for seven or eight years with a guy named Pete. Buster didn't try to keep in touch with her, but she had our phone number and occasionally called. If I answered the phone, she asked to talk to Buster. Once, when I tried to start a conversation, Buster heard me and took the phone away. We fought about that—as much as you can fight when you're the only one yelling. Pete, I at length found out, was a small-time crook, a drunk, and a woman-beater. "A carbon copy," Buster said, "of my father." He refused to have anything to do with his sister as long as she lived with Pete.

Still, I wanted to meet her. She was Buster's sister.

Beyond the kitchen window, the yard was covered with a thin layer of dirty, slow-melting ice.

"How bad could it be?" I said. In the window I saw his dark reflection. I put my arms around him, but he twisted away from me. I followed him into the living room. "I want to see the neighborhood you grew up in," I said. "I want to hear about when you were a kid from your sister. I—"

☙

"Why?" he said, his back to me. He was standing by the sofa and he picked up the book he had been reading and held it open in front of him. He looked as though he were reading, but he said: "Why? Why do you need to know those things?"

"Because," I said. I was surprised. I didn't know how he could ask such a question. "Because we're married," I said.

He looked at me then, squinting a little, as if I were far away, someplace in the distance and he could barely make me out. Then he sat down and positioned his book in the light from the floor lamp, and he really did start to read.

I sat down next to him. "Look," I said, "Buster. What's the big deal? I want to meet your sister. Is that so unusual? After all, we've been married two years," I said. I said, "It's not normal, Buster! It's not normal for a wife never to have met a single family member from her husband's family. Is that normal?"

Buster didn't answer. He appeared absorbed in his reading.

I pulled the book out of his hand.

"I'm reading," he said emphatically, as if only a monster would interrupt someone's reading.

I said, "I'm trying to explain something here, Buster. I'm trying to explain how important it is to me to meet someone from your family. After all," I said, "it's only natural for someone who loves someone to want to know all about them, isn't it? Isn't that just natural? " I said. "Buster?"

Buster sighed. He let his head fall back against the wall. He said, "There's no need for you to meet my sister."

I said, "I don't see how you can say that, Buster. Didn't I take you to meet my family? Wasn't that one of the first things we did when we decided to get married? It was. Of course it was. Because it's just natural," I said. "It's what people do," I said. "If they're getting married, first thing, they meet each other's families. It's only human." I said, "I can't see why you can't understand this, why you can't understand why I want to meet your sister. Buster?"

He didn't answer.

⑤

DRIVERS

"Buster," I said. "I only—"

"All right," he said. Then he said it softly, as if to himself, "All right." He got up and took his jacket from the hall closet and went out for a walk.

"All right, " I said—as soon as he was out the door.

We live a few miles outside of Ithaca, in a countryside of long, rolling hills and quiet lakes and ponds. We have a nice house, with an acre of cleared land behind it and a view of Song Mountain in the distance, and on the morning we were leaving for Brooklyn everything everywhere, from Song Mountain to the ground at our feet, was covered in a thick morning mist. As we drove away, our house appeared to be floating on the mist.

Buster wouldn't go to the wedding, which was only a few weeks away, at the end of April, but he agreed to a short visit. When we left I was still a little mad at him because he had refused—though I could hear his sister begging on the other end of the line—to spend the weekend at her apartment. Instead, he had told her we'd visit for lunch on Saturday. "Saturday lunch," he told her, "and no more." That meant a five-hour drive down to Brooklyn and another five hours coming back upstate, which would be hard on Buster, especially with his leg. It seemed unreasonable to me and I was sullen about it for the whole ride down—until I saw the part of Brooklyn where his sister lived. Then I was glad we were only staying a few hours.

I suppose it was the cramped and hampered atmosphere created by the closeness of the buildings that was affecting me, but the neighborhood seemed nightmarishly seedy. The streets were in disrepair—it was not possible to drive more than a few miles per hour without damaging the underside of our car—and lining the sidewalks on concrete stoops were groups of mean-looking teenagers dressed mostly in denim. The place made me nervous, and I don't think I stopped talking for an instant from the time we hit the Kosciuszko Bridge until we parked in front of his sister's building.

I was still talking as we locked up the car and climbed the steps to the foyer, where the stench of urine was so thick it made me nauseous.

꩜

"Lord," I said as Buster looked for his sister's name under three rows of bells. "This place smells like a giant urinal."

Buster, alongside me, was as quiet as always, his lips pressed together a little tighter than usual. He rang the bell and few seconds later a loud, jangling buzzer sounded and unlocked the door with a loud click.

We entered the building together and Buster paused for a second, looked around, and started climbing the stairs. In front of us, along side the stairway, black plastic bags full of garbage were heaped in piles. On the way up the steps, holding the back of Buster's belt because I didn't want to touch the banister, I couldn't decide which smelled worse, the foyer or the hall. When we reached the fourth floor, Buster's sister was waiting for us in the doorway of her apartment. She was short and dumpy, which I hadn't expected, and she had her hands shoved awkwardly in the belt of her skirt, but I knew it was his sister because she had the same blue eyes and dirty-blond hair.

"Busta," she said. "Son-of-a-bitch." She held her arms open to him.

Buster walked slowly to her, his limp aggravated by the stairs and the ride, and she embraced him when he reached the doorway. I stood behind them, smiling idiotically. I said, "Hello Jean," and she said, "You must be Terry," and she led us in.

The apartment was neat but dirty. The furniture looked to be a hodgepodge of other people's discards. The windows had bars and the walls needed to be repaired and painted. But Jean didn't seem concerned that we might find her surroundings squalid. She looked cheerful as she marched us into the kitchen to meet her fiancé.

"This is Pete," she said. "Pete. Meet my brother and his wife Terry." Then she stood at the head of the kitchen table, put her hands on her hips, smiled, and waited.

Pete, it turned out, was no talker either. He was a skinny, ratty-looking guy with purplish lips and an adolescent's pimply complexion. His hair was wet and slicked back against his head, and he just sat there at the table, holding a beer can with both hands and looking up at me and Buster. Finally he said, "Nice lookin' wife you got there, Busta."

Buster nodded and said, "If you don't mind, I'll sit in the living room. I need to stretch my legs."

"Go right ahead," Pete said. "You want a beer?"

Buster shook his head and left the room.

I don't know what I had expected—a cheerful family reunion, baby pictures over coffee in the living room—but what I got was a quiet afternoon with Pete drinking beer in the kitchen and Buster staring at a black and white television in the living room. Jean hustled about preparing lunch and I followed her, trying to get her to talk about Buster and her parents. All she wanted to talk about, however, was her upcoming wedding, which I could understand, so I gave up trying to learn anything about their family history and settled for flitting back and forth between Jean and Buster. Neither Jean nor I tried to get the men to sit together in the same room, but we reported to them on what the other one was doing. "Pete seems to be comfortable drinking beer in the kitchen," I'd tell Buster, and Jean would say to Pete, "Busta's watchin' a movie. He's got his leg stretched out on the couch."

We got through lunch on small talk between Jean and me, and by the time it was over and we all found ourselves sitting in the living room, I was exhausted. Buster, Jean, and I were drinking coffee, but Pete was still drinking beer. By my estimate, he was just starting on his second six-pack. I was comforting myself by noting that the whole event would soon be over when Pete started to talk.

"Jean says," he said, staring at a can of beer he was rolling between his palms, "that you discovered something about the DNA."

Buster didn't respond.

Pete continued. "She says you got an award for it or somethin'."

I could see Buster still wasn't going to talk, so I explained for him, feeling like a fool because I knew they'd have no idea what I was talking about. "Buster was one of a team of scientists," I said, "who helped figure out the way DNA transmits genetic information to cells."

Pete nodded vigorously. He said, "I know about that stuff."

Jean beamed at him and folded her hands in her lap.

Pete looked up and stared across the coffee table at Buster. "Did you have anything to do with those Swine Flu shots?"

🌀

"What?" Buster said.

"You know," Pete explained. "The ones President Ford made everyone take in case of a ep'demic."

Buster shook his head.

"Good," Pete said.

Jean reached across the table and hit him hard on the shoulder. "Well, go ahead," she said. "Now you started, finish."

"Well," he said, "did you take one of those shots?" He was talking to Buster, but he turned to me when he saw Buster wasn't going to answer.

"No," I said.

"That's good. You know why? Because I think that whole thing— tryin' to give everybody the shots when there never was a ep'demic or anything—was a plot. It makes sense, don't it?"

I didn't know what to say.

"Jews and niggers," he said. He strung the words out, stretching every syllable and infusing the sounds with acid hate and disdain.

Buster turned to his sister and said, "We have to go now."

It was obvious that he was cutting Pete off, and Pete glared at Buster. He looked insulted and on the edge of being angry.

Buster returned the stare, but there was no anger in his eyes. He looked concerned, like a scientist observing something problematic in nature. They stayed like that for what seemed like a very long time, just staring at each other. Then Pete looked down. He picked up his beer can and returned to the kitchen.

Jean muttered, angry with Buster, as she went about getting our coats. We exchanged terse good-byes and left without so much as a handshake.

On the drive back neither of us said a word until we hit Route 17 in the Catskills and were well on our way home. If Buster had been upset by what happened, he didn't show it. In fact, he looked comfortable, almost pleased. But I felt terrible about the way things had gone. I kept seeing those teenagers on the stoops, and the piles of garbage in the hall, and the cracked and dirty walls, and the bars on the windows—and the way Pete said "Jews and niggers" stuck with me, leaving me with such a tangible sense of fear that I kept looking into the back seat to make sure no one was there.

Then Buster said, "I'm nothing like that bastard."

His eyes were still on the road, so he didn't see my mouth fall open.

He turned and looked at me. "He's just a younger version of my father. Did you see all the ugliness and hatred in him?"

For Buster, this was an outburst.

"My father was like that," he said. "A mean drunk, full of hate."

Then we were both silent for a long time. He must have been surprised, perhaps even worried, that I wasn't talking. He looked over at me a few times. Finally, he said, "You know, I've always lied to you and everyone else about my leg. There never was an accident. My father broke my kneecap with the butt of a shotgun. He was drunk, and I hardly cried. I was afraid he'd shoot me."

"Buster," I said. I moved closer to him. "Tell me what happened."

In the dim light from the dashboard I could see Buster's eyes carefully following the road. He hesitated for a while, and then he shifted in his seat as if trying to get comfortable, and then he started talking. Two years, and he started talking, really, for the first time. He talked and I listened, moving closer and closer to him until it was like there was only one of us in the driver's seat—and we sat that way for the rest of the ride home, close together, watching the roads turning in the moonlight.

GEORGIA O'KEEFFE,
VISION

The power of it! Her breath a score of muted color, her body like cloud, wing, fire. She was dressed all in black. I fell into her and have never. Touch me. Go ahead, put your fingers on the page.

My thoughts are. It's like falling into.

This is how it happened. I was alone in my house, a split-level ranch on Long Island, middle-of-nowhere suburbia, Montauk Point, flipping through a book of Georgia O'Keeffe prints, when I heard a noise in the house. I need to give you some background here so you'll know why I felt as if the temperature suddenly dropped, icy veins.

I used to live near a coven.

I'm a single parent. My wife left me for her own reasons, having little to do with me and much more to do with her own violent past. Now it's just me and Elaine and Annie: we live together here in Montauk. I'm an artist. A visual artist. I'm a big deal, museums all over the world. Shows. Lots of shows. Mostly now I take care of the kids. But this background I'm giving you, it happened two years ago, a year or so after Allison left, my ex-wife. I was adjusting to being the kids' main man. People wanted me to get an au pair girl or a nanny, somebody anybody to take care of the kids. They didn't understand. Work, work, that comes second. You're a genius, you're a dud, what's the difference? Besides money. Actually the kind of talent that goes with being a dud is more likely to bring in money than the kind of talent that goes with genius. I have lots of money. I also have talent. Actually, I don't know where I'm at. This is the story.

It was a year after Allison left. I'm alone in the living room, sitting in the dark. Big house. Huntington Bay. All the lights off. I'm wired, holding my head in my hands. Nights like this, emptiness sets in. Kids asleep, I'm alone. Kids asleep, I'm alone. Kids asleep. . . . And so forth. I don't understand anything. I don't know why the furniture doesn't float up and out the windows and into space. I'm ready at any moment to leave the ground. What's holding me down? I have a hard time seeing things and when I do see them, really see them, I wish I hadn't. I try never to look at them again. We won't even talk about mirrors.

I'm sitting alone in the dark, a year after Allison. I hear a noise in the back of the house, then this little music box tune. It's very strange, snaps me out of my mind state, brings me back to this house, this night. When Elaine was two I gave her an Easter bunny that played a dumb medley of Easter tunes when squeezed. That's what I'm listening to, this medley of Easter tunes, pitch black house, the kids supposedly asleep. "Elaine?" I call. "Annie?" No answer. The tune ends. I walk quietly, listening, down the hall to their bedroom, flip on the light.

The girls sleeping like angels don't stir. Annie's closed eyelids are deep blue, almost purple. She's five years old, sleeping on her side, peaceful. Elaine's seven. She's sleeping on her back, top bunk. She's my buddy. We have long talks about her mom. Their room is neat because I keep it that way. In the blue and white Playschool toy box I find the Easter bunny buried near the bottom. I decide it's just one of those things. Something shifted, another toy pressed against it. What else? I turn off the light in their room, but leave the hall light on.

I start to make myself a cup of coffee. It's around midnight now. Coffee has no effect on me. I can drink a cup and then go to sleep. It's one of those electric drip coffee makers and it begins to rumble and hiss, it issues deep sighs. Hot water starts to drip into the glass carafe, clear at first then turning dark brown. I'm standing like a zombie watching the coffee drip, and I notice my letter to Allison, the one I thought I mailed a week ago, stuck in the napkin holder on top of the

☙

coffee maker. The letter just appears, as if I hadn't been staring at it for minutes. I just suddenly see it. "Damn," I say, and I pick it up. "I can't believe I didn't mail this." The house doesn't answer.

This is when it all happens. I put my coat on, go outside. It's a dark night—no moon, no stars. I cross the lawn to the mailbox, put Allison's letter in the black box, flip the red flag up. When I turn around, when I look back toward the house, I see a shadow move through the dim rectangle of light shining onto the lawn from the kids' bedroom window. At first this doesn't register as anything frightening, but I stop and look into the kids' bedroom, and in the light from the hallway, I see the figure of a woman standing over Annie's bed, looking down at her. This is a year after Allison left. I don't understand anything. My knees buckle out there on the lawn. My first steps toward the house I'm crawling on all fours, a noise coming from someplace so deep inside me it doesn't sound like me at all. Then I'm on my feet, running, screaming my daughters' names.

When I reach their bedroom, both children are sitting up in bed. Annie appears dumbfounded, sitting on the edge of her bed, her mouth open, still more asleep than awake but trying to stand. I pick her up and she wraps her arms around my neck, tight. Elaine is hugging her pillow in front of her as if for protection and whimpering "What, Daddy? What?" I look around the room. We are all listening.

Nothing.

I whisper, "I think there was a burglar in the house."

Elaine says, "Is he gone? Is he still here?"

Annie says, "Is he a bad man in the house?"

"Shh," I say. "You guys stay here and let Daddy search the house."

Both girls start to cry. Elaine grabs my shirt and Annie clutches my neck.

"Okay," I say. "Okay. But be quiet." The girls stop crying, and after we listen for a long time to the silence of the house, the three of us make our way slowly along the lighted hall to the kitchen. There, with Annie in my arms and Elaine at my side, I dial 911 and explain what happened. Then we all sit together on the floor and wait for the police to arrive. This was a year after Allison left.

§

I'm wired, thin metal prongs shooting out of every pore: antennae. Nights like this. I don't know. I have a hard time seeing things.

That was the night the police told me about the witches. The next day I went to this witch's house, this coven place. A woman named Josephine showed me around. She was interested. She offered me a glass of wine.

"I don't think," she said, "we had anything to do with what happened."

She was a small woman in her mid-thirties, not physically attractive, but very enticing on some other level, some sensual thing. "But," I said.

"A coincidence," she said. "Probably."

I said, "I feel ignorant and empty."

She started to say something. Then she stopped.

So now you understand why the icy veins when two years later while flipping through the O'Keeffe prints I heard that noise in the house.

I put down the prints and walked through all the rooms, checking first on the girls. They were fine. The house was quiet. This was three years after Allison left. I was doing better. At the worst point, I had sat alone on a bench under a tree in a friend's backyard and cried. I couldn't help it. I didn't want to cry. It was a summer night, the girls were visiting Allison. We had moved out of our house in Huntington because of the witches, because of the woman in their room, and I was homeless, wifeless, familyless, sitting on a narrow bench under a chestnut tree on a bright summer night, one of those nights the stars are in arm's reach, and I put my head in my hands and cried. After that, things started getting better. I don't know why.

But the night I'm talking about, the O'Keeffe night, after I heard the noise and checked the house and everything was okay, I sat back in my chair and relaxed. I could hear the ocean in the distance—a constant, muted roar. Once, out on the pier at Montauk Point in moonlight I saw a circle of water turn silver and begin to dance. A woman appeared alongside me. I looked at her for a long moment, then turned away, to the water. She was very beautiful: her eyes were

🌀

dark brown, her hair black. She walked away slowly, an invitation in the slowness I didn't take, though I watched her all the way to the parking lot and when she turned and opened the door to her car, our eyes met for an instant before she got in and drove away. When I looked back to the water, the circle was gone.

So I had checked the house and everything was okay. I relaxed. I flipped through the O'Keeffe book, past a painting of bones on the desert floor to another one titled "Music—Pink and Blue, II, 1919," and then on to a famous one, "Black Iris." She was already dead a few years at that time, but I closed my eyes and saw her as if she were standing in front of my chair. If I opened my eyes she would have been there in her black hat and her black cape, exactly the way I was seeing her. I watched for a long time, and just before she covered herself behind her cape and disappeared, I stretched my arm out long into that space and touched her. My God, what power I felt there. What incredible power and beauty and mystery and fear.

THE REQUIREMENTS
OF FLIGHT

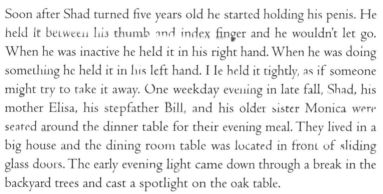

Soon after Shad turned five years old he started holding his penis. He held It between his thumb and index finger and he wouldn't let go. When he was inactive he held it in his right hand. When he was doing something he held it in his left hand. I Ie held it tightly, as if someone might try to take it away. One weekday evening in late fall, Shad, his mother Elisa, his stepfather Bill, and his older sister Monica were seated around the dinner table for their evening meal. They lived in a big house and the dining room table was located in front of sliding glass doors. The early evening light came down through a break in the backyard trees and cast a spotlight on the oak table.

Bill started eating and then stopped. "For God's sake," he said. He was leaning over his plate, an eating utensil in each beefy hand. He looked at Shad, who had just stabbed a piece of chicken with the fork in his right hand. His left hand was out of sight under the table. Shad had stick-out ears and unusually large brown eyes that made him look as though he were always just a little bit surprised. He looked back at Bill as if waiting for an explanation, as if he had no idea at all what Bill might be upset about. Bill turned to Elisa. She was sitting at the opposite end of the table. He said, "He'll give himself gangrene the way he holds that thing."

"Bill!" Monica yelled. She gave Bill a reproachful look, reminding him they had all agreed not to call attention to Shad's new behavior.

Monica was twelve years old, intimidatingly intelligent—and a master of reproachful looks.

El turned to her son. "Shad," she asked, "is there anything bothering you?"

Shad shook his head, seemingly bewildered. "Nothing's bothering me," he answered. He turned to Bill. "Do you mean because I'm holding my pee-pee?"

"Buddy," Bill said. He looked down at his plate and then back to Shad. Monica and Elisa were staring at him. "Buddy," he continued. "Can I see both your hands?"

Shad nodded. "Sure, " he said. He put his fork down and opened his right hand for Bill to see. Then he dropped his right hand into his lap and brought his left hand up and opened it.

Bill and Elisa laughed.

"What's funny?"

Monica said, "Don't pay any attention to them, Shad. They're demented."

Shad grinned, looked at Bill and Elisa, saw that they weren't angry, and went back to eating.

Later that night, when Elisa was putting Shad to bed, she asked him again. "Sweetheart," she said. "Are you sure there's nothing bothering you?"

Shad was sitting on the edge of his bed. Elisa had just put his pajamas on him. She was kneeling in front of him, her hands on his knees. She was still dressed in her work clothes: a knee-length navy blue skirt and matching blazer over a white nylon blouse with a neckline that revealed the first, slight, fleshy rising of her breasts. Shad looked out to the backyard, at a giant oak tree whose branches stretched from the middle of the yard to his window, where the leaves tapped against the glass whenever there was a breeze.

"Is it my new job?" Elisa asked. "Do you feel like I don't love you as much because I've been talking about my new job a lot?"

Shad shook his head and gave Elisa a quizzical look, as if the question confused him.

꽃

Elisa pressed on. "Is it that you're thinking about your dad, then? Is it something about your dad? You know you can call him anytime you want." She pointed to the video-phone that Wayne, his father, had given him.

Shad didn't respond. He looked up again at the tree.

"Well, I'm only asking because . . ." Elisa gestured toward his penis. "I've noticed you've been holding your pee-pee a lot. Actually, Shad," she continued, smiling a little now, adding a note of silliness to her voice, "you hold it all the time. See," she said, pointing. "You didn't used to always hold it."

"Well," Shad said. "Now I like holding my pee-pee." Then he added, "Do you think trees can turn into monsters?" He jumped up on his bed, held his free hand shaped into a claw over his head and bared his teeth.

"No, silly," El said. "Trees can't turn into monsters." She pulled Shad to her and gave him a hug as she lifted him off the bed to the floor. She pulled back his blue Sesame Street quilt, making Big Bird's bright yellow body momentarily disappear. Shad got under the quilt and she switched on the Batman night-light by the foot of his bed. She kissed him goodnight and was about turn off the overhead light when she noticed a back issue of *The New Yorker* on the floor by his closet, next to his bright red bean bag chair, as if he had left it there after reading an article. She asked, "Were you looking at *The New Yorker*, Shad?"

Shad sat up in bed and looked over to the magazine, where his mother was looking. "It's got pictures of Kiki in it," he said. Kiki was his dad's wife, Shad's stepmother—though he didn't think of her that way, because he rarely saw her. He only visited his dad's house once a year, in the summer, and then she was hardly ever there.

Elisa said, "We haven't read this issue yet." She picked it up and slipped it under her arm.

"Can I cut pictures out when you're done?"

"Same as always," Elisa said. She winked, turned off the lights, and closed the door halfway.

⑤

When she was gone, after the hall light went off, and after he heard her feet descending the stairs, Shad got out of bed and went to the door and opened it all the way, so that from his bed he could see the stairs that led down to the living room. Also, with the door full open he could bolt straight out of his bed to his mother's bed with nothing in the way, because his mother always left her bedroom door full open too, ever since the night he ran smack into it and gave himself a black eye. On the way back to his bed, he tried not to look out the window. The big tree with its long branches always scared him. It scared him a lot. When he was out in the yard and he looked up and tried to see the top of the tree, it made him dizzy, and sometimes it looked like the tree would start to lean down toward him, like it might bend over and snatch him up. He told his Mom and Bill, but they just laughed and said trees were all friendly. When he told Monica, she told him that it was probably just an illusion that made the tree look like it was bending over and that he had nothing to be afraid of. So he stopped telling them. But he was afraid of the big tree. Sometimes it banged on his window at night, like it was trying to get into his room. Sometimes it looked like the Sea Witch with all her tentacle-arms. Earlier, when his Mom was putting him to bed, putting his pajamas on him, he had seen the tree out of the corner of his eye, and it had looked like Kiki in the magazine, the way she was making an animal face with her teeth and eyes and the way her hands were like claws. Shad felt a sharp pain between his legs and he realized he was squeezing too tight. He loosened his grip but he didn't let go. He wished he would hurry up and fall asleep so that it would be the time at night when he could get up and go into Bill and Mom's bed. He closed his eyes and tried not to think about the tree outside his window.

Downstairs, in the family room, El flung *The New Yorker* into Bill's lap. It was opened to a thirteen-page, black-and-white, heavy-stock couture advertisement. The ad consisted primarily of highly stylized, super-erotic, mostly nude photos of Shad's stepmother. "Good God," Bill said, flipping through the pages.

"What?" Monica said. She was curled up on the rug in a far corner of the room reading *War and Peace.*

☙

El said, "I found it in Shad's room."

Bill said, "I didn't know *The New Yorker* published this kind of thing."

Monica jumped up. "What is it?" She hurried to Bill and looked over his shoulder at the photos. Her mouth dropped open. "Oh my God," she said. "You can see everything!"

Bill flipped the page to a picture of Kiki being held in the arms of a muscular, long-haired, stunningly handsome and totally nude man, the position of Kiki's knee functioning as a modern version of the fig leaf.

"Hey," Monica said. "How come we can see all of Kiki, but we can't see all of him. It's sexist."

Bill flipped back to the picture Monica was referring to. Kiki was standing facing the camera wearing boots that came up over her knees, holey tights that came to mid-thigh, and a see-through body-suit.

"Well," Bill said. "I mean, you can't really see everything."

"Sure you can!" Monica said. "Look!" She jabbed her finger between Kiki's legs. "What's that if you can't see everything?"

"Well, yeah," Bill said, "but— "

"Will you guys cut it out?" El snatched the magazine away from Bill. "Look at this one." She pointed to a picture of Kiki leaping into the air, her teeth bared, her hair flying wildly about her head, her hands shaped into claws. "Shad did this, this same pose, when I was putting him to bed."

"He just did it?" Bill said.

"Was he playing or anything?" Monica asked.

"He asked if the tree could turn into a monster and then he did this exact same pose."

Bill and Monica were quiet then. They both appeared to be thinking.

"You think Kiki's what's bothering him?" Bill asked.

"He's thinking about it," El said. "Why else would he connect the way the tree looks with the way she's posed." El flopped down onto the couch. "For Heaven's sake," she said. "Five years old, he's got to deal with his stepmother dancing around naked in a kinky magazine ad. How's he going to look at her when she's making him bacon and eggs, for cryin' out loud?"

෨

THE REQUIREMENTS OF FLIGHT   167

Monica scowled. "Kiki's okay," she said. She picked up the magazine from her mother and added, softly, her voice wandering off, "She's dumb as a box of rocks. . . ." She placed the magazine on her mother's lap and pointed to the date. "Shad started right after his birthday. This was out a month before."

"So?" El said. "It doesn't mean he saw it until his birthday."

"We never saw it," Bill said, discounting El's theory. "It must have wound up in his room pretty soon."

"Even if he did see it before," El continued. "He didn't have to have an instantaneous reaction."

Monica knelt behind the couch and folded her arms on the backrest. "Mom," she said gently. "Don't you think it's possible that you're really the one who's most upset by the ad?"

El didn't answer.

Bill said, "I'm getting a snack," and left the room.

"Let's be honest," Monica continued. "She's twenty years younger than you, she's got a body men die for, and she's living with your exhusband in sinful luxury. I mean, there's—"

"Monica," El interrupted. "Isn't it time for you to go to bed?"

Monica jumped up, folded her arms under her breasts, and walked stiffly from the room. "Sure," she mumbled on her way out. "Kill the messenger."

Bill entered the room as Monica walked by him in a huff. He was holding a bowl of cereal in his hand. When he sat down on the couch next to El, she got up. She said, without looking at him, "I'm going to bed," and then left the room.

Bill closed his eyes, took a deep breath, and exhaled slowly. He located the remote control and flipped around until he found CNN. He watched the news while he ate his cereal, and then he went up to the bedroom where he found El on the floor in her panties and bra doing leg lifts. He sat on the edge of the bed and watched her for a moment. He said, "I think you look great, Honey."

"Shut up, Bill."

"Darling," Bill said, his voice tender.

El sat up and crossed her legs under her. "If one more person in this house patronizes me. . . ."

"I'm—"

"I don't give a damn about Kiki."

"Then how come the exercise regimen?"

El got up without replying and went into the bathroom. She snapped the door closed precisely behind her.

Bill took off his shoes and lay back on the bed, letting his body sink into the luxurious quilts of their fat, down comforter. It wasn't cold enough yet for the comforter, but Bill had taken it down from the attic early, at the first sign of real cold. He had hoped to get more use out of it tonight than merely sleeping under it. When El came out of the bathroom with her pajamas buttoned up to her neck, he figured his chances were slim.

She got in bed alongside him, propped her head on her hand, and picked up the conversation where they left off. "Look at me," she said. "I'm forty-five years old, I've got thighs in two different time zones, a butt that drags the ground, and a family that feels sorry for me."

Bill said, "Stop being silly, El. You're not twenty-five, but you look just fine." He laughed. "'Thighs in two different time zones . . .'"

"Meanwhile," El continued, as if Bill hadn't said a word, "my ex is married to a famous model half my age, and he's turned into one of the most wealthy men in the whole damn country."

Bill said, "I thought he lost money this year."

"Not enough to matter."

"I thought he was in tax trouble."

"They're not going to catch him," El said. "They'll never catch him. He's too smart."

Bill lay back on his pillow and folded his hands under his head. He looked up at the ceiling. "You know," he said. "We're getting close to a real argument here."

El softened. She touched his shoulder.

Bill continued, still looking at the ceiling. "We both know who's better off. He's got the money, we've got the kids. He's got a wife he hardly ever sees and he knows for sure sleeps around on him; you've got me. They stay married because of money arrangements. They've got a business deal; we've got a marriage." He turned on his side and faced her again. "I may not be rich and a financial genius, but I wouldn't trade with Wayne in a million years. Would you trade with Kiki?"

El seemed to think about it. "Would I have to be named *Kiki*?" she asked.

"Stop," Bill said.

"Of course not. Of course I wouldn't trade places with her."

"So?" He undid the buttons of her pajama top and folded the silky fabric away from her breasts, which looked just fine to him, forty-five or not.

El put the heels of her hands to her forehead and issued forth a deep and deeply despondent sigh.

Bill sat up. "What is it?" he asked, knowing that she was about to tell him anyway.

"They want me to ask Wayne to endow a chair in the Humanities. They out-and-out asked me to do it."

"When?"

"Last week."

"What did you tell them?"

El didn't answer. Her eyes got teary.

"Oh, for God's sake, El!" Bill got up and walked around to the foot of the bed. He gestured toward her. "You refuse to take penny-one from this guy . . . But just because this pissant little school gives you a damned title—"

"It's not a pissant little school," El said, her face dark red now. "You told me you thought . . ."

"Elisa . . ."

"You said you didn't think Wayne had anything to do with the job."

"I didn't," Bill said. "But now—"

"Oh, come on." She threw the quilt back and got up, buttoning her pajama top. "At least I was honest. I told you they were giving me the job because they wanted money from Wayne." She walked by Bill and

꩜

to the bathroom. "Who ever heard of promoting a secretary to a dean, for cryin' out loud?" She closed the bathroom door.

"An executive secretary," Bill said, under his breath, with no one to hear him. "An associate dean." He sat down on the edge of the bed. The room was mostly dark, except for a bright strip of yellow light coming from under the bathroom door and the dim illumination of the night light out in the hallway. Outside, beyond the bedroom windows, the wind was rattling through the trees, stripping the branches of leaves and seeds. As he listened he heard the solid thud of a chestnut falling to the lawn. He got up and leaned his head against the bathroom door. He spoke into the crack between the door and the frame. "El?"

"What?"

He could tell from her voice that she was directly on the other side of the door. He pictured her staring at herself in the bathroom mirror, examining every line and wrinkle of her face. In truth, time was being kind to El. She knew it and had said so herself. She was forty-five and her auburn hair was still rich and bright, without a hint yet of gray. She had wrinkles of course, mostly around her eyes and forehead, but she still looked good. She looked like a woman. "Are you going to come out?" he asked.

"Why?"

"So we can talk."

"What about?"

"About your job. About them pressuring you to tap Wayne for a contribution."

"They're not pressuring me."

"No? What do you call it?"

"Collecting."

"What are you talking about, El? What do you mean, *collecting?*"

"I mean, Bill . . ."

Bill felt El's weight push against the other side of the door. They were leaning against each other, two inches of a hollow wood door keeping them from touching. "What?" Bill said.

꒰

El's voice was soft, not much above a whisper. "I mean I hinted that I could bring Wayne in as a contributor to the school—if I had an administrative position, with a solid future."

Bill was silent for a long time. When he spoke, his voice was soft, muted. He said: "And you never said a word about this to me?" He paused and when she didn't respond, he continued: "You've never taken a cent from Wayne, money you *deserved*. Now you do this. I don't understand. Not at all."

El was silent and after awhile the bathroom went dark. The yellow strip of light at Bill's feet disappeared. After another moment or two, she said: "You've got your own company. In ten years you want to be the biggest construction company in the valley. You're putting a bid in for this, you're putting a bid in for that. You've got plans. How many nights have we gone to bed talking about your plans?'"

"So? What has that got to do with anything?"

El raised her voice. "I hustled a little! I did what Wayne would have done. I was doing the damn job anyway! I just made them give me what I deserved."

"Is that how you see it, El? Really? Is that what you tell yourself? Because . . . That's hard. . . . Really. . . . I'm out in the fog here. I don't get this at all."

"Well . . ." El stepped away from the door. Bill could hear her as she closed the lid on the john and sat down. "Well," she repeated. "Like you said, Bill. You're no genius."

Bill stepped back from the door. For a minute he considered putting his fist through it. Then he grabbed the pillow and the quilt from the bed and carried them down to the living room, where he settled himself on the couch. Being down in the living room at night lying on the couch with his own bedding made his stomach fluttery. It made his heart beat fast, his skin feel like it was just slightly electrified. He had been married to Elisa now for a little over four years. It was legally his first marriage, but before he met Elisa he had lived for several years on and off, mostly on, with a woman who would never marry him, though he had asked her several times, until it was understood between them that it was a standing offer. In that first relation-

 G

ship, he spent lots of nights on the couch. They fought about many things, but mostly they fought about having children. Bill wanted children; she didn't. He left her for the last time just before his fortieth birthday, after he had long given up on her ever being ready to get married. Then he met Elisa; and Shad and Monica were a big part of the attraction. Now he found himself on the couch again, and he didn't like the feeling. After a time, he heard Shad wake up and run into El's bed, the way he did every night without fail. He listened, but he didn't hear El carry him back to his room. Before he fell asleep, the sky had already begun to grow light.

Monica woke him in the morning. "You guys fight last night?" she asked.

Bill turned over, looked at her, then turned over again and buried his head in the cushions.

"It's seven o'clock," Monica said. "You're supposed to be at the warehouse by eight." She spun around energetically, flipped on the living room light, and marched off to the kitchen, turning all the lights on along the way. Outside, on the backyard deck, a squirrel was gathering acorns. Monica stopped at the window by the kitchen sink and watched it for a moment before the focus of her attention shifted to her own reflection. She was pretty, but she would never be as pretty as Kiki. Kiki had perfect skin. It was like she didn't have pores or something. But then she had once heard her dad complain that Kiki could shelter the homeless for a year with what she spent on skin care. That wasn't right, and plus there was all the time she spent putting stuff on her face. Was it worth it? Monica stepped closer to the window. She touched the skin of her cheeks with her fingertips. Her skin was all right, but she definitely had pores. She could see them. And she had a little hint of a pimple right at the bottom of her nose, by her upper lip.

Monica could still remember the fights when her dad left. He was a jerk and a liar. She was seven when he left and Shad wasn't even born yet. It was a couple of months after her dad left that Shad was born. He had told her Mom that it was her fault. He told her she ruined everything because she was jealous of him. She was jealous of how important he was getting to be. Mom said he was never around anymore. He said he was never around because she was a bitch: a complaining, nagging, jealous bitch. Monica was only seven at the time, but if she closed her eyes she could still see them in the old house, fighting. She could still hear some of the arguments. The words were stuck in her memory. She guessed they would be forever.

But her dad was a liar. He left because of Kiki. Mom found out later that he was already living with her. He had bought her an apartment in New York and half the time he was away he was with her there. She hated him for blaming it on her mom. For calling her mom the things he called her, when it was all just an excuse to run off with Kiki. She could understand his leaving them for Kiki. She was so beautiful. Monica could understand that he wouldn't want to live with her and her mom when he could have Kiki, even if thinking about it made her feel sick to her stomach. But he should have just said that. And he should have come to see her and Shad more often. He was a jerk if he thought a video-phone and a trust fund would make everything just fine.

"Thanks for getting me up," Bill said. He had stumbled into the kitchen and was fishing around in the refrigerator.

Monica watched Bill's reflection in the window. He closed the refrigerator door and held a bag of coffee beans in his hand as if he were displaying them on a TV commercial. Monica said, "So what'd you guys fight about?" She turned around. "You slept in your clothes?"

Bill looked down at his rumpled pants and shirt, at his half-off socks, the toes of which flopped in front of his feet. "Looks like it," he said, and he shambled to the counter by the stove and plugged in the coffee grinder.

"So?" Monica pressed. "What did you fight about?"

Shad walked stiffly into the kitchen, his thumb and forefinger clamped over his penis, and he climbed up on a counter stool.

"Morning, Shad the Bad," Monica said.

Shad said, "I wet the bed again."

"My bed?" Bill said, spinning around.

Shad didn't answer for a moment. His lips were pressed together and he appeared to be a little frightened. Finally he said, weakly, "Mom's bed."

"Great." Bill turned back to the coffee grinds. He pressed a button and a loud ugly buzzing filled the kitchen for a moment.

El came into the room carrying a bundle of wet bedding. "Did he tell you?"

Bill said, without turning around. "I'm surprised it was possible, the way he holds that thing clamped shut."

"Biiillll!" Monica pleaded. "We said!"

El started for the basement with the bedding. On her way out of the room, she said: "Bill's decided to be a prick lately."

Monica's face turned red. Bill slammed the coffee grinder lid down on the counter.

"What's a *prick*?" Shad said.

Bill said, "It's a bad word, Shad." He was stiff and motionless, his back turned to the room. Then he smacked the coffee grinder across the counter, spilling ground up beans everywhere. Monica took a step back and Shad started to sob. Bill motioned for Monica to take care of Shad, and then he followed El down into the basement.

El was standing with her back to the washing machine, waiting for him. She was wearing a white quilted robe pulled snug around her body, the belt pulled tight as a saddle cinch. She spoke as soon as she saw Bill come off the stairs. Her voice was a harsh, whispered hiss: "What the fuck's wrong with you? We agreed not to call attention to Shad, as per Dr. Wilk's and everyone else's recommendation!"

Bill stood directly in front of El, toe to toe with her. "What the fuck's wrong with you!" he said. "You call me a prick in front of the kids?"

"Would you lower your voice!"

"No." Bill leaned over her. "I want the kids to hear! I want them to know that no one can talk to me like that!" He was shouting.

El stepped away from him. "Are you trying to intimidate me?"

"Are you trying to intimidate me?"

๑

"I'm not shouting. I'm not standing on top of you."

"You're just calling me a prick in front of the kids."

El's voice dropped to a hiss again: "What are you doing calling attention to Shad?"

"What are you doing lying to me?"

"What are you talking about, lying to you?"

Bill sneered and turned around as if to walk away, and then turned around again. "I'm *not* a genius," he said. "But I'm not dumb, god-damn it. The way you pretended to be upset about their motives for hiring you, when you were hustling it all along. . . ." He mimicked her voice, "*I know they're just hiring me because of Wayne*, like you're so upset about it, like *they're* so corrupt. How could you put on such an act?" He shook his head, disgusted; then went back up the stairs. El leaned over the washing machine, resting her elbows on the white enamel surface and her head in her hands.

In the kitchen, Monica was handing Shad a piece of toast. Her hand was shaking slightly. Shad's eyes were full of tears. Bill came into the room and watched them both for a moment. He shoved his hands into his pockets. "Guys," he said, a pleading note in his voice. "Grown-ups have fights sometimes. That's all."

Monica shrugged, attempting a look of indifference. She went about doing something at the sink.

Shad had turned around completely, so as not to have to look at Bill.

Bill was standing awkwardly in the doorway. "Shad, Buddy," he said. "Turn around and eat your breakfast."

Shad pointed out the window at the oak tree. He said, "I had a bad dream and the tree and it made me wet the bed." He spoke haltingly, as if trying to find words for something that was difficult to say. Then he punched at the air in front of him as if he were pounding his fist into a wall and he shouted: "I hate that tree! I hate it! I hate it!" He covered his eyes with his arm and cried loudly.

Bill heard El on the stairs behind him and he stepped out of her way. When she came into the kitchen, both children ran for her. Shad grabbed her around the knee and Monica around the waist. Bill

🌀

backed out of the room as El explained that everything was all right, that everything was perfectly fine.

He went up to the bedroom and got ready for work.

§

El took the day off to stay home with Shad. They spent the morning together in the family room, watching *Shining Time Station* and *Mister Rogers*, and *Barney*, before starting on a few hours of pretend, wherein Shad was a pirate and she was a princess to be saved. In the late afternoon, when Monica arrived home from school, her denim jacket pulled half off her shoulder by the weight of her bookbag, El suggested they all go out to the mall to buy a pirate hat and an eye-patch and a hook for Shad, and some new jeans for Monica. They were on their way out the door when the phone rang.

Monica said, "Let the answering machine get it."

"Yeah," Shad seconded the idea. "I want my hook."

El picked up the phone in the kitchen. She was expecting to hear from one of Wayne's lawyers, a guy named Harden something. She was surprised when it turned out to be Wayne on the line. "I was expecting Harden what's-his-name," she said. "I'm honored. I get to talk to the man himself." She was smiling. The kids were watching her from the doorway. She waved for them to come in and then covered the mouthpiece with her palm and whispered, "It's your father."

Monica and Shad both pulled long faces and made gestures of exasperation, upset that they would have to wait now before heading out to the stores.

"Listen, Wayne," El said. "The kids are standing right here. Why don't I put them on the video-phone?"

Monica rolled her eyes.

Shad folded his arms under his chest. He said, "I want to go get my hook!"

El pointed upstairs with her thumb, indicating that Shad and Monica were to go get on the video-phone and not give her any argu-

§

ments. She watched them trudge up the stairs. "They're on their way upstairs," she told him. "I'll talk to you when they're done." She put the receiver down and hurried to her bathroom, where she quickly changed into a new blouse, applied fresh make up, and straightened out her hair. When she went into Monica's room, she found Monica on the floor, her feet propped up against the wall, lying on her back and holding the phone to her ear. Shad jumped up and down on her bed, his free hand reaching for the ceiling. The screen on the video-phone was filled with a black and white picture of Wayne from the shoulders up, holding a handset to his ear and smiling.

"Dad," Monica said, as soon as Elisa came into the room. "Here's Mom. She wants to talk to you."

El took the phone, positioning herself in front of the camera.

"Nice blouse," Monica said, sneering.

El flashed her a look and then turned her attention to the phone. "So," she said. "Was Harden able to work it out?"

"Absolutely," Wayne's voice came back. Then his picture began to disappear, eaten up by a new shot that snapped onto the screen piece by piece from the bottom up. In the new shot, he was wearing the intense-and-serious-Wayne look. "It's a done deal."

"Great," she said. She smiled and pushed the button that transmitted a picture of herself across three thousand miles to Wayne's office phone.

"Hey," Wayne said. "You look great, honey."

"Thanks. Tell Kiki she looked great in *The New Yorker.*"

"Oh, God," he said. "Did you see that?" Then he added quickly, "The kids didn't see it, did they?"

"Afraid so."

"Bitch," he said. "She's screwing that long-haired faggot model."

"Faggot?" El said. She wished he would transmit a shot of himself as he looked at that precise moment. She could hear the anger and hurt in his voice and would have liked to have seen it etched in his face.

Wayne laughed quietly. "I guess *faggot's* not right, huh?" He laughed again. "Are you enjoying this?"

☙

"No, Wayne," El said, her voice thick with sincerity. "Why don't you get a divorce?" Behind her, Shad stopped jumping on the bed.

"Because I'd lose too much money."

"Money," El said, "isn't everything." On the other end of the line she heard Wayne's sharp, derisive laugh.

"Look," he said. "I've got to go. I just wanted to call and tell you myself that the deal is done. They've got their endowment, I'm happy to be a contributor, and they can keep me on the A-list."

"Great," El said. "Good for your taxes, no?"

"Good for my taxes, absolutely," Wayne said. "And you? How's it feel not to be a lackey anymore? Can I still call you Ellie, or do I have to call you Dean now?"

"Dean Ellie," she said. "Call me Dean Ellie."

"Hey," Wayne said. "Send me one more picture before you hang up. Show me a little cleavage."

El grinned, bent slightly over the phone, opened the top two buttons of her blouse, and transmitted the picture.

"Mom!" Monica shouted.

El hung up the phone. "What?"

"How could you?"

El looked back at the video-phone. "You mean the cleavage? For God's sake, Monica. I was married to the man for twelve years. It was just a little joke."

Monica's face was red and there were tears in her eyes. Shad was leaning against the wall, looking away from both of them. El sighed and buttoned up her blouse. "For Christ's sake," she said. "Let's just go shopping."

§

At the mall, Shad couldn't find his pirate's outfit, but settled happily for a suit of armor and a mace. Monica refused to buy a thing. On the way back, in the van, Shad changed into his knight's outfit. Monica helped him adjust the metallic gray plastic helmet on his head. She snapped the face guard in place over his chin before strapping on the breastplate. Shad couldn't do it himself because he wouldn't let go of

§

his penis. He was holding on with both hands, worrying El and Monica. He wouldn't even let go to hold onto his new mace.

On the street approaching their house, Monica leaned close to El in the driver's seat and whispered in her ear. "You know, Mom, we're going to have to do something if he doesn't quit this." Then, before El could respond, the car rounded a curve and their house came into view. Bill and a half dozen of the guys who worked for him were loading equipment of some kind into the back of one of his vans.

Monica said, "What's going on?"

Shad yelled, suddenly and tremendously excited: "Look! Look!"

"What is it?" El parked the car by the driveway, behind Bill, and twisted around in her seat toward Shad, who had let loose of himself with one hand and was pointing to the top of the house, shouting: "Look! Look! Look!"

"What is it?" El repeated, looking up at the house.

"Oh my God!" Monica said.

"What?" El shouted.

Shad opened the van door and jumped out. He ran to Bill, who was standing in the middle of the front lawn with a big grin on his face. The other men were leaning against their van, all bright and happy, looking over to El and Monica.

"The tree," Monica said, getting out of the van. "They cut down the tree." She slammed the car door shut and walked toward Bill, who had picked up Shad and was carrying him on his hip around to the backyard.

El looked up to where the crown of the big oak tree should have been towering over the roof, and saw nothing but blue sky and clouds. She laughed, amazed she hadn't noticed it, and surprised such a big tree could be cut down so quickly. She got out of the van, exchanged greetings with the crew, and then they all walked down to the backyard, where Bill was standing, looking at the fallen corpse of the big tree, his arm around Monica. Shad was jumping up and down alongside them, one arm waving wildly in the air, yelling, "Hooray! Hooray! Hooray!"

As El approached Bill, he said: "It would have had to come down in a year or two anyway. It was—"

⑤

"Fine with me," El said. She picked up Shad and then leaned over to Bill and kissed him on the cheek. "Now maybe we'll get enough sun to put some plants in the living room."

Bill touched Shad's elbow. "You think you might sleep a little better now without that old tree tapping on your window, Buddy?"

Shad nodded vigorously. "Can I walk on it, Bill?" he asked.

"Sure," Bill said.

Shad wriggled out of El's arms and ran down to the yard where the body of the oak tree lay scattered. In one corner of the yard, the branches were piled several feet high. In another corner, logs a foot and a half or so long and of various widths were lined up and stacked in rows. In the center of the yard, the massive trunk of the oak lay cut up into several sections. Shad headed straight for the biggest section of tree trunk and climbed up on it.

"Hey," Monica said. "That looks like fun." She trotted off after Shad.

For awhile, Bill and El and Bill's crew watched the kids playing on the tree. Then El went back into the house, and the men all drove back to the warehouse, except Bill, who said he would join them in a half hour or so. After they had driven away, he watched Shad and Monica for a time and then climbed up the stairs to the deck and went into the dining room.

El was standing at the kitchen sink with a copy of *The New Yorker* opened to Kiki's ad. When she saw Bill, she said, "The kids don't need to see this," and she dropped it in the garbage.

Bill closed the sliding glass door behind him. Without the tree to block the sun, the kitchen was noticeably brighter. The floor's white tiles were whiter than normal, and the black, mirror-like surface of the refrigerator soaked up light.

"Hey," El said. "Look at this." She was pointing out the window to the yard.

Bill joined her by the sink. In the yard, Monica was sitting up on the biggest section of the tree's trunk, her elbows on her knees and head in hands, looking off pensively at the sunset. Alongside her, Shad had taken off his armor, dropping the breastplate, mace, and helmet to the ground beside the tree, and he was walking one foot in front of the other, carefully, like a tightrope walker—and like a tightrope walker, his arms, both arms, were stretched out parallel to the ground for balance.

Bill said, "That was easy."

El leaned against him. She said, "I'm sorry that I did this thing the way I did. I should have just out and told you." She wasn't looking at him as she spoke. She was looking down into the sink.

"But," Bill said. "The thing itself, doing it, you don't regret that?" He had his arm around El, and the way he was holding her and the tone of his voice made it clear that the question was an honest one.

El shook her head without hesitating. "No," she said. "I don't." She kissed him on the shoulder. She said, "I've got some phone calls to make," and she left the room.

Bill remained awhile leaning over the kitchen sink, looking out into the yard. Monica was in the same position, almost motionless, looking off at the sunset, and Shad was still playing the tightrope artist, walking carefully back and forth between Monica and the edge of the tree. From where Bill watched, looking down, he felt like a bird hovering over his nest. He laughed at himself for the feeling, but it was still a good one. It made him feel good, as did watching Monica, who looked so grown up and serious—and Shad, who was managing to keep his balance, his arms still spread out wide to either side of his body, like a nestling stretching his wings, getting ready to learn the difficult requirements of flight.

GIFTS

for Raoul Vezina and Jay Walter

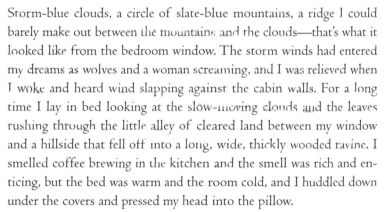

Storm-blue clouds, a circle of slate-blue mountains, a ridge I could barely make out between the mountains and the clouds—that's what it looked like from the bedroom window. The storm winds had entered my dreams as wolves and a woman screaming, and I was relieved when I woke and heard wind slapping against the cabin walls. For a long time I lay in bed looking at the slow-moving clouds and the leaves rushing through the little alley of cleared land between my window and a hillside that fell off into a long, wide, thickly wooded ravine. I smelled coffee brewing in the kitchen and the smell was rich and enticing, but the bed was warm and the room cold, and I huddled down under the covers and pressed my head into the pillow.

A week before, our house had burned. Ellie and I lost most of what we owned, but we were thankful for our lives, and so I worked things out with the court and my clients and my partners, and took two weeks off from being a lawyer so I could take this vacation at Howard's cabin. Actually, it's our cabin: Howard willed it to us when he died. Howard was our son. He was twenty-six when he died six years ago, and since then we've only been to the cabin twice, both times in the last year. It's situated on a little peninsula of land that juts out into the ravine, and it's not a very valuable piece of property because it won't be around much longer: the land it rests on is slowly eroding. In another ten years the cabin will sit on the edge of the ravine, and in another twenty it'll be gone. But the view . . . The view is magnificent. More so now than when Howard was alive.

The first time we saw the place was 1969. Those were hard years. The world was changing before my eyes, and I didn't like what I was seeing. Howard did, and we were always at odds. In college he let his hair grow long, and he came home for holidays with hair like a girl's reaching down to his shoulders. I tried not to look at him. I tried to tell myself it was a fad. He always had a delicately handsome face, and then with that long hair he looked so feminine, he looked so much like a girl that I wanted to smack him and make him get his hair cut. I can still hear myself yelling at him, telling him to act like a man. He was full of ideals—and all I could see was long hair and a face that seemed too pretty.

But 1969. That spring he had graduated from college and with money he had borrowed for grad school he bought this cabin. We found out, not from Howard—we had given up trying to keep track of him—but from his girlfriend's father. His girlfriend's name was T.J., and though he had been seeing her for a couple of years, we had never met her. One night that summer her father called and threatened to shoot Howard if he didn't send T.J. home. After I got him calmed down he told me about the cabin, and I promised I'd go up there and talk to Howard. By the end of the phone call, though I don't think my voice showed it, I was angrier than T.J.'s father, and not about Howard and T.J., but about the way Howard had spent his grad school money—money he had gotten from a loan I cosigned.

I had wanted to go see him alone, but Ellie insisted on coming.

"We really should let him know," she said.

I glared at the rutted dirt road. This was not the kind of driving my Buick had been designed for, and every time a rock clunked against the frame I cursed the mountains and grew angrier at Howard. "How?" I said, trying to sound even-tempered. "How do we let him know we're coming?"

Ellie didn't answer. She turned and looked out the window at trees that crowded the road.

❁

"No phone," I said. "No mail delivery. How am I supposed to let them know?"

Ellie touched her fingertips to her forehead, just above her eyebrows—which is something she always does right before she cries.

"Don't cry, Ellie," I said. But the tears were already falling. Ellie is a frail woman with delicate features. I knew we were only a short way from the cabin, and I didn't want Ellie crying when she saw Howard—so I tried my best to calm her. By the time we got there she was feeling better. I had agreed to walk the half-mile trail to the cabin first, and then bring Howard back to the car. This, Ellie reasoned, would give T.J. time to straighten out her house before we all arrived. I didn't argue. It still makes me smile to think of how concerned Ellie was that T.J. have enough time to straighten out her house for guests.

I was glad for the half mile walk. It gave me time to compose myself and rehearse what I wanted to say. The sweet smell of the woods was calming, though I was constantly annoyed at the overhanging branches and the uneven path. I was going to tell Howard about how much Ellie and I had sacrificed for him, and what he owed us: first of all, to live someplace civilized, and then to contribute something to society, to give something back in return for what had been given to him. I remember rehearsing that speech when the path opened onto a clearing and I saw the cabin. It's a big log cabin with a slate roof, and there's one large bay window in the front that brings the morning light into the living room; and there's a little three-step stoop that leads up to the front door. The way I was standing at the edge of that clearing, with my legs and arms so stiff, I must have looked like just another tree, because no one noticed me. The cabin door was open, and I could see in through the living room to the kitchen. Howard was sitting at the kitchen table smoking a pipe, and a much older man—he looked to be in his late forties to early fifties—was sitting across from him. T.J. was sitting on the table between them with her legs crossed and folded under her. Her eyes were closed and her hands were resting palms up on her knees. All three were naked. I stood there a long time taking in this sight: T.J., with her boyish chest and skinny body, with her long, straight hair that reached down to the tabletop; the older man, whose face was lost somewhere under a disheveled mop of curling, mouse-brown hair and a beard that grew wildly over his face; and my son . . . my son Howard, who, if not for the evidence of his sex, could have been mistaken for a pretty, flat-chested girl with silky, dark hair falling over her shoulders. I had just about decided to turn around and leave, and to tell Ellie no one was at the cabin, when a huge chow that had been lying on the cabin floor under the bay window saw me. He was a dopey-looking dog with a full ruff of long, silver-gray hair. When he saw me, he jumped right into the window. I'm still surprised it didn't break.

All three naked bodies at the table turned at the same time. The older man stood up, and Howard and T.J. leapt for the chow, who had regained his bearings and was about to make it out the front door. Howard caught it by the collar and T.J. had it by the tail, and still the thing carried them halfway out the door before they managed to pull it back into the kitchen and tie it to a short leash. I could hear Howard explaining over the chow's barking, "It's okay! It's okay! He's my father!" and then T.J. closed the front door and ran through the living room to the bedroom. The older man—whom I later learned was an ex-lawyer, ex-stockbroker, ex-corporate executive named Tom McGuinn—must have left through the back door because I didn't see him again. Then the front door opened and Howard, dressed in a white robe with a black silk rope for a belt, walked across the clearing and joined me.

"I'm sorry you didn't let me know you were coming," he said. He was looking me in the eyes—something I taught him to do when he was a boy. He said, "I'm sorry about how this must make you feel, Dad."

I nodded.

Howard looked away and we were both silent awhile. Then he started talking casually. "Lieberman loves T.J.," he said. "He's such a big, dumb puppy."

I guessed that Lieberman was the chow.

"A couple of weeks ago T.J.'s father came busting in the cabin and Lieberman bit him." Howard smiled.

I nodded again.

"He sent you up here, didn't he? T.J.'s father."

"He's threatened to kill you."

"He's told me in person. T.J. says he won't do it."

"That's nice to know. If she were my daughter, I don't think you'd be so lucky." As soon as I said that, I felt like a jerk.

Howard said, "I love T.J."

"So you let her sit naked in front of another man?"

Howard looked at me defiantly. "She sleeps with him too. In fact —"

I grabbed his robe and pulled him close. When he didn't resist, I pushed him away and turned and walked down the path, half expecting him to follow. He didn't, and I remember cursing him as I followed the trail. When I got back to the car I told Ellie no one was at the cabin. She looked at me and knew I was lying. "What happened?" she asked. I didn't answer. I started the car and we drove in silence until we found a motel where we could spend the night.

After I carried our suitcases into the room and stretched out on one of a pair of double beds, Ellie asked me again to tell her what had happened. I told her and she kept shaking her head through the whole story. When I finished she asked, "Are you sure about the other man?" I hadn't told her what Howard had said, or even that we had argued. I just told her I had been upset with them and had left. She wanted me to go back. "You have to go back," she said. "We can't leave things this way."

I agreed. Ellie had meant for me to go back in the morning, but I was too upset to wait. After the TV news was over, I left her alone in the motel room and drove back to the cabin.

By the time I arrived it was dark. There was no moon that night and as soon as I turned off the lights and stepped out of the car I couldn't see a thing. I held my fingers in front of my eyes and I still couldn't see them. I got the flashlight out of the glove compartment and let its thin beam of light guide my way. The woods were full of strange noises: at one point as I walked along the trail, I must have surprised an owl or some other large bird, because I heard a great, thick flapping of wings from a tree limb only a few feet in front of me. Then, after my heart-beat slowed somewhat, I began to hear an irregular clicking noise, like someone sending Morse code; and as I continued walking the clicking got louder, until, standing once again at the clearing in front of the cabin, I saw T.J. sitting at the kitchen table typing.

I remember how intent she looked at her work. She stared at that typewriter as if it could talk to her, as if she were waiting for a mes-sage to come whispered from its innards. Then suddenly, as if she heard what she was listening for, she'd type furiously for a minute or two, and then stop again to listen. I must have watched her there for ten or fifteen minutes. Occasionally she'd rub her nose with a bent forefinger, or pull a long strand of hair across her lips and bite at it—but always she'd return to her listening and typing. Lieberman was sleeping on his back in front of the bay window, and McGuinn was sitting on the couch reading a thick, dark book.

I walked around to the back of the cabin. There, through the bedroom window, I saw something that it took several minutes to make out. It appeared to me—standing alone in the darkness outside the cabin, looking in through the bedroom window—that Howard was floating naked through space, and it took me the longest time to take the pieces of that optical illusion apart. When I eventually did, it seemed somehow tremendously funny. Howard had painted the room black—floors, walls, ceiling, everything. He had covered his bed with a black blanket. And then, in the manner of Jackson Pollack, he had splashed the room—floors, walls, ceiling, bed, everything—with splotches of luminous white paint. Somewhere in the room he had hidden a black light; and with the darkness outside and the black light shining inside, and with him lying on the bed, he appeared to be float-ing naked among stars.

The way Howard had decorated his room reminded me of when he was nine or ten years old and a Boy Scout: when he camped out, he loved to fix up his tent. He liked it better than anything, and he was always stealing things from around our house to use as decorations. I associated that wildly painted room with his old Boy Scout tents, and it struck me as so amusing that I suddenly felt at ease. I approached the window and knocked at the glass as if I were standing at the front door. "Hey, Buck Rodgers!" I called, and this also struck me funny. I bent over and folded my hands across my stomach and laughed so hard my cheeks and jaw and sides started to hurt. When I finally looked up the light was on in the room, and Howard was tying a knot in his black belt. He was flanked by T.J. and McGuinn, and Lieberman was standing on the bed. They were all staring at the window.

I smiled.

Howard opened the window. "Dad," he said, "What are you doing?"

I shrugged and then we smiled at each other. Howard motioned for me to go around to the front of the cabin.

He and T.J. met me on the steps, and I heard McGuinn and Lieberman walking out the back door.

T.J. held out her hand. "I'm very sorry about this afternoon," she said. "I'm really terribly embarrassed."

Her voice was so sweet and her manner and tone so intelligent that I liked her immensely as soon as I heard her speak a few words. It didn't hurt that she was apologizing—which, at the very least, was an effort at courtesy. I shook her hand. "There's no need to apologize," I said.

"Oh," she said. "I just wish our first meeting had been different." She was barefoot and wearing a pair of baggy jeans and a man's blue cotton workshirt. She clasped her hands together behind her back. "Let's go in," she said, and she stepped back through the door.

Howard started to follow.

"T.J.," I said. "I hope you won't mind, but I'd like to talk to Howard alone for a while. Out here. I'll feel more comfortable out here."

"I understand," she said. "Can I make you some coffee or tea?"

"Coffee," Howard said. "My dad's a big coffee drinker."

T.J. closed the door, and as Howard and I sat alongside each other on the cabin's steps and listened to her, she went about making a pot of coffee.

ᔕ

"She seems like a nice girl," I said.

Howard said, "I love her, Dad. If this were a different time we'd be married."

I looked away. I didn't want to get into serious matters so quickly. I had hoped we might at least start out talking about the past and sharing memories. I wanted to talk first about those things that joined us before getting to the matters that divided us. But there we were after our first few words and my son was indirectly attacking marriage and the family. I took a deep breath and let it out slowly. "Howard," I said. "I don't understand you, and I really want to. Where can we start?"

Howard shrugged and we were both quiet for a long time. T.J. brought me some coffee, and then we both listened as she went back to her typing. Finally, I asked him what T.J. was writing. She was working on a novel, he told me. That got us started talking, and once we were started we talked through the night while T.J.'s typewriter clattered behind us. Howard believed, he truly believed, that he could love everybody, that we are all beautiful, God-like creatures—and I couldn't make him see it wasn't true. I tried to tell him what poor, desperate animals we all are at heart, but he didn't know what I was talking about, and after awhile I began to feel deranged and unhealthy for trying to make him see things as I saw them.

At dawn T.J. joined us and we walked around to the back of the cabin and watched the sunrise over the ring of mountains. It came up bright and red and it turned a thin line of clouds red all along the horizon. I could almost see Ellie at the motel stumbling out of the bed and shuffling groggily toward the bathroom. Ellie has gotten up at dawn every morning for as long as I've known her. I said, "I've got to go now."

"You're thinking of Mom, aren't you?" Howard said. "She's getting up now."

I laughed and Howard added, "I wish she were here so I could tell her I love her."

The sun had risen clear of the mountains. It was a big, red circle floating above us and casting a red glow over the trees. "I love her too,"

☙

I said. And we all three sat there quietly a little while longer before I shook Howard's hand and T.J. hugged me, and finally I left. On my way to the trail I passed McGuinn and Lieberman sitting on the front steps. McGuinn was wearing a bright green vest and he had dressed Lieberman in a blue flannel shirt, putting the chow's legs through the sleeves and buttoning it under his belly. Around the dog's neck he had tied a red bandanna. I waved and McGuinn waved back, but Lieberman just stared intensely. He's never been a very trusting dog.

I've dreamt of that sunrise a number of times since Howard's death, and I must have been dreaming of it again the night of the fire. I awoke to the high-pitched, piercing sound of the smoke alarm, and I don't remember dreaming of anything, but I was groggy and a little dizzy and the living room was filled with a thin haze of smoke and an eerie red glow. For a second before I realized what was happening I thought I heard Howard's voice. I thought I was back at the cabin watching the sunrise. Then I came to my senses. It was a cold night, but the living room was so hot, sweat fell off my body. Ellie was more unconscious than she was asleep, and I had to pick her up and carry her out on my shoulder. When I opened the front door and stepped out into the cold night air, the house seemed to explode behind me. Within minutes there were flames hurrying behind every window, and several hours later the house had burned to rubble—and I watched it burn with Ellie, at first shivering in the cold, and then warm behind a neighbor's window. And all I could think of was Howard. Watching the house where we raised him burn down was like watching his cremation.

He had gotten sick in 1973 and died early in 1974. During those last days in the hospital, he had grown so frail and emaciated that it was hard to look at him. He was twenty-six and he looked like a little old man, his skin sunken around his skeleton, his eyes looking like they might pop out of his head. It took all the courage I had to sit beside him and talk in a normal tone. Ellie couldn't do it. She tried, but toward the end she couldn't look at him without burying her face in her hands and crying, and so she sat in the lounge and waited, trying to build up her strength.

꒱

The night before he died, Howard said something to me that I thought I understood but didn't really until the night of the fire. It was late. I had stayed past visiting hours because Howard seemed more alert than usual. He was able to understand what I was saying, and if I bent down and put my ear near to his mouth, I was able to understand his occasional whispered replies. I was trying to tell him, amidst the sickening hospital smells and the fluids dripping through tubes all around us, that his life was the greatest gift Ellie and I had ever been given. But each time I tried to speak all my emotions rose up and choked off the words. Finally I said, "Howard— your life— your life is like a gift—" and I couldn't go on.

Howard motioned with one finger for me to come closer, and he whispered in my ear, "Death is a gift too." When I backed away and looked down at him he said, loud enough for me to hear, "From me to you," and he managed a weak smile.

I thought I knew what he meant then. I thought he meant death would be an end to his suffering, and to my having to watch him suffer. But now I don't think that's what he meant at all. The night of the fire, watching thick flames consume our home, seeing everything I owned drifting away as smoke, I was struck with a physical beauty so solid I could feel it. Death came to me suddenly as a fact, because I saw everything turning in time to dust and ashes—me and Ellie and our house . . . and Howard. I looked at the flames and felt all through me the uniqueness and the beauty of things in time—and often now I feel sure that's what Howard was talking about when he said death was a gift too. It was a revelation when I thought my time of revelations was long gone.

Ellie called from the kitchen. "Joseph, get up!" she yelled. "You've got to see this."

I sat up in bed and looked out the window. The storm clouds were so thick it looked like night out there, but I knew it was midmorning. Still, I didn't feel like getting out of bed. Alongside my pillow, on the mahogany night table, was a copy of T.J.'s first novel. It had just been published by a small press and it wasn't getting much attention, but she was excited about its publication. I hadn't

ᔕ

read it yet: it had come in the mail with a long letter the day after the fire. I remember meeting the postman on the street and how we both laughed as he delivered the mail to an acre plot of debris. T.J. said the book wasn't getting many reviews, but the reviews it was getting were good. McGuinn, she told me, had gone back to being a lawyer. He made lots of money these days and dressed very conservatively. She said I wouldn't believe it to see him, but I did. It was 1980 and the country was back to normal. It was like the '60s and '70s had never happened. I hoped McGuinn was happy.

"Joseph!" Ellie called, "Come out here! You're going to miss this!"

I grumbled to myself. I still didn't feel like getting up, but I struggled out of the warm bed and put on my robe and walked out to the kitchen.

For a moment I was disoriented: sunlight poured into the cabin through the bay window and the front door. It was an exceptionally bright day. Then a violent gust of wind slammed the front door closed, and I turned and looked out the back window and the back door, and it was dark as night.

"Wow," I said. I had never seen anything like this and neither had Ellie. Even Lieberman, who had quietly watched our house burn from the distant seclusion of his doghouse and who seemed to want nothing more out of life than to lie somewhere and grow old in silence—even Lieberman was trotting back and forth between the front and back of the cabin and sniffing wildly at the doors.

"Isn't it magnificent!" Ellie said. "Isn't it glorious!"

I nodded. Through the back window I could see the darkness of the storm, and through the front window I could see the mountains rising up around us in bright sunlight. I could see the sky clear and blue beyond the mountains' ridge and I could see the crisp play of light and shadow between the hollows and rises.

"Yes," I answered. "Yes it is."